THE MUNICIPALISTS

A NOVEL

SETH FRIED

PENGUIN BOOKS

PENGUIN BOOKS

An imprint of Penguin Random House LLC

ISBN 978-1-64385-260-7

Printed in the United States of America

This book is dedicated to Julia Mehoke
and to the city that brought us together.

On August 7 of 1904, a flash flood hit the No. 11 Missouri Pacific Flyer as it crossed a trestle bridge on its way to Pueblo, Colorado. A wall of water carried off four of the train's six cars and the remains of finely dressed men and women were found caked in mud as far as twenty miles away. The superintendent of the train's dining service was in the forward sleeper when he saw the other cars go down and later offered the following account to the *Colorado Springs Gazette*: "I have never experienced anything like the awful sensation that came over me when I saw the cars, packed with human beings, floating down that flood. The water surged into the coaches so quickly there was not a sound from the passengers. I heard no calls for help." Ninety-seven people were killed that night, making it the deadliest derailment of a long-distance train in US history.

The honor of second place goes to the No. 48 Lake Shore Limited, which jumped the tracks in western New York on August 12 of 1998. The train ran at full speed over a damaged length of rail, causing the first six cars to roll down a twenty-foot embankment and plow into an empty field. The rest jackknifed into one another and scattered themselves along the tracks.

I can't help but remember the words of the man from the Flyer and imagine the scene as eerily quiet once the wreck settled. Torn steel. Clouds of dust rising up. Maybe at the edge of the field above the cottonwoods a flock of birds that had been startled from their branches by the sudden disaster were already beginning to circle back down to rest. Eighty passengers died that day, securing the Limited its second-place rank. If my parents hadn't been on board, it would have only come in third.

I mention it because when a ten-year-old boy loses his parents, it makes him see things differently. So much of his world vanishes so quickly that he may be surprised to notice afterward that there are still telephone poles and traffic lights. The roads don't peel themselves back in horror. The familiar buildings are all still standing. For instance, Becker's Independent Grocery where he once walked alongside his mother. In his memory there's the horsefly hum of fluorescent lights and his sneakers squeaking on the scuffed acrylic of butter-colored floors. The air is close with the round, earthy smell of produce and fresh bread. He remembers it well, but when he passes Becker's on a gray day while sitting in the back of his foster parents' dented minivan, the place seems to have forgotten him. The flat, glass storefront stares straight ahead without so much as a glimmer of recognition. Encounters of this sort at first feel like deepenings of the same loss, as if bit by bit the world was denying that the life he lost was ever real. If the boy is lucky, when the pain becomes too much, he will begin to see through this childish perception all the way to the truth. Then he will know what I know: The stubborn and impersonal resilience of the built world is in fact a force for good.

When the Lake Shore Limited derailed, it was rushing

through the idyllic countryside of western New York. Any of my colleagues will tell you that victims of trauma in rural areas are far more likely to die before they reach the hospital than their urban counterparts. To see why this is the case, one doesn't need to subscribe to the *Journal of Demography and Health Care*—though I do and can confirm it is an excellent publication. Rural health care administrators are dealing with a low number of calls spread out over large distances, and so are forced to reduce the quality of EMS care to achieve an acceptable cost per call. Keeping that in mind, it becomes clear that roads and buildings are not the villains here. The closer trauma victims are to population centers and dense infrastructure, the more likely it is that their lives will be saved.

It's understandable why some people might still choose to strike out for the country, fleeing the frustrations that can result from so much proximity with other people. The choice can even seem obvious. Pavement and foul-mouthed strangers are traded for trees, a view of the lake, rolling fields. But the fact of the matter is that the farther you get from the infuriating crowds that might offend your sense of solitude, the more your risk increases. This is a notion you're free to scoff at until the day that I hope never comes for you finally does, a severed finger in your beautiful kitchen, a drunk driver swerving the wrong way down a dark country road.

And believe me when I tell you that traumatic injury is the least of it. City dwellers have a lower risk of death from heart disease, cancer, stroke, drug overdose, and suicide. They enjoy more employment opportunities, transportation options, and cultural amenities. Contrary to popular perceptions, urban areas are also better for the environment than lower-density sprawl, and their school systems tend to produce better outcomes. That is the power of cities. The economy of agglomeration.

In the course of my profession, the important work I do, I fly to municipalities all over the country in the hopes that they can benefit from my expertise. When I look out the plane's window on a clear day, I can see both the cities and the sticks. Urban landscapes surrounded for miles and miles by a broad patchwork of empty fields. Never is it easier to see these two ways of life as physical realities in conflict with one another. The desire to come together and the desire to escape one another. Density and dispersal. It's a war we fight with our own lives every day. And as long as I can remember, there's never been any question about what side I was on.

1

In Suitland, Maryland, just outside DC, there is a large gray building that is home to the United States Municipal Survey. The main building boasts over 2 million square feet of assignable space. It houses research laboratories and data centers where our technicians utilize fleets of aerial drones to monitor most US cities in real time. In our Traffic department, serious men and women use VR rigs to investigate congested roadways, while down the hall the folks in Weather are busy running hurricane-force winds over manhole covers to determine at what point they get sucked up and turn lethal, cast-iron Frisbees whistling with a thud into the reinforced glass. Nearby there's also the compound containing our supercomputer, OWEN, which ingests data from over two hundred satellites. Our headquarters is by all accounts an impressive facility, though my small office on the fifth floor is a bit more modest in scope.

There's just enough room for a desk, two chairs, and a narrow bookshelf of binders. I find it cozy, but the lack of space can occasionally exacerbate an awkward situation. Like when Agent Marcuzzi stomped in that morning, taking a seat across from me without a word.

I had asked him to stop by for a friendly meeting, but his attitude was so immediately hostile that at 7:00 A.M. I was already forced to wonder what sort of day it would be. He hunched forward in his seat, causing the shoulders of his blazer to bunch. His hands were folded in his lap and he was knocking his thumbs together like he was waiting for a bus he didn't want to get on.

He glanced at the model locomotive on my desk and I hoped for a moment he might smile. Next to my nameplate, I had placed a 1:64 scale model of an eight-axle C8 Manley & Wrexler. I had a reputation at the agency for being somewhat joyless and so I'd brought the model from home to liven up my workspace. It was from a series of collectibles called Trains of Yore, which depicted classic locomotives in scrupulous detail. They were generally marketed toward the elderly, but I was thirty-two and owned over two dozen of them. I liked the look of that handsome little locomotive on my desk and the C8 never had an accident while in use. So there was also an inspirational element. Yet when Marcuzzi saw it, he grimaced.

"I'm sure you know why I asked you to come."

"No," Marcuzzi said. "I have no idea."

This surprised me.

"Fort Collins," I continued. "You reported 4.73 percent added efficiencies."

He nodded.

"The group's goal," I said, "was 5 percent per target municipality."

"I know what the goal was."

"Then you know that 4.73 percent is unacceptable."

Marcuzzi let his mouth hang open, as if he couldn't believe what he'd just heard.

"Thompson, are you joking?"

"About this? Of course not."

"That's insane," he said. "That—that's well within the margin. Those numbers are just to give you a general sense of—God damn it, I *achieved* my goal."

"Peter," I said. "On the projects I run, numbers are numbers. I asked you here so we could talk this through and get your efficiencies up."

"A third of a percentage point? What do you want me to do? Head out to the wind farms and blow?"

"So you agree," I said, "that making up the difference wouldn't be hard to do."

I had been trying to insert some humor into the conversation, but Marcuzzi must have read my smile the wrong way.

"Honestly, Henry. Go fuck yourself."

He almost knocked over his chair as he left the room.

If I were less accustomed to this sort of friction with my colleagues, then a display of that sort would have been a minor scandal. But as it was I simply made a note to head out to Fort Collins myself at the first opportunity. I also took a deep breath and turned the C8 around on my desk so it faced me. In the cab stood a lone engineer staring ahead soberly, his little eyes taking in the seemingly endless plains to be traversed. I smiled down at the man. Yes, life wasn't easy, but luckily there was always much to be done.

I'd blocked off an hour for Marcuzzi, so now there was time to attend the meeting for the Port Oversight Committee happening down on the third floor. It was hard not to regain your confidence when you were walking with purpose through the halls of headquarters. The speckled white granite floors were always polished and glassy, while the dark wood paneling along the walls gave the place a warm, collegial air. It was early still, but the broad corridors were already resounding with the dressy heel clacks of so many agents, all of us looking sharp in our matching, agency-issued suits—navy single-button blazers with thin lapels and the option of pencil skirts for any female agents who preferred them. I passed men and women gathered in the open work areas to discuss infrastructure problems. They rearranged 3-D projections of subway tunnels and took notes while model dams buckled from the force of simulated earthquakes. A group of junior agents passed me in a huddle, grabbing fist-sized data sets from their agency phones and tossing them onto each other's screens as they argued among themselves about carbon emissions in the Rust Belt and the legalities of federal intervention.

The agency had begun seventy years back as a plucky arm of the DOT, a few dozen policy wonks who took pride in punching above their weight. But at the rate the world was urbanizing, cities had become the new space race. Our budget had exploded and we now coordinated with state and local governments to fund and advise thousands of major city improvement projects every year. We were in the middle of the golden age of American urban planning and for me the atmosphere of collective optimism never failed to produce a pleasant sense of belonging.

I remembered I had some fieldwork coming up in Wisconsin so I took out my agency phone and asked for the five-day forecast in Madison. The animation of a handsome young agent with startling blue eyes appeared on the screen.

"According to GPS," OWEN said, "you're at USMS headquarters in Suitland, Maryland."

Our chief technology engineer, Dr. Gustav Klaus, had put a lot of time and energy into OWEN's artificial intelligence interface, but the more humanlike the interface became, the more trouble I had interacting with it.

"I'll be flying out later this week, just . . ." I held the phone closer to my mouth and half barked into it, "Weather conditions. Madison, Wisconsin."

My voice was louder than expected and a fellow agent frowned at me as she passed.

"You sound stressed," OWEN said.

The animation's eyebrows arched slightly to demonstrate its concern. "While you're in Madison, you should take some time for yourself and check out Lake Monona. It's supposed to be nice."

"The weather, OWEN, I just need to know the weather."

"Oh, it's the middle of June," OWEN said. "I bet it's gorgeous."

I closed out of the interface in frustration. Between Marcuzzi and my own phone, the morning seemed off to a poor start. As I entered the meeting, I tried to focus on my eagerness to hear Agent Steinbelt's report on Norfolk and the proposed regulations the agency would attach to any new funding. Steinbelt planned to start with a virtual tour of Lambert's Point and so we were in the windowless central boardroom with one of the better 3-D projectors. I took a seat at the long conference table and told myself there was time enough for this day to be a good one. A productive one.

But almost as soon as Steinbelt brought up the simulation, the projector sputtered out and the waters that had just begun to lap at our feet faded from the room. The fire alarm let out a single shrill whoop and then went silent as our agency phones began to emit a high-pitched tone. The devices lit up the dark room as committee members removed them from their pockets and briefcases. The screens all displayed a dense block of characters:

```
!#~#K#~y1878~#@#~#!/!#~#@#y#!9!#~#@#~#!
!#~#@#~#!%!#~#@`~#!8!#~#@#~#!%!#~#`#~#!
!#~#@#~#!%!#~#@`~#!8!#~#@#~#!%!#~#`#~#!
!#~#@#~#!%!#~#@`~#!8!#~#@#~#!%!#~#`#~#!
!#~#@#~#!%!#~#@`~#!8!#~#@#~#!%!#~#`#~#!
!#@#~{LA_URBOJ_ESTAS_FROSTIGITAJ}~#!
!@^!~.>Kt&*`87@/8^8Kt%!#~#@#~9P/{788##!
!87@/~#!%!#~#@87@/~#!%!#~#@@/888Kt&*!
!@^!~.>Kt&*`87@/888Kt%!#~#@#~9P/{888##!
!#~#K#~y1878~#@#~#!/!#~#@#y#!9!#~#@#~#!
!#~#@#~#!%!#~#@`~#!8!#~#@#~#!%!#~#`#~#!
!@^!~.>Kt&*`87@/8^8Kt%!#~#@#~9P/{788##!
!87@/~#!%!#~#@87@/~#!%!#~#@@/888Kt&*!
```

I stared down at the message in confusion while the other committee members held up their phones like flashlights and shouted questions to one another.

I excused myself and hurried out of the room to report the

issue to a technician. In the hall, the sunlight coming through the windows only emphasized that the whole building had gone dark. A few nearby faces were illuminated as agents examined their phones. Elsewhere people flipped unresponsive light switches and tapped the dead call buttons on elevators. Some half leaned from their office doors as if waiting for someone to wander by with an explanation. Meanwhile, shouts began to come from behind the doors of the secure rooms whose passcode-protected entryways were sealed shut without power.

The noise from my phone grew more piercing and then abruptly stopped. I held it up to check the screen and it exploded. There was a flash of sparking blue flame and something hit my face like a fist. All at once my palm was bleeding and there was a sharp pain in my cheek. The hall was filled with the smell of burned plastic and I felt dizzy. All around me there were blurred figures stumbling forward and covering their mouths or clutching their hands to their chests. The shouts from the sealed rooms grew more frantic and I could hear people begin to pound on the doors.

My breathing felt unsteady as I removed my necktie and wrapped it around my palm. I could feel my pulse where it was hurt. When I noticed how fast it was, it went faster. There was an old panic welling up in me, a childish sense of helplessness at the world's ability to go suddenly upside down.

Something jostled me and I looked up to see a group of agents rushing past. One of them noticed me standing there and shouted, "Come on!" The urgency in his voice broke through my fear and I joined them as they dragged a desk out of the secretary pool. We used it to ram down the heavy double doors to a conference hall where we could make out people crying for help.

The rest of that day was a confusion of darkened corridors as we agents divided ourselves into groups and rushed through headquarters, prying open doors and tending to people's injuries as best we could. I eventually found the agency's director, Theodore Garrett, just outside his own office, improvising a bandage for a young woman's hand out of one of the spare dress shirts he kept in his desk. I tried to get him out of the building, but he just gave me a serious look and told me to make myself useful.

Even after the north lawn had become a frenzy of strobing lights from the arriving ambulances and fire engines, Garrett refused to leave. Around two in the morning I brought him a mug of instant coffee. He was standing under a work light in the main entryway to the first subbasement, talking a team of firefighters through a map of the floor's access tunnels. His shirtsleeves were rolled up to his elbows and he had a determined look on his face that caused even his mussed white hair to inspire confidence. The left side of my face had started to swell up from where the shards of my phone had lodged themselves and when I approached him with the coffee it seemed to take him a moment to recognize me.

When he did, he dismissed the firefighters and took my head in his hands, tilting it back so he could get a better look. He whistled the way he did when I showed him troubling data from a town where the employment rate was starting to stagnate or where the high school test scores continued to drop. It was an oddly comforting sound, indicating that things were indeed bad but it was nothing he hadn't seen before.

"Can you still see out of this one?" he said, waving a hand in front of the eye that was nearly swelled shut.

I told him I could and he stepped away.

"You'll be fine," he said, like a father playing down a scraped knee.

Strangely, it did make me feel better.

He took the mug of coffee, then thanked me. The dark hall was cluttered with upended chairs and dented waste bins. From the floor above us we could still hear shouting and the rhythmic banging of doors being smashed in.

Garrett sighed and looked down. His foot was resting on a printout bearing the cryptic block of text that had appeared on my phone. Before the building lost power this message had shown up on computer monitors all over headquarters. It was spit out again and again by copiers and printers. Garrett moved the printout right side up with the toe of his shoe and examined it.

"'La urboj estas frostigitaj.'" He recited the words slowly and then took a sip of coffee.

"What does it mean?"

He ignored the question.

"It's in Esperanto."

"You know Esperanto?"

"I don't," he said, "but I know someone who does."

o———o

Within hours, we started to hear the news coming from the city of Metropolis. While the attack on headquarters in Suitland was in progress, over three hundred miles away the agency's Metropolis station had already been burned down and its underground data center in the West Side had collapsed in on itself, leaving a building-sized sinkhole in Eleventh Avenue. Both incidents took place during the station's hours of operation and yet first responders reported no casualties at either site. Then of course there were the drones.

It didn't take our technicians long to identify that the havoc at headquarters was the result of a virus that was uploaded to the agency's supercomputer. OWEN managed most of our day-to-day operations in Suitland, everything from the building's lights and security passcodes to the automated espresso machines in the break rooms. The rest of our surveillance fleet was unaffected, but the virus had deactivated our drones over Metropolis in midflight, causing over seventy of these titanium orbs, each roughly the size of a basketball and covered in carbon-fiber strakes, to fall from the sky over the most populous city in the Western Hemisphere, crashing into buildings and wounding over a dozen people.

In the days that followed there was a fair amount of public outrage directed at the agency. Garrett accepted full liability and started arranging for the USMS to pay hospital bills and damage settlements. Despite being the director of one of the most powerful government agencies in the country, Garrett saw himself first and foremost as a public servant. He always made it clear that his driving passion in life was shortening people's commutes, haggling with zoning boards for more parks, finding the government loopholes that would send funds into the coffers of community centers and public libraries. He spoke of every city in the country with an affection and familiarity that suggested he had family there. He could tell you if the museum was any good and what parts of town to avoid after dark, where to try the pancakes and where to try the pulled pork, what kind of winter they had last year, and if it looked like the school levy was going to pass. Garrett was in his late sixties, but usually bounded around the agency like a much younger man, putting his agents to shame with his sheer exuberance. Now he was sitting in his office making call after call with his shoulders slumped and his face frozen in an expression of stunned, inarticulate grief.

I came to the agency as a civil engineer with no grasp of policy and Garrett had taken it on himself to mentor me personally. I did my best to pay back this generosity through my devotion to the agency and as a result I often found hand-drawn cartoons in our break rooms of me gingerly sniffing air from a jar labeled "Garrett's farts" or sitting in Garrett's lap as if he were a department store Santa and telling him that for Christmas I wanted a personality. But the other agents could think what they wanted. I genuinely admired the man and he was the closest I'd come to making a friend at the agency. It pained me that I had no idea how to assist or comfort him during the difficult times that were now upon us. The idea that he even needed comforting was in itself a disorienting thought.

To make matters worse, our station chief in Metropolis, Terrence Kirklin, had gone missing and was now being sought in connection to the disappearance of Sarah Laury, the mayor of Metropolis's eighteen-year-old daughter. Even with government drones raining from the sky, the news cycle was dominated by concern for Sarah, a bona fide American sweetheart. She had been a favorite of the press since her infancy. In the popular imagination, the fact that one of the most powerful families in Metropolis had adopted a child through the city's own foster system had all the charm of a fairy tale. By the time she was eight years old, the iconic photograph of her volunteering in a soup kitchen (smiling with her hair in blond ringlets, ladle filled with soup, the homeless man in the picture also smiling) was already being sold on postcards in souvenir shops in Archer Square. At age sixteen, she was on the cover of *Sports Illustrated* in the equally iconic photograph of her receiving an Olympic gold medal in individual show jumping (hair straightened, bangs, the bronze medalist looking up at her with something like awe). By seventeen, she had retired from the sport as well as a brief modeling career in order to focus on her studies and philanthropic work.

Her story had always been important to me personally. As an orphan myself, I found it encouraging to see one of my own become such a success. Though, at the agency she had recently become a bit of a controversial figure after leveling a spate of public criticisms against her father's administration and attending a few fringe political rallies throughout the city. It was unfortunate, since Mayor Laury was known for being pro-infrastructure. And now, as if her public repudiations of her own father weren't troubling enough, she had apparently taken up with a bureaucrat who was over twice her age.

Shortly after Laury went missing from the residence hall at Newton College, the young socialite uploaded a video to the internet in which she declared her love for a public servant named Terrence Kirklin. She then requested that the authorities not attempt to find her. Laury did not appear to be under duress and seemed quite sincere in her sentiments. But it wasn't long before the media started speculating that she had undergone some sort of brainwashing. This belief was most likely influenced by the fact that Sarah Laury was a blond-haired, green-eyed beauty, whereas Kirklin was known to the public only in his connection to the agency that had accidentally imploded a portion of Eleventh Avenue and sent a fleet of drones raining down over the city. Kirklin was also six foot five with a goatee and an eye patch over his right eye from an injury he had sustained in the Coast Guard. Whole television segments were devoted to the fact that he was suffering from male-pattern baldness and was perhaps a bit overweight. In person Kirklin was, though not quite handsome, a striking older man. He was tall with an intense, quiet way about him. But in the picture that the press used, Kirklin's bare scalp was shining awkwardly bright. The dark hair around his ears, usually well-groomed, was stringy and unkempt. His good eye was bloodshot and his lips were parted in a way that made him look demented.

For the agency, Kirklin's abrupt absence was a problem in itself. Certainly, everyone had always known him to be a moody and defiant station chief. His annual meetings with

Garrett were dreaded in Suitland for their tempestuousness: One year, the two got into a shouting match over optimal sidewalk width that ended with Kirklin throwing a small bookcase through the window of Garrett's office. Nevertheless, he was without question the best station chief the agency had ever seen.

For two decades he had managed the infrastructure of a city roughly the size of Rhode Island during a period of rapid and sustained growth, the population swelling to 35 million people. More electricity, water, and freight flowed in and out of Metropolis in a single day than it did in the entire state of South Dakota in six months. Kirklin's combined system of turn restrictions, one-way streets, pedestrian crosswalk intervals, street-cleaning schedules, temporary through streets, detours, bus lanes, and bike lanes was a mad symphony that allowed more people to move simultaneously across the streets of Metropolis than was ever thought possible. Kirklin liaised with every public office, utility, and public benefit corporation within the greater metro area. As a result, the city's Department of Health and Mental Hygiene reported that in the last decade life expectancy in Metropolis had increased by 2.7 years. According to the Environmental Protection Agency and the Bureau of Economic Analysis, pollution and commercial growth in the city had gone down and up, respectively. Dealing with the loss of such a man would have been a nightmare for the agency during the best of circumstances, let alone during the crisis in which we now found ourselves.

The turmoil in Metropolis and Suitland prompted our board of directors to form an oversight committee that put the majority of our projects on hold while they conducted an audit of Garrett's leadership. Already they were trying to keep any investigation of the cyberattack private despite Garrett's requests for outreach to the FBI. After the PR disaster of the crashing drones, they were anxious to keep any details of the attack from getting picked up by the press as a potential data breach. When these severe-looking men and women weren't interrogating Garrett, they could be seen wandering through headquarters, taking in all of the fallout from the attack with colicky disapproval.

Garrett asked me to meet with him in his office later that week, and I expected a war council of sorts, an urgent discussion on how to defend the agency against the destructive influence of the oversight committee. As I took my usual seat, I noticed on his desk one of the printouts with the block of text produced by the virus. After Garrett had tipped me off about the line in Esperanto, I'd typed it into a translation engine, which rendered it as: "The cities are frozen." A vague threat or warning I didn't understand. Before I could ask him about it, he told me the committee had instructed him to step down as director by the end of the month.

For a moment the floor attempted to switch places with the ceiling, but I surprised myself by rising from my seat and saying with confidence, "No."

Garrett looked up at me with a question on his face.

"I can put together a dissent channel," I said. "Give me some time to write the memo."

"Sit down."

"I know the agents don't like me, sir, but everyone will sign it if they know it's for you."

He waved me off.

"Henry, if there's so much as a whiff of opposition, they'll gut this place. Do you understand?"

"Without you, this agency—"

"Stop," Garrett said. "We're talking about an irreparable loss of institutional memory. Not just the people who sign that memo. Anyone who's ever sat in on a meeting with you is out the door. The agency as you know it will be finished."

I was standing in front of his desk. I wanted to leave and put together that memo without delay, but didn't see how I could without his permission.

"Sir, what am I supposed to do?"

He looked up at me until I sat back down.

"You don't want to hear this," he said, "but their decision makes sense. You don't have all the facts."

I asked him what the facts were and he told me not to get ahead of him. He then surprised me by taking a pack of cigarettes from his desk and offering me one.

"This is a federal building, sir."

Garrett laughed and wagged a finger as if he thought I might say that, then lit the cigarette with a book of matches from his blazer pocket. I'd never seen him smoke before and the tobacco smelled stale.

"Do you remember an agent named Stuart Biggs?" he said.

I did. He'd been an undistinguished agent in Sewerage with a geekish demeanor that was extreme even for the agency. In other words, he had as few friends as I did. When I was alone with him in the elevators he once told me, apropos of nothing, that a lifelong dream of his was to revolutionize sewer systems using electric turbines he called waste mills.

"Bit of an odd duck," I said.

Garrett nodded.

"I suppose that's why no one noticed he was reassigned to Metropolis eight months ago."

Garrett took another pull on his cigarette and let me take in this detail. Kirklin never accepted transfers from Suitland because he assumed the agent in question would be sent by Garrett to keep tabs on him. He liked to recruit his agents from Metropolis, specifically from programs for troubled youths, a stark contrast to the tweedy men and women that composed Garrett's core staff in Suitland. My first two years at the agency, I had sent in requests every few weeks for permission to contribute to various projects being run in Metropolis. After my twentieth rejection, I received a note on Kirklin's letterhead asking me to tell Garrett he said hello.

"That seems strange given Kirklin's paranoia."

"He wasn't paranoid," Garrett said. "I was spying on him."

Garrett put his cigarette in the side of his mouth and pulled a file folder as thick as a phone book from a shelf behind him. He seemed to admire its heft before dropping it onto his desk.

"Whenever I tried to sneak candidates directly through Kirklin's recruitment process, he'd end up having them shadow his interns. So last year I entered Biggs into the station assignment pool with an internal note that I didn't think he was right for policy work. Kirklin hired him a week later. Since then I've had Biggs monitor Kirklin's behavior to report on anything strange."

He pointed to the file folder on his desk.

"This is January to February of this year."

"Biggs was comfortable with this?"

"He was excited to work in Metropolis. I also approved some sewerage project in Tucson for him. I thought he was going to do a cartwheel on his way out. But now he's gone quiet along with the rest of Kirklin's people. We need someone to make contact with him. The attacks in Metropolis and on headquarters are connected and I think Biggs might know enough to convince the board to open our investigation to outside law enforcement."

Garrett ashed his cigarette into a mug bearing the agency's seal. I didn't appreciate the gesture, but I told myself that these were difficult times. He wasn't himself.

"That means I need someone in Metropolis," he said. "It has to be someone I trust, because the board can't know I'm going around them on this. And this Biggs thing has to be worked fast. Because whatever this is"—he held up the printout of Esperanto—"it isn't over."

I started to understand why I was sitting there. Despite my unpopularity, I knew the staff at headquarters down to the mailroom. Every once in a while Garrett liked me to help him pull a name for an assignment. To find Biggs he'd need an agent with experience in the field and enough discretion to keep the board from finding out, but one young enough to be unphased knocking on strange doors for an out-and-out goose chase. It'd be tough putting together my recommendations on such short notice. And with the board challenging projects left and right, no one was going to want to leave their desks until they were sure their portfolios were safe.

Garrett didn't need to know the details, so I just told him I'd take care of it.

He thanked me with a rasp in his voice I attributed to the smoke. As I excused myself and rose to leave, he started to go through Biggs's file.

"And don't worry," he said, a moment before I realized I'd misunderstood, "I won't be sending you out there alone."

2

The agency maintained a small airfield just inside the Beltway near Marlow Heights. Garrett had sent instructions for me to meet him there at 9:30 A.M. so he could brief me on Biggs and introduce me to whatever agent would be coming along as my second. At a quarter to nine I was already sitting on one of the red plastic benches in the small lounge attached to the control tower.

I faced the window overlooking the runway, which glowed a ghostly white under the overcast sky. The air in the lounge was stale and mixed with the pinch of burned coffee coming from the old percolator in the corner. There was an uneasy flutter in my stomach and in the dim reflection of the lounge's window I could see the desperate look of a fitful night's sleep.

Not only had Garrett's demeanor in our meeting left me worried, but in all my time at the agency I had never been assigned a task so completely outside my expertise. Most of my work fell within the scope of improvement implementation and project management. The most investigative work I'd ever done was when I helped evaluate a water treatment center in Duluth and ended up proving that improper sanitation practices were responsible for the mysterious uptick in beaver deaths in the surrounding area. But testing the gums of a beaver corpse for toxicity levels wasn't the sort of preparation I expected to help me investigate an apparent act of terrorism.

I tried to stoke my optimism by reminding myself that I'd finally been assigned to agency business in what was without question the greatest American city. I wasn't the type of agent to conduct a personal errand while on official business, but I hadn't been able to keep myself from packing my old Nikon. Over the past few weeks my fellow enthusiasts on the Trains of Yore message boards had been raving about a special exhibit on model trains at the Metropolis Transit Museum. Whenever I was in the city, I made a point of visiting the MTM, with its collection of retired railcars displayed in a beautifully renovated ironworks. I loved to wander between the cars, watching decades of engineering genius unfold with the satisfying inevitability of a bedtime story. Due to the urgency of Garrett's request, this might have been my first time to Metropolis without such a visit if it weren't for the fact that this new exhibition included one of the rarest model locomotives in existence. It was the 1:64 DR-88, or "Steam Beetle," as the actual train had been known due to its low, rounded appearance. Manufactured in a limited run by the O'Neil Brothers in 1898, there were only a few dozen models in circulation and one in mint condition was worth upwards of $250,000.

When he was alive, my father kept a Steam Beetle on the desk of his little office at home. The model had been gifted to him by his father. He had no idea it was worth more than our entire house or my parents' modestly successful dessert shop, Thompson Family Frozen Yogurt, which they owned and operated in our hometown of Steubenville, Ohio. As a boy I had loved that locomotive. Partly because it was beautiful, but mostly because it belonged to my father. I knew perfectly the weight of that engine in my hands, the brisk chug of its coupling rods when you pushed it, the faint scent of oil that someone long ago must have carefully rubbed on its axles.

When my parents left in the summer of 1998 to attend the National Restaurateur Conference in Rochester, my father lent me the model to console me over my fear of being left with our only living relative, Great-Aunt Juniper. As he handed it to me, he crouched so we were eye to eye and told me that he and my mother would be on a train just like it. Something about this comforted me at the time, though looking back the memory betrays my father's shocking ignorance about trains, since the Steam Beetle had about as much in common with a modern passenger train as a human being does with a lungfish. Nevertheless, I remember putting the train under my arm and hugging his leg after he rose. The light pressure of his palm on the top of my head. My parents were supposed to be back in six days but instead were crushed to death in that wrecked passenger train an hour outside Buffalo.

Two months later Great-Aunt Juniper died of what was believed to be an aneurysm-related tumble down the stoop of her old bungalow on her way to fetch the mail. I was apparently the one to discover her and call the ambulance, but to this day all I remember of my time with her is a stretch of worn orange carpet, a sunlit hallway, and an unfriendly calico cat with a clouded eye. I managed to keep the locomotive with me for a year or two in the foster system before I made the foolish mistake of taking it to school one day for show and tell. An older boy on the bus, amused to see me holding it, took it from my hands and threw it out the window. I heard it clink distantly in the street as the bus rushed between cornfields and the boy laughed as if he'd just done the most natural thing in the world. I got off at the next stop and hurried into an unfamiliar road to where I thought it'd been thrown, but I never found it.

I knew Garrett's assignment deserved my full attention, but the remaining Steam Beetles were mostly in private collections and the chance to see one in person was rare. I planned to ask someone at the MTM to take a photograph of me with it, a prospect that felt genuinely exciting to me, a reclamation of something long lost.

I was brought back to the airfield lounge by the sound of a car door slamming. I stepped outside to see Garrett and an agent I didn't recognize already standing on the tarmac. There was a healthy wind and I had to hold on to the fedora that Garrett liked all us agents to wear when we were on duty out of doors.

Garrett was standing in a trench coat looking up into the clouds, while the agent he had brought with him watched me approach. The agent seemed unimpressed and soon looked down to inspect his own tie.

I put down my bag and said good morning to them both. Garrett turned to me and nodded, pulling an envelope from inside his coat and handing it to me.

"Some details on Biggs. Find him and get him to tell you whatever he can."

He stepped to the side and gestured to the other agent.

The wind was picking up and he had to shout in order to make himself heard.

"This is your partner, so to speak. He'll explain everything to you on the plane."

I greeted the man, but he continued to observe me without comment. Garrett took the envelope from my hand, tucking it into the inside chest pocket of my blazer.

"I need you to keep this all as quiet as possible, Henry. The board can't know what we're up to."

Then, in what seemed like an odd gesture, he removed the tie clip he was wearing and slid it onto my tie.

"Thank you," he said. "The agency thanks you."

He slapped me on the shoulder and headed back toward his brown Crown Vic in the parking lot without looking back, his body hunched forward in the wind. He gave an all clear sign to the tower, after which I heard the whine of engines starting up. The man who was to be my partner stood with his hands in his pockets, watching the plane taxi over. He was handsome with a healthy tan, the sort of person you didn't often see around headquarters. He had a thick head of blond hair that was a little longer than I liked to see on an agent, though it was parted neatly, giving him a slightly classic look. I supposed this must have appealed to Garrett's nostalgia enough that he wasn't bothered by the fact that this man was walking around without his hat. All agents hated the fedoras, with the exception of Kirklin's people, who never wore them, but it was precisely because the rest of us hated them so much that it was seen as poor form to shirk wearing them.

These thoughts distracted me so that it took me a moment

to realize he and I were staring at each other. Embarrassed, I looked away and began to examine the tie clip Garrett had given me. It was made from a silver-colored alloy and was ordinary looking except for its size. It fit the width of my tie nicely, but the front bar was a full inch from top to bottom, making it look like I was wearing a money clip. When I looked closer I also saw several small apertures across its front. I ran my finger over them and noticed that the clip was warm to the touch.

"Don't play with that," the man said. His voice was filled with such sure authority that I obeyed him even though the rebuke seemed ridiculous.

"Sorry," I said. "I'm Henry."

He turned to face me and I noticed that his eyes were a bright and familiar shade of blue. I took a step forward and held out my hand.

"Nice to meet you," he said, keeping his hands in his pockets.

The plane pulled into its boarding position and I wasn't able to make out what he said next over the noise from the engines. It sounded like he was trying to tell me something about OWEN. I asked him to repeat himself, but the jet's automated door was already opening, its small flight of steps gently touching down on the runway. He gestured for me to pick up my bag, then walked toward the plane ahead of me. The clouds had made it dark enough that the tower decided to flip on the edge lights along the runway. They flashed with a jolt just as the agent was stepping over them. I was startled to see his body flicker and briefly become transparent before adjusting to the dramatic change in light. That was what he had been trying to tell me over the sound of the jets.

It was his name. OWEN.

The only plane available on such short notice was one of our four-seaters, so OWEN and I were forced to sit uncomfortably close, facing one another in two of the cramped cabin's disproportionately large white leather armchairs. Among other things, I was busy mulling over the convincing groan of leather that had sounded as OWEN took his seat as well as the way the seat's padding seemed to give beneath him as if it were supporting real weight. I was also trying to determine, the way one might when left alone with a dog or a small child, just how aware of me this image of a man was and to what extent he and I would be able to interact. As the pilot chatted with the tower, OWEN was busy looking around the cabin inquisitively.

"I know everything there is to know about planes," he said, after some time. "But I've never been *on* one."

I was surprised by his tone, which was boyishly self-assured. Before I could think of anything to say in response, the plane started to take off. As we shot up the runway and began our ascent, OWEN turned around in his seat to watch the pilot with guarded enthusiasm, like someone interested in seeing a card trick performed despite the fact that he already knew the secret that made it work. Once we reached altitude he chuckled to himself and turned back around, satisfied with either the performance of the pilot or the nature of flight in general. He then exhaled deeply and clapped his hands together, the sound of it echoing sharply in the small cabin.

"Okay," he said, sounding reluctant to get down to business. "How can I be of assistance?"

"Actually," I said, "could you start by telling me what you are exactly?"

He considered the question.

"What am I? Well, I'm a 3-D projection of the agency's supercomputer. And what you are is a bipedal ape with high manual dexterity and a brain that's only really impressive if you take into account the fact you grew it yourself. Now maybe you'd prefer to ask a slightly less insulting question, like *who* am I?"

"Oh," I said, "I didn't mean any offense. Who are you?"

"I already told you. The name's OWEN. Try to keep up."

I told him this all seemed remarkable and he smiled.

"Now you're getting it," he said.

The technical wonders involved in allowing me to converse with OWEN on an agency jet as if he were a fellow passenger seemed staggering, not least of all because the technicians at headquarters had only recently gotten OWEN back up and running.

Even after everyone was given the all clear to resume using OWEN-linked technology, we were all reluctant to do so. Agents who worked on the top floors had been taking the stairs instead of risking getting stuck in the elevators and, despite several memos I circulated reminding everyone that it was a fireable offense, no one had any compunctions about keeping our secure doors propped open with office chairs.

For research queries, the physical archives had become suddenly popular, its once empty stacks now abuzz with agents who felt more comfortable compiling their reports and analyses the old-fashioned way.

Garrett had released a statement apologizing for the fact that the virus had exploited a secret self-destruct function in our phones, which was supposed to have been used only in individual cases to protect confidential agency data. Replacement phones with the self-destruct function removed had already been distributed, but most agents had opted to pay out of pocket for their own private cell phones. I had gone to the Iverson Mall myself to purchase a mobile phone that was in my bag still waiting to be activated. In short, trust in OWEN was at a nadir and I wasn't sure how I felt about the fact that Garrett had sent me on such an uncertain mission with some OWEN-tech as my only ally.

Before the virus, OWEN had been working almost at capacity on a constant basis, but now he said his usage was practically down to zero, something he seemed to take personally. He described the aftermath of the virus with some embarrassment. From his point of view the whole thing had been like a terrible fever in which he was both himself and not himself, his own components performing tasks without him while he looked on in horror. Though the way he used the phrase "human error" to describe the various security loopholes that had allowed a virus to be uploaded in the first place made it clear that he directed blame more at the agency's technicians than at himself.

According to OWEN, the whole situation couldn't have come at a worse time. The agency's R&D division had been working on his projected interface for years, combining the latest developments in optics, deep learning, sonic projection, nanotechnology, and more. The attack had happened just as they were entering the final stages.

"I'm still not feeling entirely myself," OWEN said. "But Gus felt that given the recent unpleasantness it was important to demonstrate my effectiveness."

The Gus he referred to was the aforementioned Dr. Gustav Klaus, a renowned mathematician and computer engineer whose seminal work on parallel processing had earned him a Nobel Prize and the coveted Sterling Motherboard from the Kilbe-Klanck Institute. He was OWEN's creator and developer, though OWEN spoke of him with the sort of irreverent familiarity that one might use when describing an eccentric relative. It wouldn't have surprised me if Klaus had encouraged this attitude. OWEN's name purportedly stood for Object-Oriented Database and Working Ekistics Network, though many suspected that Klaus had just retrofitted the acronym so he could name the supercomputer after a beloved younger brother.

Klaus had personally designed the hardware for this new interface, which OWEN pointed out was the large tie clip I was wearing, containing a series of projectors as well as an array of sensory equipment. Klaus had also developed a complex system of parameters that OWEN referred to as "verisimilitude protocols." These parameters controlled everything from the way his projection automatically adjusted to surrounding stimuli to his basic disposition when interacting with others.

To hear OWEN tell it, his introduction to human

interaction had consisted primarily of talking to Klaus and watching movies with him. It was common knowledge that Klaus's preferred genre was old gangster films, his lab walls decorated with large color posters of *Pépé le Moko* and *Each Dawn I Die*. OWEN spoke fondly of the films of Kurosawa and claimed to have a great admiration for Charlie Chaplin, but it was nothing compared to the way his face lit up when he talked about James Cagney or Edward G. Robinson.

Klaus's love of mobsters could be seen in his massive pompadour of gray hair and penchant for loud suits. This vanity seemed to be a gift that had been passed down to his newest creation. As we spoke, OWEN grew preoccupied with his own physical appearance, looking down to adjust the pattern of his tie or the cut of his suit through an apparent act of will. He would frown with concentration and sprout cuff links and pocket squares and boutonnieres, his voice becoming distant while he answered my questions, as if anything I said was clearly of secondary importance to his deciding whether or not his blazer looked better with a peach carnation or a plum-colored pocket square in a four-point fold.

When I asked him if he could focus on our conversation, he asserted that he was able to focus on everything in his immediate vicinity at once. With the aid of sonar, infrared, satellite relay, and all the other complicated sensors and data feeds managed by the clip on my tie he was able to see everything from the back of my head to the pilot's mustache and the plane's position over the Atlantic. He was able to combine all of this sensory data into a single synthesized impression while continuing to sit across from me and fiddle with his tie.

Apparently there were hundreds of identical tie clips back in Suitland waiting to be distributed to the other agents. OWEN explained that the ultimate goal of the new interface was for each agent to enjoy the service of someone who not only had access to our database but *was* our database, someone who could check the status of every electrical grid in the country in real time, report on traffic conditions, and cite building codes off the top of his head. These clips would also be able to capture an unimaginable amount of raw data just by means of that agent going about his or her normal duties throughout the city. Working in conjunction with our existing drone program, our agency could come closer than ever to a perfect system for monitoring the progress and needs of our nation's cities. It was an undeniably thrilling vision for the future of the agency.

Though, he was also rather frank about the fact that the project had missed several important deadlines and gone severely over budget. After all the additional setbacks that followed the virus, it was obvious why Klaus had jumped at the chance to use the interface to impress Garrett.

In terms of how useful it actually was in its present form, I remained skeptical. But OWEN seemed confident enough in himself for both of us. As our conversation returned to his various abilities, he became much more animated and even stopped adjusting his clothes awhile. When I asked how his body managed to make an impression on his chair, he demonstrated that it was an optical illusion by creating a similar indentation on one of the cabin's empty seats. As far as the groan of leather was concerned, he pointed to one of the apertures on my tie clip and told me that it was able to throw sound up to one hundred feet at over 180 earsplitting decibels. When I asked him how this was possible, he waggled his fingers like a magician and switched subjects, pointing to another aperture that he explained could project images around obstructions. He had me hold my hand three inches in front of the tie clip to show how, using just the silver clasp of my watchband, the lens was able to continue projecting his image sitting across from me without interruption. I also knew from my own experience that he'd had to step directly over a 200-watt runway light before his projection had been forced to carry out any perceivable adjustments. Even more incredible was when he projected light onto my person, camouflaging me to the cabin's interior so that I appeared almost invisible. Pleased by my astonishment, he went on to perform impressions of Garrett and Klaus, taking on their shapes and voices with an amazing degree of accuracy. OWEN referred to these skills as "emergent capabilities," meaning they weren't intentional consequences of his design but were simply possible given the makeup of his interface. While Klaus had been aware of some of them, OWEN had stumbled upon most of them himself.

However, these fascinating displays soon degenerated into him cycling through a few dozen hairstyles, asking for my opinion on each. I mentioned that I never worried much about my hair when I was out in the field since Garrett preferred us all to wear our hats. I gestured toward the fedora resting on my bag near my feet in an effort to use our present conversation as a teachable moment, but OWEN only looked down at the hat and laughed.

"Oh, I know," he said. "You all look like idiots."

I was surprised by this comment, as I was by the fact that he was now holding what appeared to be a tumbler of whiskey, its cut glass glinting in the soft light of the cabin.

"It's a program I wrote for myself," he said, noticing my interest. "When I take a sip, a series of complex math problems are generated that overwhelm my interface's processors. It diverts resources away from my less essential functions like social intelligence and inhibition."

He described this process with pride, as if drinking on the job were an innovation that rivaled the lightbulb. Not wanting to take too much credit, he admitted that he had come up with it by watching Klaus drink in his lab late at night. When I asked OWEN what purpose this program served, he only frowned as if it were the wrong question and took another sip before smacking his lips and saying, "It relaxes me."

"But do you think it's appropriate?"

"Ah," OWEN said, winking. "Don't worry about that. Your boss doesn't want an official record of any of this because he can't have the board find out. He had me put up a memory partition, so you're the only one at the agency who has access to the data I gather while we're in Metropolis. We can do whatever we want."

He held up his glass, toasting our good fortune.

"All the same," I said. "I'm going to have to ask that you not drink while you're assisting me."

He stared at me blankly for a moment and then began to laugh so loudly that I saw the pilot turn around and look disapprovingly back into the cabin. As OWEN's laughter subsided, he congratulated me on what he seemed to have mistaken as a witticism.

"I was a little worried about you, Thompson," he said, pointing a finger at me and squinting. "I mean, you've got all those complaints in your personnel file about what a pill you are."

He immediately held his hands up to distance himself from this comment, adding, "Their words."

"Complaints," I said. "There have been official complaints about me?"

OWEN shook his head.

"The important thing is that you and I are going to have a fine time," he said.

I didn't respond to this last bit of encouragement and made plans to draft a report to Garrett on my concerns regarding this new interface. While it was certainly an achievement in many ways, it had also already proven itself to be incredibly self-indulgent and rude. I also thought it might be a good idea to start dropping a few hints to Garrett about Klaus drinking in his lab.

OWEN misinterpreted my silence as anxiety over our mission.

"Don't worry," he said, polishing off the rest of his drink and leaning toward me. "Whatever's going on out there, I'll figure it out. I'm literally the most intelligent entity on the planet. I have the equivalent of 4,239.23 human brains."

"Is that right?" I said. Even though he was only a projection, I still felt his face was a little too close to mine.

"Yup," he said, settling back in his seat. "I did the math." He began to refill his glass with a flask that appeared in his hand out of nowhere before adding, "I *am* the math."

For the rest of the flight OWEN seemed content to drink,

change the cut of his suit, and experiment with different facial expressions in a large handheld mirror that he pulled from one of his pants pockets. I figured once I got to my room in Metropolis, I could ditch the tie clip someplace safe and go about my business.

In an effort to avoid any further small talk, I turned to face one of the plane's windows and thought about seeing Metropolis again. Over the past few years I had been to the city only a handful of times for conferences and the like. Though, I did have a nice collection of guidebooks on the city, which I enjoyed flipping through from time to time. As a USMS agent, one couldn't help but have an affection for the place.

I remembered seeing it for the first time when I was nineteen years old. The National Engineering Academy had closed its dormitories for the winter holidays and the students with families had climbed into their parents' cars while I loaded up my book bag with a loaf of white bread, two packs of bologna, an extra sweater, and a few of my favorite textbooks. I walked through the snow to the nearest bus station, where I bought a ticket to see the city that the social philosopher Pierre Abernacky had once called "the great crucible." I planned to spend my vacation staying in youth hostels and stomping around in the cold, examining storm drains and bridge abutments. During the long bus trip out, all around me people dozed and farted and complained about the bus's broken heater. I was perfectly happy making sandwiches on my knees and reading Andre Denard's *The Anatomy of a City* for what must have been the tenth time. When Metropolis finally appeared on the horizon, massive and startling, a woman sitting behind me gasped. I felt the surge of significance only a teenager can feel. In that moment I had been certain that Metropolis was somehow wrapped up in my destiny, that it would be the place where I would show the world who I was.

The years since then gradually tempered this certainty. By the time I received Kirklin's final refusal to let me work in Metropolis, I wasn't even sure if I wanted to anymore. Metropolis had already become the pinnacle of everything an American city could be, whereas all over the country there were smaller, struggling places that could use my help.

During our plane's descent, all that could be seen stretching off in every direction was a dense mass of glass towers, the complexity of it all beautiful and nightmarish. My task of understanding any aspect of what had happened here seemed absurd. To distract myself from the fact that I was alone, I looked over at OWEN, who was too occupied with his outfit to notice me. Arching an eyebrow, he tried switching his navy necktie to a plaid bowtie and then, horrified, switched immediately back. I was left with nothing to do but watch as the towers of Metropolis grew closer, eventually swallowing us up. When we touched down I thought once more about that youthful fantasy of mine in which I saw the city serving as some grand stage where I would demonstrate my true worth. Only now I found myself hoping it wasn't true.

3

Many cities impress and please us because they are such perfect examples of human order. Here one thinks of the great European capitals, the streets of Paris lined with orderly rows of five-story Haussmanns or the open-air museum of Rome, where it feels as if not one building has been erected without first considering the argument of the city as a whole. The occasional flourish or internal variation in which one of these places self-consciously attempts to step outside of itself only reinforces the impression that everything there is in fact the product of a single unified thought, a calm and artful expression of humankind's mastery over its environment.

Metropolis is no such city. Described by former poet laureate Anaya Davis as "the million-city city," Metropolis is a clash of competing visions. Art deco skyscrapers dating back to the rise of the automobile stand alongside modern glass spires and sidescrapers that run along whole avenues. Buildings with programmable facades adjust themselves into pleasing shapes under the shadow cast by the knobbed steeple of a two-hundred-year-old cathedral.

The perfect grid of broad streets occasionally gives way to labyrinthine tangles where cobblestones still push up through the pavement, cramped streets winding through old neighborhoods of two-story brick buildings that tempt those passing through to imagine a thousand rainy afternoons in the 1800s or drunk sailors getting lost on some bleedingly hot summer night. These reveries are inevitably interrupted by the sudden sight of buildings stretching vertiginously overhead or by the powerful rush of air from a vent underfoot as an express bullet train races uptown.

This mix of old and new was a major aspect of Kirklin's legacy. Of the 623 skyscrapers in Metropolis, over seventy of them were built during his time as station chief. Through his influence he streamlined the city's once complex and restrictive zoning codes and also balanced out the power of the Landmark Preservation Office by helping establish the Office of New Works. Just as the LPO worked tirelessly to protect the city's architectural treasures, the ONW worked equally hard to seek out low-density buildings of less significance that could be demolished to make way for higher-density structures. Through the healthy tension between these two offices the city had managed to maintain its twentieth-century charm while still keeping its housing prices relatively affordable, allowing a greater number of people to enjoy the city. And Metropolis was first and foremost a place to be enjoyed.

Now that the Industrial Age was largely over in the United States, Metropolis had survived by becoming a pleasant, exciting place to live. Most employers had become so mobile that the most effective way for the city to attract citizens was by offering a seemingly endless variety of amenities, so that what had once been merely a by-product of the city's thriving economy was now one of its most reliable anchors.

This wasn't terribly different from the progress of other

consumer cities. What made Metropolis unique was the sheer scale and rapidity with which it had embraced this version of itself. The number of bars and restaurants alone was enough to overwhelm, many of them offering highly specialized and unique experiences. When browsing through my collection of guidebooks I was often forced to wonder what it meant when an establishment described itself as a "post-apocalyptic cabaret" or a "calypso-style hookah cantina." The city offered everything from casual vegan dining to internationally acclaimed bistros that served only live seafood. Depending on the neighborhood, you could find street vendors selling pork buns, sabich, cups of borscht, skewers of meat dipped in yellow sauce, and small spotted eggs with their tops broken off, served raw and with a dash of ink-black hot sauce.

Those seeking entertainment could participate in augmented-reality bus tours, gawking through headsets from open-topped buses. There were television tapings, holo-theater murder mysteries, fringe improv clubs, warehouses occupied by guerrilla art happenings. There was jazz on the roof of the Hamilton, musicals in the Tort Amphitheater, the enormous indoor water park at the Bertram Center, the forty-story botanical garden towers standing on either side of Fourth Avenue, connected to one another with sloping glass walkways made to look like a cascade of vines, and the lake in Coldicott Park, where tourists could take rowboats to a lush island and explore its cool, stream-fed grotto with its transported ruins of an ancient Greek village.

Of course, all this extravagant fun lent itself to the perception that Metropolis was just a playground for the rich.

But the city's progressive social programs—most of which had also been aggressively expanded by Kirklin in recent years—as well as its wealth of opportunities had also made it an ideal place for those starting out. When the middle class began its mass exodus to the suburbs in the 1950s, the population of Metropolis was sustained by the underprivileged and a massive influx of immigrants. First-generation Americans made up roughly half of the workforce and the city was home to the largest Russian, Greek, Lebanese, Indian, and Chinese enclaves in the Western Hemisphere. To this day, foreign-born citizens accounted for over $700 billion in economic activity and they did so in both skilled and unskilled roles. They made up half of the physicians in the city as well as half of the retail workers. They were more than half of the licensed nurses, half of the hospitality industry, and a third of the executives. And the grandchildren of many of those middle-class suburbanites who left behind city life for their wood-frame split-levels were now doubling back, abandoning the monotony and high unemployment rates of low-density living, selling their hand-me-down SUVs and pickup trucks to put down deposits on studio apartments in the East Side.

With over 35 million people squeezed onto 1,200 square miles of land, there had never been any question of trying to manage Metropolis the way we did other cities, monitoring them from afar and sending out agents like me whenever necessary. Garrett had once asked me half-jokingly what I thought would happen if Kirklin were to get hit by a bus. He sounded a little intrigued but mostly troubled by the idea of a Center City–bound K1 bus sending Kirklin to his final reward. His concern was that there was no way for us to know how to take responsibility for Metropolis in the event of an emergency since we had almost no idea how the station was run.

But while those of us in the analog world were forced to piece together most of our information about the station through gossip and Kirklin's oblique updates, OWEN was able to speak about operations in the city with a surprising familiarity.

"His people had been acting weird for a while," OWEN told me as we waited to be taxied to our gate at Bixley, a relief airport in the North Side. He still seemed a little tipsy, but I thought it might be a good idea to see if he knew anything useful before I ditched him at the hotel. I asked him what he meant by "weird" and he carefully fed his glass, still half-filled with booze, into his chest pocket as if saving it for later. He then rubbed his hands together and projected a document in the air between us.

"Look at this," he said. "Not only did they request two hundred gallons of nitric acid last June, but they put it on the same form as a bunch of caving harnesses and back-mounted chemical sprayers." He shook his head at the form and clucked his tongue. "Now there's a hole in Eleventh Avenue and you chumps never saw it coming."

"Wait, you're saying our people in Metropolis destroyed their own facilities?"

OWEN laughed before realizing I was serious.

"Henry, the station burned down in the middle of a weekday. Don't you think it's strange no one found any bodies?"

"Does Garrett think they were involved?"

"I'm guessing that's why he put you on a plane to Metropolis."

OWEN's theory seemed far-fetched. Garrett's interest in Biggs made it clear he had some suspicions about the Metropolis branch, but OWEN was talking about sabotage as if it were a foregone conclusion.

"If you knew the request was suspicious," I said, "why didn't you warn us?"

"My contextual intelligence was still underdeveloped," OWEN said. "When this request was submitted I was basically a filing cabinet. An amazing, amazing filing cabinet."

OWEN brought up a set of spreadsheets and pointed out several budgetary irregularities he'd found by independently auditing the reported expenses for Kirklin's station. He said he'd uncovered hundreds of expense reports from Metropolis in which costs seemed to have been deliberately inflated. A purchase request for two hundred parking cones had been billed to the agency for $17,000, or $85 per unit, which meant unless those parking cones had been encrusted with semiprecious stones, they'd been less than a bargain. And Kirklin had recently doubled his station's expenditure on uniforms without hiring a single person. OWEN estimated that upwards of $400 million of agency money was unaccounted for, and possibly much more.

I wasn't sure how seriously to take the analysis of a supercomputer who by my count was seven drinks deep, and so I told him that for the time being I was only interested in the task at hand.

To prove that he knew what he was talking about, he started to analyze all the travel requests I had ever submitted. From that information alone he was able to tell me that I was single and had no siblings, information that wouldn't have been included in my personnel file. When I confirmed that he was correct, he smiled and added, "And both your parents are dead?"

A look of pain or anger must have moved across my face, causing him to pump his fist in victory.

"See?" he said.

Convinced he'd earned my trust with his dead-parent gambit, his voice took on a more conspiratorial tone.

"If I'm right, we probably haven't seen the worst of it," he said. "We should be careful out there. His people could be everywhere."

"This isn't one of Klaus's movies," I said. "We're just here to ask some questions."

OWEN shook his head.

"You won't be able to ask anyone anything if Kirklin's agents slit your throat and leave you in a dumpster."

"What?"

OWEN shushed me and peeked out one of the plane's windows to watch the airport's line crew as they marshaled us into position.

"I don't like it," he said. "Too many eyes."

I tried to protest, but he shushed me again.

"Don't worry," he said. "I've got an idea."

Suddenly I was sitting across from a white French bulldog.

"Kirklin could be watching the airports," the dog said. "We'll have to disguise ourselves."

He waved his snout toward one of the airplane's windows,

inviting me to take a look. When I saw my dim reflection in the reinforced plexiglass I noticed that I was a large muscle-bound man with a red perm.

"OWEN, this isn't necessary."

"I wish I agreed with you."

"Get this off me," I said.

"You don't like it?"

"Off."

"You could offer some constructive criticism," he said. "If you don't like the disguise, we can tweak it."

He squinted up at me as my pecs began to grow larger.

"Stop it!"

"We have to go bigger," he said. "The masking works better if the projection is larger than your actual body. And try to be more deliberate in your movements—it will help with consistency."

In response, I stood up from my seat and shook myself violently. The projection began to bend and warp but managed to stay attached. OWEN nodded thoughtfully as the projection caught up with my movements.

"I think we've got it," he said.

I finally pulled the tie clip off and threw it. When it hit the front of the cabin, OWEN's projections flickered for a moment but didn't disappear. He stared up at me with his dog mouth hanging open in shock.

"This is ridiculous," I said.

He looked down at his paws for a moment, then raised his head and squared his small shoulders.

"Henry, you're hurting my feelings."

He saw that I wasn't going to be moved on the subject and the image of my disguise disappeared. He wagged his tail hopefully when he asked if he could stay a dog, but I shook my head no. Once he restored himself to his previous shape, he looked at me as if he expected me to apologize or thank him for changing back. But I just stepped through him, cursing under my breath and reluctantly picking up the tie clip on my way off the plane.

As we walked through the terminal, OWEN sulked, regarding with suspicion the crowds of fellow travelers passing all around us. Outside arrivals, a man selling tickets for a shuttle service shielded his eyes in the bright afternoon sun and asked us where we were headed. OWEN squinted at the name of the shuttle service on the man's T-shirt as if it were a fake detective's badge.

"Yeah, right," he said.

Then he stopped, thought for a moment, and told the man pointedly that we were going to Hershey, Pennsylvania. The man frowned and repeated this information aloud to himself as OWEN led me over to a line of self-driving cabs. Once we were inside, he refused to give the car's computer our destination, instead telling it which way to go a few streets at a time.

Beyond that he didn't say much. Garrett had told me not to worry about arranging my own accommodations in Metropolis, but it wasn't until OWEN told the cab to take the Matlin Expressway all the way down to Alpine and Block that I realized he had meant OWEN would be making the arrangements for me, meaning my hotel had been selected by a computer that was currently giving me the silent treatment.

We drove along the Lawrence River on Center City's eastern edge, eventually leaving behind the high, glinting office towers and luxury apartments of Center North for the lively, lower-density neighborhoods that spread out to the south. According to the dossier Garrett gave me back on the tarmac, Biggs lived not too far from Bixley, and I would have preferred to stay someplace close so I could interview his neighbors. I might have mentioned this to OWEN if he hadn't been sitting with his arms folded, turning in his seat every so often to look out the back window, a passive-aggressive gesture demonstrating his belief that we were being followed.

OWEN got us off the highway as soon as he could and kept us to small streets, where I noticed in store windows the various printed and handwritten signs that read FIND SARAH. Men and women on the sidewalks wore white ribbons pinned to their chests, a symbol of solidarity with the Laury family. The news program on the cab's video monitor was showing old footage of Sarah giving the commencement address at Metropolis University when she was only twelve years old. She looked self-possessed and dignified, even though the sight of a child in a mortarboard giving advice to her elders was almost comical. In the video she spoke of the importance of public service, her voice wavering with such obvious passion that it wasn't difficult to understand the city's sadness at her strange disappearance.

OWEN told the car to let us out just as we hit Chinatown. From there we proceeded on foot, navigating through crowds of tourists who were too busy snapping pictures of the fast-food signs written in hanzi and the red and gold paper lanterns hanging in shop windows to notice that OWEN was occasionally forced to drift right through them. He moved quickly, away from all the novelty shops displaying cheap Metropolis hoodies and knockoff handbags. It was several blocks before we reached what I thought of as Chinatown proper, where the locals browsed the fresh markets and old men sat in small parks, betting cigarettes on games of chess.

But after we turned down a few more side streets, the stillness of the neighborhood took on a more unsettling quality. OWEN came to a stop in front of a run-down brick building, the first floor of which was occupied by an abandoned take-out place with a half-torn awning that read FRIENDS FOREVER DUMPLING HOUSE. It was surrounded by desolate-looking apartment buildings and across the street was a warehouse with the words GAO FAMILY INDUSTRIAL RUBBER FLOORS painted above its loading bay. OWEN looked down the empty street in both directions to make sure we weren't being watched, and then waved me over to a windowless door adjacent to the main entrance of the late dumpling house.

"Buzz 2G," he said, sounding less than pleased to break the silence between us. "Bao-yu will let us up."

I hit the button and asked OWEN how he had found the place.

"The internet," he said, smiling up at the building with what looked like pride in a job well done.

I gave the place an uncertain look and asked him what travel website he had used. He rolled his eyes and said he "wasn't talking about *that* internet."

The entrance opened halfway and a woman in a blue tracksuit stood there holding the door as if she were getting ready to slam it shut again. OWEN quickly addressed her in Mandarin and her expression brightened. He then gestured toward me with his thumb and said something that caused her to laugh and open the door the rest of the way.

OWEN and Bao-yu continued to chat as we followed her upstairs. OWEN turned to me briefly on the second landing to explain that this building was an underground safe house for illegal immigrants. When I asked him if we were breaking the law by staying here, he frowned as if I had just reminded him of exactly what it was he didn't like about me.

On the third floor, Bao-yu took us down a narrow hallway, where the only light came from a window looking out on an alley. The hallway was crowded with shelves covered with dusty stacks of take-out menus and boxes of unused plastic bags with smiley faces on them. I had to help her move a broken cash register and half of a restaurant booth out of the way before she could open the door to my room. OWEN described it as a studio, but the space we were shown was clearly once a utility closet. Its plaster walls had been painted black and the room itself was empty except for a twin-sized bed in one corner, a small dark wood bureau, and a shadeless lamp resting on a folding chair near the door.

OWEN was standing at the window in the hallway, taking in the view of an opposing brick wall.

"This place is perfect," he said.

I placed my hat on the bureau and opened the top drawer. Inside was a small pile of men's white briefs.

Bao-yu said something in Mandarin and OWEN relayed the message.

"It's $1,500 for three nights and the bathroom is on the first floor."

"You're joking."

"She's doing us a favor," he said. "We're not her typical clientele and you look like a snitch. Also, she usually only accepts cash, but has graciously agreed to accept a wire transfer from the agency. I've already taken care of it."

"It's $500 a night and there's not even a bathroom up here?"

OWEN looked confused.

"Do people pay more to be closer to the toilet?"

"Sort of."

"Sorry, but you have to admit that's a little counterintuitive." He paused. "I could ask her to bring you a bucket?"

"OWEN, why am I staying here?"

"It's secure," he said. "I'm in charge of keeping you safe while you're here and this isn't the type of place anyone would expect you to stay."

"Listen," I said. "No one is looking for me."

Just then a buzzer sounded from downstairs and Bao-yu excused herself. OWEN waited for her to leave, then stepped into the room and put a weightless hand on my shoulder.

"Henry, I didn't want to scare you, but our cab was being observed."

OWEN brought up a satellite image of a city street. He pointed to the roof of a car making a turn through an intersection.

"That's us twenty minutes ago," he said.

He then pointed to the roof of a building in the upper-right-hand corner.

"And what do you see there?"

The image was pixelated, but I was just able to make out a circular shadow.

"That could be anything."

"Are you joking?" he said. "This is the exact outline of an H-311 surveillance drone. We're the only agency that uses them."

"All our drones in the city crashed."

"Except the ones in the Northeast Supply Hangar, which housed two reserve fleets and enough hardware to set up their own navigational relays."

"You think someone is watching the city with our drones?"

"I don't think they're ours anymore."

"OWEN, this is—"

"Serious, I know. But I think we lost them once we ditched the cab. It would have been easier if I had been allowed to use disguises."

There seemed to be no use trying to convince OWEN against the possibility of such complex forces at work, and so I decided it was time to carry on without him. The room had already been paid for and I figured he could continue to enjoy the hospitality of Friends Forever Dumpling House while I found a real room uptown. It was early still and there was enough time for me to swing by the transit museum to get my picture with the Steam Beetle before starting the hunt for Biggs.

From downstairs came the sound of Bao-yu yelling and slamming the front door.

"That could be trouble," OWEN said. "I'll see if I can get satellite visual on the street out front."

"Sure," I said, giving that preposterous room one last look and trying to decide if I wanted to walk to the museum or get myself pumped up for it by taking the subway.

OWEN looked up at the ceiling in concentration and I took the opportunity to reopen the top drawer of the bureau. I pulled off the tie clip and wrapped it tightly in one of the pairs of underwear before dropping it into the drawer. I shut the bureau and turned around just in time to see OWEN flicker out of sight. His voice was still able to move about the room, but was so muffled that his confused and urgent protests were barely discernible.

Bao-yu's shouting continued downstairs and was now accompanied by a loud banging. I grabbed my bag and hat as I made my way to the stairs. In the foyer, I found Bao-yu with her hands pressed flat against the front door, shouting at whoever was pounding on the other side. The door shook violently with each blow and Bao-yu leaned in as if to bolster it.

I was just asking her if everything was all right when the tip of an axe blade poked through the door. She screamed at the sight of it and fled up the stairs back into 2G. The door received two more massive thwacks before it collapsed into the foyer in a heap.

Standing outside were two men dressed in matching suits, which I was surprised to notice were the USMS cut. The men could have been mistaken for field agents except that their suits were black instead of the usual navy and they weren't wearing fedoras. The bigger one must have been at least six foot, five inches and had a thick beard as well as blond hair that came to his shoulders. He stood holding his axe at the ready and looking down at the demolished door as if to intimidate it into further submission. The other one was leaning forward as he brushed splinters and dust from the broken door off his pant legs. When he stood up and adjusted his thin black tie, it occurred to me with surprise that I was looking at Stuart Biggs.

As soon as he spotted me he tilted his head back and smiled, showing a mouth of large, perfectly white teeth.

"Henry Thompson," he said, "as I live and breathe."

"Stuart?"

He spoke rapidly to his companion in an odd-sounding language.

"Sorry, Henry," he said. "Nothing personal."

The blond man grunted in response and stepped toward me, lifting his axe. I fell back into the stairs as he took a wide, heavy swing, the axe blade narrowly missing my head and sinking into the wall.

I scrambled up the stairs as he started to tug the axe free, and it wasn't long before I heard them both heading up after me, their pace slow and deliberate.

On the third floor, I slipped into my room, shut the door, and began digging through my travel bag for my new cell phone. Once I found it I got down on the floor and did a quick army crawl under the bed. Luckily, OWEN had gone quiet in the drawer and I was hopeful that it would take the two men a while to find me hiding under the sagging twin bed.

When I hit the phone's power button, the screen lit up with a series of loud-but-welcoming chimes before asking me to register my Newtech mobile device.

Below I could hear the footfalls of the two men making their way up the stairs as they talked to one another in their foreign tongue. Their tone was casual; they could have been discussing anything from baseball to their plans for that night once they had finished killing me.

I pressed the button indicating that I did not want to register my phone. An hourglass appeared, rotated, and then disappeared before a message flashed onto the screen: "You must register in order to use your Newtech mobile device."

It sounded like the two men were walking down the third-floor hallway, smashing things indiscriminately as they went.

The phone asked me for my preferred username. I pushed random keys on the screen's keyboard until I had entered the required number of characters. When I hit submit the resulting text was autocorrected to "Salad daughter urine gut."

The hourglass reappeared and rotated. A new message: "The username Salad daughter urine gut is not available. Please select any one of the following usernames: Urine_Daughter912, GutSalad727, Daughter_Gut613!, _SaladUrine4, Daughter_Salad212, or Gut_Urine474."

I selected Gut_Urine474 and was immediately prompted to create a password. I mashed the keyboard again and hit enter, prompting another message: "This password is weak. Are you sure you would like to continue?" I selected yes.

The men's voices sounded close.

The hourglass reappeared and was followed by a flashing screen that congratulated me on registering and asked me to reenter my password. In the same moment, the door to the room flew off its hinges. The blond man pulled me out from under the bed by my ankle and rolled me onto my back.

Biggs stood in the doorway with his hands in his pockets. My phone had fallen to the floor and the blond man crushed it under his heel before raising his axe as if to bring the handle down onto my face. I instinctively brought my leg up and kicked, planting my heel into the man's crotch as hard as I could. He dropped the axe and fell to his knees.

Biggs gasped at the sight of his partner on the floor. He ran to his side and began to rub his shoulders.

"Spiru," he said. "Spiru."

I grabbed the axe as I stood up and held it in front of me, more as a partition than a weapon.

"Biggs, what's going on?" I said.

He turned to me as he continued rubbing his partner's shoulders, his eyes wide with anger and righteous disbelief.

"Can you give us a minute? Can you?! You kicked Teddy right in the testicles, which is a pretty cheap shot."

I was taken aback by the anger in his voice. There was also something strange about his enunciation that I didn't recall from our interactions at headquarters, a slight sibilance that wasn't quite a lisp.

"He was going to hit me with an axe."

"Yeah, with the handle," he said. "You would have been fine."

"He—on the stairs, he swung the blade at me."

"So he got carried away a few minutes ago. Does that mean he deserves to be kicked in the nuts for the rest of his life?"

Teddy moaned at the mention of his testicles. When he winced, baring his teeth, I noticed that his too were incredibly white.

"You mean you're not trying to kill me?"

"Not *here*," he said, sounding irritated. "We're supposed to throw you off the Lennox Street Bridge."

I was still unsure whether I was prepared to hit someone with an axe when Teddy rose to his feet with the pained expression of an athlete who knew he would be expected to tough it out. He took a deep breath and stepped in a slow circle, looking for his axe. As soon as he noticed I was holding it, he took a few steps forward and unceremoniously punched me in the face, taking it from me as easily as if I had handed it to him. I stumbled back toward the bed and Biggs resumed his position near the door, watching the proceedings with a look of grim satisfaction that suggested I probably wouldn't make it to Lennox Street.

Teddy lifted the axe and gave it another broad, heavy swing in my direction. I fell back onto the bed, which collapsed under me—making the blade land too high. As Teddy once again struggled to pull his axe from the wall I kicked him in the crotch a second time. The look of astonishment on his face was indescribable.

Biggs rushed forward and lifted me by my collar, then hit me in the mouth and threw me into the bureau, which splintered beneath me. The underwear came spilling out and I saw the tie clip slide across the floor.

Biggs wrenched the axe out of the wall and looked ready to bring it down on me himself, but suddenly OWEN appeared in the doorway and shouted for everyone to freeze. He was holding a samurai sword, which he leveled at Biggs.

"Drop the axe," OWEN said. "It's the nerd or your life."

He chopped the air with his sword and his interface produced a simultaneous whistling sound that was a little too loud to be realistic, though neither of the men seemed to notice. Biggs tossed the axe to the floor and put his hands up. Teddy was still on the ground and had to push himself up to his knees before following suit.

OWEN gestured for me to stand up, then ordered the two men to sit in the middle of the floor with their backs together.

"All right, Thompson," he said, pretending to be careful as he slid his sword into the scabbard hanging from his belt. "Tie them up."

Having just narrowly escaped a beheading, I found it difficult to match OWEN's poise.

"With what?"

"Oh, I don't know," he said, his voice taking on a certain sharpness as he pointed toward the demolished bureau. "How about some of those disgusting pairs of underwear over there."

"Or," Biggs chimed in, "you could use our ties."

OWEN silenced him by pulling his sword a few inches from its scabbard and slamming it back down.

I tied their hands behind their backs and noticed that their fingertips looked as if they had been burned. OWEN noticed it too and tried to ask the men about it. Teddy kept his head bowed in silent prayer over his genitals and Biggs just laughed, saying that they'd both been doing some ironing.

"How did you find us?" OWEN said.

"This is our city," Biggs answered. "No one sets foot here without us knowing."

"Who's us?" I asked.

OWEN shook his head like I'd just embarrassed him, then took a step toward Biggs.

"Where's Kirklin?"

Biggs smiled.

"Kirklin who?"

OWEN unsheathed the katana and raised it over his head before letting out a blood-curdling howl. He kept the sword overhead for a moment, observing Biggs for any sign that his resolve had been weakened. When Biggs only looked confused, OWEN frowned and put the sword away again.

He told me to get my things together and stepped out into the hallway before adding, "And don't forget your tie clip."

I stooped to pick up the clip and felt a sharp pinch in my back as well as a stiffness in my calf from when I'd been thrown through the bureau.

"Wait a second," I said, trying not to limp as I followed him into the hallway. I waved him away from the door and lowered my voice.

"Can you contact the police or something?"

"No," he said, crossing his arms in front of his chest.

"But aren't you, like, a . . ."

"Technological marvel capable of contacting every single police station in the world in one-billionth of the time it would take you to fall down a flight of stairs?"

"Yes?"

"You're right, but I'm not calling the cops."

When I asked him why not, he shrugged.

"Oh, a couple reasons," OWEN said. "First of all, on the plane you insulted my disguises and when I told you that my feelings were hurt you persisted in being rude."

I started to stammer out something in my defense, but OWEN cut me off.

"And when those goons showed up, I couldn't do anything about it because you put me in a drawer, and judging from the smashed, low-end cell phone in there I'm guessing when you needed help I wasn't even your first choice. So while I am obligated to help you get out of here alive, I'm not going to be taking orders from someone whose attitude is so completely toxic and unhelpful."

There was an awkward silence between us before I came out with the only thing I could think to say, even though it felt absurd saying it to a computer. "OWEN, I'm sorry."

He considered my apology a little while before accepting it.

"Wonderful," I said. "Can you call the police now?"

"No."

I took a deep breath. Keeping OWEN's apparent vulnerability in mind, I felt it was probably for the best that I remain calm.

"Why not?"

"Well," OWEN said, "I still don't really feel like it, because that was a terrible apology. Also, we were sent to the city to find out what Biggs knows, which we can't do if he's in custody. And lastly, according to police scanners, Bao-yu called 911 about seven minutes ago. So get your bag, get Biggs, and let's get out of here."

Biggs and Teddy had left a black Buick sedan at an angle in the middle of the street with its engine still running. OWEN's sword kept Biggs docile while I popped the trunk and loaded him inside. Once I was behind the wheel, I saw OWEN standing by the passenger-side door. He shoved his sword up the sleeve of his jacket, then cleared his throat. I followed his eyes down to a black soft leather briefcase on the passenger seat. I had to stare at it for a moment before I understood. I threw the briefcase into the back and he appeared in the seat next to me as I straightened the car out and pulled off down the street.

◦———◦

OWEN directed me to Velmer Hill, a dozen blocks of high-end office and residential buildings in the West Side. Taking a nervous right onto Quillent Street, I asked OWEN what in the hell was going on and why he had been asking Biggs about Terrence Kirklin. He glanced back toward the trunk and projected his voice into my ear as a whisper.

"Keep your voice down," he said. "And if you'd listened to me on the plane, you'd already know."

OWEN used satellite imaging to confirm no drones were

following us. He also managed to locate a federally owned building in the area that was closed for the day, its empty rooftop parking lot ideal for an interrogation. As we pulled up, I saw a large brass placard over its main entrance identifying it as the regional office of our colleagues at the United States Census Bureau. The agency enjoyed a good relationship with the USCB and so I was reluctant to follow OWEN's suggestion to ram through the steel security gate blocking the ramp to the building's roof. Only after he promised to help allocate $6,500 of agency funds to reimburse them did I finally rev the engine and plow through the gate, sending it sparking up the ramp in a twisted heap.

When we reached the roof, I drove through the lot to the far row of spaces marked for visitor parking. As I navigated our stolen Buick neatly between the painted lines of Visitor Parking 0001, OWEN looked around at the empty lot.

"You know," he said, "sometimes you exhibit what a psychologist might call 'internalized oppression.'"

"What's that supposed to mean?"

But he had already projected himself out into the lot, where he was peering over the roof's barrier wall down into the street. Even though he must have been using a combination of infrared, sonar, and satellite imaging to check if anyone had noticed us breaking past the building's security gate, the projection of OWEN was looking down into the street with a large pair of binoculars and occasionally licking his index finger to test the wind.

When he was satisfied we wouldn't be disturbed, he returned to the passenger seat and regarded me for a moment before again projecting his voice softly into my ear: "We have to interrogate him now. Are you up to it?" I hesitated before telling him I was. "You might have to punch him. Do you know how to punch people?" I thought for a moment, then shook my head no. OWEN shrugged as if to suggest he hadn't thought so and brought up an animation that hovered above the dashboard. It depicted a man's face opposite a floating, disembodied fist. Flashing arrows highlighted the fact that the thumb was curled outside the fist and that the impact should fall on the first two knuckles. There was a series of quick diagrams on appropriate stance and follow-through; then the fist began slamming into the man's face again and again, a thumbs-up icon appearing at the center of each impact. I held my clenched fist up to OWEN to demonstrate my form and he examined it for a moment before projecting a thumbs-up icon onto it.

"Are you ready?" OWEN said.

I nodded, then stared blankly at OWEN.

"You have to get out of the car and open the trunk," he said.

"Right," I said. "Sorry."

As we walked to the back of the car, something occurred to me. I took a few steps away from the trunk and lowered my voice.

"OWEN, are you going to pull out a samurai sword again?"

"Absolutely," he said, stepping away from the car himself and half pulling the sword from his sleeve as if he were trying to reassure me.

"Why a sword?"

"I told you," he said, taking the sword the rest of the way

out and slicing the air with it as he spoke. "I'm a Kurosawa fan. The katana is an elegant weapon."

"OWEN, did Klaus ever show you *The Magnificent Seven*?"

He lowered the sword and gave my question some thought, eventually snapping his fingers.

"You think a gun would be scarier?"

I nodded and he looked down at his sword briefly before whipping it off the roof.

"Okay, I'll try it," he said. "Also, can I just say? I really appreciate how you communicated that feedback. When you locked me in that drawer I started to feel pretty low, so I read through some of the self-help books available online. I finished about eighty thousand, and more than half of them suggested that discussion and compromise are the lifeblood of a successful relationship, whether personal or professional."

I told him that seemed perfectly interesting, but he ignored me when I tried to remind him of the bound man in our trunk.

"I read a book called *Excuse You*," he said. "It mentioned that it's important to be clear and honest when someone has hurt your feelings. That's what I always do, because I have what the book calls 'healthy impulses.' But it also said you need to communicate clearly when someone has behaved in a way that makes you feel valued and respected. So that's what I'm doing right now, Henry."

OWEN paused and then said expansively, "I'm communicating that to you."

"That's great," I said. "Maybe we can talk about this some more after we've interrogated Biggs."

"Oh, definitely, I'd like that," he said, sounding excited by the possibility of further discussion. "Also, if we have time later maybe I could summarize the compare-and-contrast essay Gus had me write on Sturges and Kurosawa. He said I managed to draw some very subtle parallels."

I wondered whether OWEN might actually be a more effective partner when he was upset with me, but I settled on telling him that sounded fun as I moved toward the trunk.

I opened it and inside Biggs was lying perfectly still, staring up at us without expression. Once I pulled him from the trunk, he stood behind the car, looking off into the middle distance with fatalistic resignation, as if he understood he was in danger but simply wasn't impressed by the fact. I took his elbow and jostled him, drawing his attention to OWEN, who was standing across from us.

"Henry just learned how to punch people," OWEN said. "He couldn't be more excited to give it a try. But if you answer our questions, I can make sure it doesn't come to that."

Biggs looked over his shoulder at the view of the city behind us and OWEN snapped to get his attention. When that didn't work, he pulled a gun from inside his jacket and cocked it. Biggs turned to face him, slow but obedient. I was discouraged to see that the gun OWEN had chosen was a pearl-handled Smith & Wesson that looked at least a hundred years old.

Already the interrogation was going poorly and I was dreading the possibility that I might have to punch someone.

"I'll start with an easy one," OWEN said. "Where is Terrence Kirklin?"

Biggs shook his head once and then smiled with his disturbingly bright teeth.

OWEN motioned for me to hit him. I steadied myself by grabbing his shoulder and brought my fist back a little too far, but otherwise I was pleased with how I carried the whole thing off. The punch landed squarely against his jaw with what felt like substantial force. However, the sense of relief I felt at having successfully followed OWEN's instructions was quickly replaced by horror when I saw that Biggs's teeth had come out. Not individually. All of them, together. His full set of teeth clacked once on the pavement and then fell in two halves, straight and shining, connected to a pair of glistening pink gums. The unexpected sight caused me to shriek briefly, but OWEN was fascinated. He bent down on one knee to examine them before calling out, "They're dentures."

Biggs stood with tendrils of drool hanging from his soft, empty mouth.

His words were slurred when he spoke, but I was able to make out, "Not bad for a first punch."

"Interesting," OWEN said, still examining the teeth. "No fingerprints. No dental records."

He looked up at Biggs and said, "You're staying right here until we know everything. I can have Henry work on you all day if that's the way you want it. Or you can end this now and save yourself the discomfort."

Biggs seemed to consider OWEN's threat for a moment before shrugging to himself and head-butting me in the temple. My vision blurred, but I heard his quick steps moving away from the car and OWEN shouting for him to stop. My eyes refocused in time to see him make it to the low concrete barrier separating the parking lot from the building's ledge. He paused there to shout something in another language and then rolled himself off the building.

There was a long silence before we heard the impact down below. OWEN let his revolver disappear and buttoned the top button of his blazer.

"Well, that was a weird thing to do," he said.

I pulled myself up and walked over to the barrier. OWEN appeared next to me and we both looked down into the street at Biggs. His hands had stayed tied behind his back and he had pitched himself forward like a diver so that his skull received the brunt of the force. We stared down at the resulting gore in disbelief.

"He didn't seem depressed to me," OWEN said after a while. "Did he seem depressed to you?"

I turned away, feeling sick.

"What was that language?" I said, trying to make sense of what Biggs had just done. "What was he saying?"

OWEN projected himself back toward the car and seemed to be examining the scene of our interrogation.

"Esperanto. He said Kirklin would find us before we found him."

OWEN might have taken that moment to point out that he was right, whatever was going on had something to do with Terrence Kirklin. But at the moment he was otherwise engaged. He had moved to the roof of the Buick with his binoculars and was analyzing automobile and foot traffic on nearby streets. He predicted we had ten minutes before the police showed up. He suggested we flee the scene unless I was confident I could convince the authorities we had tied up a man and taken him to the top of a building with no intention of throwing him off.

"Then what?" I said, still trying to understand how OWEN's mad speculations could be true. "Biggs was our only lead."

"Biggs was *your* only lead," OWEN said as he jumped down from the Buick. "I've got hunches enough for the both of us. Now let's move."

I grabbed my bag from the car, along with Biggs's briefcase. After searching the rest of the vehicle for anything of significance, OWEN projected another animation into the air between us showing a man using the cigarette lighter from a car's dashboard to light a necktie that had been inserted into the filler neck of a car's gas tank.

OWEN must have sensed my reluctance after the animation repeated a third time.

"The police will be here before you would be able to wipe the car down," he said, pushing his face through the animation. "And you humans get your DNA and greasy fingerprints all over everything. It's disgusting and incriminating."

On OWEN's recommendation I also picked up the man's dentures and threw them into the backseat as I was grabbing the lighter from the dash. When the spare necktie from my bag caught fire, OWEN shooed me away from the car. The stiffness in my calf that I'd noticed earlier was getting worse, but I managed a quick limp, carrying my bag and the briefcase toward the edge of the parking lot. By the time we reached the stairwell leading down to the street the car was awash in flames.

"Hey, look at that," OWEN said. "You got it on your first try."

There was a series of loud pops as the tires burst in the heat, followed by a wail of sirens in the distance.

"What do we do now?"

"We should find a cab and get out of here," OWEN said.

He pointed back toward the thick column of black smoke rising up into the clear sky.

"The cops frown on this sort of thing."

4

We found another self-driving cab and OWEN told it to head uptown. Thanks to my bad leg I almost fell as we climbed into the backseat, and so OWEN insisted on giving me an impromptu medical examination. He confirmed that there were some large slivers of wood in my leg and upper back, but assured me the wounds were minor and recommended I treat them myself once he found us another room. He then immediately launched into the introduction from his compare-and-contrast essay on *Seven Samurai* and *The Magnificent Seven.* Despite trying to sort through everything I'd just seen, I followed along in an effort to avoid the risk of hurting OWEN's feelings—a dangerous prospect, as I had learned. I was so focused on feigning interest that I failed to pay attention as he occasionally stopped to give the cab directions. I was therefore surprised when we arrived at Eldrit Plaza.

As the city's premier luxury hotel, it was certainly an improvement from the converted utility closet he had expected me to stay in a few hours ago. Yet I couldn't help but wonder what folks in Suitland would think when a five-star hotel showed up on an expense report. I didn't look forward to explaining why I had stayed at a hotel that *Zagat's* described as "a little slice of Dubai right in Center City Metropolis."

As we pulled up between the series of faux Persian columns leading to the hotel's bright glass entrance, OWEN told me we could come back to his paper later—he had just been in the middle of describing "the synthesis of Kikuchiyo and Katsushiro into Chico"—and explained that he had booked us one of the villas on the top floor. According to him, it was a necessary extravagance. The suite would come with its own security detail, and since lying low in Chinatown hadn't worked out he felt our only option was to place ourselves in the care of professionals. He read aloud a paragraph from the hotel's website boasting the number of foreign leaders who had stayed in the Eldrit's villas while they were in the city.

"It'll be safe as mansions," OWEN said.

"The expression is 'safe as houses,'" I said, pulling my bag and our stolen briefcase from the backseat.

"I have access to all of the crime statistics currently available," he said. "'Mansions' makes more sense."

He did most of the talking once we were inside, flirting with the AI clerk on the slender monitor at the front desk, an image of a young woman whose hazel eyes and dark hair swept up in a loose bun were clearly not lost on OWEN. I watched as he made himself gradually taller and handsomer as he arranged to pay for the suite with another wire transfer. She seemed to find him charming and laughed when he abruptly interrupted their transaction to try to impress her with some close-up magic. When she laughed and asked him how he had turned a deck of cards into an egg, he admitted that if he told her it would ruin it.

Meanwhile I was holding on to a nearby kiosk of travel brochures in an effort to keep weight off my right leg.

OWEN had insisted on disguising me and so I was wearing dark sunglasses, a leather duster, and a long, dirty beard. My appearance seemed to be cause for concern among the Eldrit staff. While I waited for OWEN to finish checking us in, I was asked to leave the building by two different hotel employees. Each time, OWEN turned from the front desk to explain that I was with him, and the employee in question would shoot me one last unfriendly look before reluctantly walking off.

The clerk must have noticed me staring impatiently at OWEN, because she eventually asked him in a half whisper if I was all right, to which he replied, "He has his moments."

OWEN called me over to register my thumbprint on the counter's scanner. As I did so, he asked the clerk if we could have a first aid kit sent to our room.

She looked concerned but said only, "Certainly."

She might have been about to say something else, but was stopped when we turned to leave and I accidentally tripped over a luggage cart and toppled down with it. Unable to help me up, OWEN instead bent at the waist and shouted down encouragement while I struggled to get back to my feet. When we made it to the elevator, the clerk was watching us with her mouth hanging open.

"She seemed nice," OWEN said as the elevator doors closed. He then whistled for the rest of our ride up to the thirtieth floor.

In a testament to the Eldrit's level of service, a first aid kit was already waiting outside our room when we arrived. I picked it up and touched my thumb to the door's biometric lock, which caused the room to open automatically. Inside was a massive suite with marble floors and a south-facing wall that was all glass, offering a panoramic view of the city. Just off the foyer was a large open kitchen and a lounge area with modern-looking furniture and an indoor pond complete with water lilies and ornamental koi. A recording of a woman's voice welcomed us to the Eldrit while I put down my bags.

"OWEN, how much did this cost?"

"A lot," he said, admiring the winding staircase that led up to the master bedroom. "I had to fudge the agency's budget a little. If anyone asks, this money went toward a community center in Little Rock."

There was a lot about this statement to give a conscientious agent pause. For the time being I was comforted by the knowledge that OWEN's continued financial breaches were not being reflected on my expense account.

Near the kitchen was a small guest bathroom, where I brought the first aid kit, placing it on the white quartz countertop next to the sink's raised ceramic basin.

OWEN appeared behind me, sitting on the closed lid of the toilet with his legs crossed and his hands folded over one knee as if he were there to help me get fitted for a tuxedo. He said he had a wealth of medical information at his disposal and that he was there to assist. I even found his presence comforting until I stripped to the waist and he seemed to blanch at the sight of the large splinters in my back. I then lowered my pants carefully, revealing a piece of wood in my calf roughly the size of a pencil. I turned to OWEN to get the benefit of his medical advice, but he just looked unhappily down at my leg and said, "Yuck."

With no expertise forthcoming, I yanked the wood out of

my calf without a problem. More difficult were the splinters in my shoulders, which I had to dig out with the first aid kit's tweezers while looking behind me into the vanity mirror over the sink. By the time I was finished, my back and leg were running with small rivulets of blood. OWEN was sitting with his hands covering his face. The tie clip on the counter was making a whirring noise and his projection began to flicker.

"You're so—vulnerable—I mean—I understood—on an intellectual level—but this—"

It seemed the films he watched with Klaus had only managed to prepare him for casual violence. He'd barely been phased when Biggs jumped to his death, but now watching me bleed from a few minor puncture wounds in that bathroom seemed to be more than he could bear.

He stood up and stepped through me toward the door.

"It looks like you've got this covered," he said. "So I think it'd be best if I just—"

Before he could finish his sentence, he turned into a French bulldog and fainted.

He lay there motionless in his dog's body with his tongue hanging out. Above him in bold white text was a slowly rotating error message. I decided not to try to wake him, in the hopes that I might get out of having to hear the rest of his compare-and-contrast paper.

I cleaned my wounds with rubbing alcohol, then took off my underwear and stood in the shower, letting the cold water stanch the bleeding. After drying myself off, I applied a large bandage to my calf and grabbed one of the hotel robes out of the linen closet, wrapping it around me as tightly as I could to apply some pressure to my back. I moved into the lounge, where I began to feel light-headed myself. I crawled onto one of the hard, armless sofas and, though it was still early, fell almost immediately asleep.

o———o

I was sitting at a desk in the middle of a warehouse. A large open space filled with rows of metal filing cabinets. On the desktop in front of me under the light of a small lamp was a stack of forms I was in the process of filling out, ticking boxes and writing complicated figures into empty columns. Once I had finished the last of them, I pushed the neat stack of forms toward the center of the desk, admiring my work. Then, *thunk*. A hand reached down and placed a pair of bright white dentures on the stack. I watched with some irritation as a pool of saliva steadily spread from beneath the dentures, making my writing run and become illegible. I looked up and saw a man in a dark suit standing over me. He laughed, showing me his empty mouth. Behind him, the drawers to the filing cabinets had all been opened and their contents were in flames.

I woke to the sound of OWEN sighing heavily and pouring himself a drink. When I sat up on the sofa, I saw he was standing by one of the villa's large windows, holding a glass of his dark liquor and staring out at the skyline. It was morning and the day was overcast, most of the buildings rising straight up into the clouds. I tied my robe and joined him where he stood.

"I'm working on a patch," he said as I approached, his voice sounding a little defensive.

"A patch?"

"A software update. One that will allow me to withstand the sight of your blood without further . . . incident."

"Are you embarrassed because you fainted?"

"Don't be stupid," OWEN said. "I'm a computer. I don't faint. The interface was just overwhelmed by the intensity of the situation and I inadvertently shut down for a moment."

OWEN's mood seemed to be deteriorating so I chose not to point out that he had more or less just described the act of fainting.

"Don't be too hard on yourself," I said.

He looked down into his drink.

"What kind of computer faints?" he said, though now it wasn't clear whether he was rejecting my choice of words or lamenting his performance.

I still had what I felt were legitimate concerns about OWEN's interface, but whatever was happening in Metropolis was beyond anything I'd anticipated. OWEN's assistance, as erratic as it was, seemed like my only chance to make sense of it. I thought it would therefore be in my best interest to keep him in a positive mind-set.

"You also stopped those men from killing me with an axe," I said.

OWEN turned from the window and regarded me with what looked like gratitude.

"That's true. I did do that."

"And then you helped me set that car on fire."

He chuckled and looked down at his shoes. "You probably could have figured out how to set it on fire yourself—"

"OWEN, I wouldn't have known where to start."

He was smiling now. "You really don't mind that I fainted?"

"Honestly," I said, "I'm more worried about your drinking."

He laughed and downed the rest of his drink, then projected himself around me in a hug. I took a step back, but his image remained fixed to me and I was forced to stand there until he was finished embracing me.

"This actually reminds me of one of the books I read yesterday," he said.

He released me from his hug but kept his hands projected onto my shoulders.

"*The Syntax of Friendship* by Dr. Eleanor Pomodoro. She says you have to think of a friendship as a paragraph and that when a friend expresses an insecurity, you should always try to reassure him or her without dismissing the feelings that he or she is trying to express. She says it's all about acknowledging the content of your friend's sentence without trying to correct his or her emotional grammar."

"Is that what I did just now?"

"Yes! And you also reassured me by bringing in a subordinate clause that highlighted some of my strengths and caused me to view my failings in a larger context. You made me see myself as I related to the . . ."

The excitement in his eyes suggested that he expected me to complete the phrase he had in mind.

I ventured a guess. "The rest of the paragraph?"

He nodded vigorously.

"Henry, you have to read this book. I just ordered a copy and had it sent to your apartment. Consider it a declaration of friendship."

Just my luck. The first colleague I'd befriended at the agency and it was an alcoholic supercomputer.

"It sounds to me," I said, doing my best to keep us on task, "like the sooner we find out what's going on, the sooner I can go home and read it."

OWEN considered this. And while he had already seemed more or less committed to our task, it was not until I suggested it was preventing me from being exposed to the work of Dr. Eleanor Pomodoro that he really came alive on the subject of investigating the attacks. He changed the pattern on his tie to a series of tiny daggers with drops of blood dripping from their blades.

"I swear to you, Henry, we will find Terrence Kirklin and make him eat his own eye patch."

I didn't know about that sentiment exactly, but the agency I loved was in crisis, my mentor's career was over, and the previous day I'd seen a coworker fling himself off the roof of a building after trying to kill me. The man at the center of it all was apparently Terrence Kirklin and I wanted to know why.

I grabbed the briefcase that had belonged to Biggs and dumped it out onto the glass coffee table in the lounge. Together we examined its contents: a roll of breath mints, a silver ballpoint pen, a hardbound book titled *Conversational Esperanto*, a bottle of prescription pills, and a yellow legal pad that was blank except for its first page, which was covered in some hastily written notes. The book on Esperanto was clean except for a few notations in the margins that looked innocuous enough and a stamp on the inside front cover that read EX LIBRIS SFEM. The label of the pill bottle didn't reveal much, just the drug name Ketaconazole. I read the name to OWEN in the hopes that he might be able to determine its significance. He was busy examining the notepad and I had to read the drug name a second time before he turned his attention to the bottle.

"Antifungal pills," he said. "His dentures must have been new, probably not fitted properly yet. Explains the breath mints."

Then, with the gracious tone of an adult who has decided to include a child in a serious conversation, he pointed toward some numbers in the upper-right-hand corner of the man's legal pad and asked me to take a look at them:

1000–2100

1000–2100

1000–2100

1000–2100

1000–1730

1000–1730

When I wasn't able to make sense of them, he looked pleased with himself and suggested that they were most likely a series of durations written in military time.

"Ten a.m. to nine p.m., Monday through Thursday. Ten

a.m. to five thirty p.m., Friday and Saturday. Null on Sundays. Those are the hours of operation of almost every public building in the city. Now look over here."

He pointed to a pair of sketches at the bottom of the page. One was an arrangement of adjacent squares that created a horseshoe pattern while the other was just a progression of intersecting lines marked with a series of Xs.

"I checked that pattern of squares against the floor plan of every government-owned building in the city. The scale is off, but I'm pretty sure this is the first floor of the Metropolis Museum of History."

He pointed to the second sketch.

"These Xs match the route for the Civic Pride Parade this Sunday, which will be passing one block north of the museum, closing down the surrounding streets."

"Yes?"

"On a day that the museum itself will be closed."

He looked at me as if the conclusions to be drawn from this were too obvious to mention. Though, when I asked him what it all meant, he shrugged.

"Oh, I have no idea," he said. "But if Biggs was interested in the history museum, then so are we."

5

The Metropolis Museum of History, MetMoH for short, is a beautiful ten-story building at the head of Attleman Park in Center City. It serves as the focal point of what is informally referred to as the museum district, a fifteen-block radius containing a dozen of the city's best cultural centers, home to some of the world's most beloved displays of art, science, and history. The MetMoH is by far the largest, with over three hundred exhibition halls featuring reconstructions of whole city streets as they appeared in bygone eras as well as a constantly changing array of the museum's over four hundred thousand cultural artifacts, including everything from Arthur Tyler's upright bass to the mummified remains of Spanker, a French spaniel that belonged to the city's first colonial mayor.

The building itself is also a notable work of art, the last to be designed by that great American Renaissance man Charles L. Webber. Its wide apron of granite steps leads up to a large portico with high vaulted ceilings and columns with neoclassical reliefs depicting prominent citizens of Metropolis throughout history; visages of former politicians and social reformers who had clashed angrily in real life now stand arm in arm, smiling serenely at patrons as they enter the museum.

OWEN and I were staked out in the natural history exhibit on the first floor, watching the crowds for any suspicious activity. The hall was a large rotunda with its walls covered in smoky murals of ancient forests and marshes. Arranged throughout the space were platforms bearing stuffed elk and mountain lions along with elaborate re-creations of the area's ancient megafauna. A stampede of life-sized mastodons dominated the center of the room. Nearby a massive short-faced bear glowered at nothing, while toward the grand entrance a six-foot-long giant beaver was frozen with alarm as if it had stumbled upon the museum patrons in a clearing. It was one of MetMoH's most iconic spaces, encapsulating the grand drama of the place as a whole and reminding visitors of the city's transformation from coastal forest to cultural epicenter.

It was also positioned just off the main entrance on the first floor so that all visitors were required to walk through it before branching off into the other exhibits. I had been skeptical about the idea of a stakeout, but OWEN insisted.

After entering the exhibit as museum guards, we found a nice location in one of the many blind spots of the museum's surveillance cameras. Across from us was also a surprisingly graphic display of a moose giving birth, which was driving enough patrons away from our general area that we were able to get settled without anyone noticing. OWEN was inspired by the impressive appearance of some of the megafauna, and so disguised us as a fake species of giant skunk that he named *Mephitis giganteus*. He brought up a low platform around us along with what he determined to be that skunk's ideal, leaf-shrouded habitat, allowing us to scrutinize the flow of patrons into the museum.

Hours passed and we still hadn't seen anything out of the ordinary. Dozens of children were led through the hall by nervous schoolteachers busy making sure their students were paying attention to the docents. Since Sarah Laury's disappearance was still popularly regarded as a kidnapping, many of the children were made to wear plastic whistles that hung from their necks with string. Every so often a child would blow experimentally into his or her whistle and consequently receive a sharp, whispered reprimand. There was also the expected throng of tourists as well as young couples out on lunch dates, using the more peculiar dioramas as an excuse to tap one another gently on the arm and point. There were the art students who sat on the low mahogany benches making sketches, and finally the dozens of elderly patrons who had only come to the museum for the exercise, pairs of them walking in slow, aimless circles.

OWEN's capacity for detective work had been quite impressive earlier that morning, but, perhaps because his social intelligence was still developing, his ability to draw helpful conclusions from his direct observations of the museum patrons seemed limited. He was intensely suspicious of the elderly patrons, a fact that became apparent when two women in their seventies power walked by our habitat. They were looking straight ahead, focusing on their low-impact cardio. OWEN perceived this lack of interest in the museum's displays along with their expressions of grim resolve as indications that they were up to something diabolical. He was also wary of two young boys who had broken off from their class and stopped in front of the moose birth. They were leaning on the velvet ropes surrounding the scene and howling with laughter.

"Two o'clock," OWEN said, waving his snout toward the boys. "I've got some patrons acting strangely."

"They're just kids, OWEN."

"So? Terrorists use kids all the time. They give them heroin and turn them into killing machines. Don't you read the news?"

"Is there anything to suggest they're working for terrorists besides the fact that they're children?"

"Well, somebody must have given them drugs at least," OWEN said. "They're laughing at that moose's vagina, but there's nothing funny about it. The artist rendered it perfectly."

"That's normal, OWEN. Kids think bodies are funny."

There was a prolonged silence in which I could feel OWEN looking at the moose's vagina and straining to see the humor in it. He was eventually distracted by the return of the septuagenarians as they completed their circuit around the hall and slowly approached our position. They stopped twenty feet away and began bickering while one rifled through the other's bright purple fanny pack. OWEN was no longer bothering to maintain the integrity of his disguise and was now watching the two with his eyes wide and his skunk nostrils flared. He seemed certain that one of them was about to reach into the pack and produce a hand grenade.

"Get ready to tackle those two," he said.

I whispered for him to get ahold of himself, but he was already counting down from three.

Fortunately that was when a tall man in a black agency suit entered the hall. He took a steno pad from his jacket and started to look up unabashedly at the museum's security cameras, taking notes.

The septuagenarians had resolved their argument and now appeared to be dividing an assortment of vitamin supplements between the two of them.

"OWEN," I said. "Over there."

"Don't worry," he said, keeping his eyes fixed on the women. "I see them."

"No, over *there*."

The man in the dark suit was now tucking his notepad back into his jacket and walking toward the exhibit on the Dutch fur trade.

"Oh, him?" OWEN said.

He seemed reluctant to give up his suspicion of the women, so there was no little disappointment in his voice when he recognized that the man I'd spotted was clearly suspect. Once we were certain no eyes were on our display, OWEN turned us back into guards and we headed over to the fur trade exhibit, where the man in the black suit was already taking the stairs up to the next floor. We half ran through the crowds gathered around reproductions of beaver felt hats and rusted muskets, then crept up the single flight of broad cast-stone steps after him. Heavy black drapes hung over the next exhibit's entryway and after I pushed my way through, we found ourselves surrounded by photographs of 1970s Metropolis: vandalized subway cars strewn with garbage, burned-out buildings, a group of children playing on the roof of an abandoned car.

We slowed down and pretended to browse when we saw that the man had stopped in the middle of the room to take more notes. A sign near the exhibit's entrance labeled it THE FORGOTTEN CITY. The room was documenting those days when all US cities were seen as little more than accumulations of blight. It was a time when the country as a whole was still convinced that low-density homeowners were somehow the solution to every societal ill and struggling urban areas were left to rot. A photo near the entrance showed an elderly woman crying on a fire escape. In the reflection of the frame's glass, I saw that OWEN had changed my disguise yet again. I was now wearing baggy carpenter jeans with holes in the knees and a stained undershirt.

"We're tourists," he said. "Newlyweds."

Beside me OWEN had taken on the shape of a beautiful young woman wearing cutoff jean shorts and an oversized Mickey Mouse sweatshirt. My reflection in a glass case revealed that I was also sporting a Toledo Mud Hens cap and had thick blond sideburns that looked like they'd recently been used to mop a floor.

"You know, I'm from Ohio," I whispered. "This depiction is a little ungenerous."

"I hate to break it to you, pal, but it's an averaged composite of all the obvious out-of-towner data I just collected downstairs. If you want a more realistic tourist disguise, you'll have to go back down there and skin one. Now follow my lead."

We sidled up to a series of screen-printed posters and

pretended to admire a handbill for some band called the KickMurders. It was an edgy collection by the MetMoH's standards, tucked away in one of the smaller exhibit halls. The place was empty except for our man. He had been studying one of the room's support columns and writing in his notebook, but now seemed distracted by a photograph of an underweight homeless man, shirtless under his army jacket and scowling at the camera. The man lowered his notebook and turned to face the picture, regarding it with what looked like concern.

"Excuse me," OWEN said, suddenly standing directly behind him. "Can you help me?"

The man turned and frowned.

"Help you?"

OWEN waved me over.

"Honey," he called out. "He says he can help us."

Before the man could object, OWEN launched into a long explanation about us being on our honeymoon all the way from Toledo.

"We got turned around," OWEN said. "And now we don't know the way back to where we're staying."

The man looked around the room as if remembering how much work he had to do, but, perhaps deciding it would be easier to send us on our way than risk any unpleasantness, asked OWEN for the name of our hotel.

"We forgot it," he said, the delicate face of the projection taking on an exaggeratedly pitiful expression with eyes that now seemed almost comically large.

"Well, if you don't—how am I supposed to—"

"It's nearby."

The man pinched the bridge of his nose and, to my incredible surprise, began guessing the names of hotels. When he mentioned the Tennison, OWEN squealed and clapped his hands.

"Oh! That's the one!" He pointed down to the man's notepad. "Do you think you could draw us a map?"

The man shook his head in disbelief and proceeded to draw the intersection of West 48th Street and Seventh Avenue. OWEN gave me a matter-of-fact look and pointed discreetly over the man's shoulder, where he was projecting the same punching animation as before.

When OWEN saw I didn't want to do it, he raised his eyebrows and began running the animation at twice its previous speed. The man was almost finished with his map when OWEN projected "DO IT" against the far wall in letters a full story tall. The words moved closer, began to flash.

The man looked up from his notebook and I hit him in the face as hard as I could. When I made contact with the bridge of his nose I felt the cartilage give way and I inadvertently shouted out an apology as he fell to the floor with his face in his hands, blood streaming through his fingers.

OWEN shouted at him, telling him to stay out of the history museum, then ordered me to grab his notebook. I tucked it into my suit coat and we ran toward the heavy tarp at the far end of the hall that was blocking off the adjoining exhibit, closed for renovations. I lifted the tarp and crawled underneath a few moments before the museum guards showed up, drawn by the commotion.

I stood by the covered doorway and listened to the guards

ask the man if he was all right. They encouraged him to stay still, but as soon as they radioed down for assistance, I heard him pull himself up and flee the room.

OWEN and I snuck out unnoticed into an exhibit on jazz, where patrons gathered around various 2-D projections of famous musicians and listened to them perform through rented headphones. OWEN had already transformed us into another pair of patrons. He had taken my criticism of his tourist disguises to heart, but only in the sense that he was now deliberately attempting to get a rise out of me. I looked down to see that I was now the attractive young woman, though her Mickey Mouse sweatshirt had been replaced with a baggier one bearing in hot pink letters the enigmatic slogan JUST PLOPPIN'. OWEN was a tall, gangly man with buck teeth and freckles. He wore cargo shorts that came down nearly to his ankles and a black, tight-fitting sleeveless T-shirt. Despite the signs everywhere prohibiting flash photography, he stopped every so often to raise a gigantic camera and snap pictures with a flash that made a powerful walloping sound.

He approached a projection of Nathaniel Tate in the middle of a ferocious drum solo and called over to me in a nasal exaggeration of a Midwestern accent.

"Hey, Tammy, look at 'im go!"

None of the museum employees seemed to take any special notice of him. He even paused to snap a picture of two nervous-looking guards as they patrolled the room.

"It's a good thing we're keeping an eye on this place," he said to me. "The security stinks."

He kept snapping pictures until we reached the cafeteria,

a sunlit room on the fourth floor with café tables and large tropical plants. We found a table out of sight and I pulled out the notepad. The first few pages were stained with the man's blood, but as I continued to flip through I saw that it contained a list of physical observations about the museum. He had almost every room mapped out by hand and had dutifully identified which were load-bearing walls and which were only dividers. Several rooms contained central pillars and for these he had labeled the position of each with a check mark.

We only had to glance at the notes briefly to know what they were. The various calculations and focus on internal supports suggested that these were the plans for a demolition using explosives planted inside the building. One page bore the museum's address and the date of the parade under the phrase "Laŭ ordono de T.K." OWEN translated it, "By order of T.K." I recognized the initials right away.

There it was, plain but befuddling. One of the most brilliant civic planners in the country was organizing a plot to destroy a beloved institution in his own city.

OWEN leaned back in his chair, looking lost in thought.

"What are we supposed to do?" I said. "We know what these drawings are, but the police won't."

He took a moment to send a few warnings to the MPD, though he knew I was right. We had no proof. No real details.

OWEN went quiet, concentrating, before eventually breaking into his toothy, tourist grin.

"I'll tell you what we'll do, Tammers," he said. "We'll stop 'em ourselves."

He raised his camera and the flash went off, blinding me for a moment.

OWEN's plan to protect the museum was surprisingly simple. If Kirklin's people were going to plant explosives in the building, what better way to stop them than if we were already inside? We checked out of the Eldrit and when no one was looking we stashed my bag in a model tenement on the museum's seventh floor. I planned to sleep there for the two nights leading up to the parade on Sunday. During the museum's hours of operation we wandered around the exhibits, keeping our eye on the place using OWEN's never-ending supply of disguises.

At night we investigated key points in the building's infrastructure to make sure no explosives had already been planted. OWEN had hacked into the museum's security system, a complicated exertion on his part, during which his only instructions to me had been to "shut up for a minute." But ultimately he was able to turn off the museum's alarms as needed and loop feeds from all the security cameras so the museum appeared to be empty in all the footage. This allowed me to climb into air ducts, pry open maintenance closets, and comb through some of the museum's more complex exhibits.

When I needed a break, OWEN and I tried to pass the time by playing cards with a deck I borrowed from the gift shop. But he was too good at counting them for there to be any real chance or fun involved. We even came up with a special set of rules to address what OWEN kept referring to as my "human handicap." I still lost. We toured the gift shop looking for other distractions and the closest we came was a chessboard, which we both lingered over if only to contemplate the staggering degree to which OWEN would have walloped me at a game of chess.

We ended up talking for the most part. About movies at first, but when we came to Gorcey Hallop's performance in *The Orphan Gang* the conversation turned to my upbringing. He and I stood in a room that was dark except for the low orange security lights. One could just make out the interiors of old textile factories and ironworks. As I began to describe the circumstances of my youth, I realized I had never said any of it out loud before.

It certainly hadn't all been bad. While the succession of foster parents to whom I was assigned often seemed ill equipped to deal with children, I ended up falling deeply in love with the foster care system as an abstract entity. No matter how often I was transferred from one house to the next, the rules that governed my care always stayed the same. The complex set of regulations regarding doctor visits, clothing allowances, religious freedom, nutrition, and closet space was a source of relentless consistency throughout my otherwise itinerant childhood. My foster parents were required to install locks on their medicine cabinets and conduct quarterly fire drills. I can still remember one of my foster families standing outside at eight in the morning in their pajamas, the parents swearing under their breath and consulting a stopwatch, their biological children glaring at me as the morning dew on the lawn dampened all of our socks. To me the scene was heartwarming. Because while my caretakers themselves were often ambivalent about such precautions, complaining about all the hoops that had to be jumped through in order to do a good deed, the rules always stayed rigidly devoted to my well-being.

When I was thirteen years old, I was moved to a home in Akron, Ohio, where on the living room coffee table I found a small packet of papers explaining my rights as a foster child. The first few items caught my eye:

1. The foster parent will adhere to the following:
    a. Permit the child to eat meals with the family, and to eat the same food as the family unless the child has any dietary restrictions.
    b. Allow the child to participate in family activities.
    c. Treat the child with dignity.

The list went on, but I was affected so deeply by item 1(c) that I had to put the packet down. After the death of my parents, I had become a serious and inward child, so the mention of the word "dignity," as I stood in another strange living room, filled me with an intense welling up of gratitude toward the benevolent, rule-generating body that my foster parents often referred to bitterly as "the goddamned government."

"So now you're the goddamned government," OWEN said.

He might have meant it as a joke, but I told him I was proud of it. He had referenced my personnel file on the plane and long before that I'd known I wasn't exactly well thought of among the other agents. I explained to OWEN that it was difficult to work with people who didn't truly understand the consequences of rules. If my foster parents had picked and chosen what rules they followed, what sort of life would I have had?

"Sure," OWEN said. "I get it."

He put his hands in his pockets as we strolled, looking up as if he were trying to recall something.

"There's only one thing I don't understand," he said. "I still have access to all the data from my old interface."

"When you were on our phones?"

"Right. Did you know that when the interface was at peak usage, over 90 percent of your colleagues regularly engaged with me in what could be described as small talk?"

"No," I said, not sure where the question had come from.

OWEN waved his hand to tell me he was being rhetorical. "Half your colleagues gave me nicknames. Some of them called me Odie. Others called me O-man. On account of my eyes, Emma Ackerman in Renewable Energy got her whole department calling me Deep Blue."

"I never realized you were so popular."

"You didn't notice that the team who won the agency's softball league last year called themselves the Supercomputers?"

I looked at OWEN seriously. "The agency has a softball league?"

He laughed.

"I guess that's what I'm trying to say. Henry, you were always yelling at me when I was a phone. Over a third of our interactions ended abruptly in a manner that I was programmed to interpret as anger. So my question is, if you're passionate about the work you do for the agency, if it's meaningful and important to you, then why don't you seem to be enjoying yourself?"

I was surprised by the question and told him that I liked the work just fine, but when it came to the people . . . My voice trailed off and I noticed OWEN looking at me, his eyes steady.

"I shouldn't have been so glib about your parents on the plane," he said.

It was a simple statement of fact, the way someone might say they didn't like fish or that the turnpike would have been faster. I knew it was probably as close as OWEN would ever come to offering up an apology on the subject, or any other for that matter. I thanked him.

"Come on," he said. "There's something I want to show you."

He led me to an exhibit on the history of technology and we stood there in the soft glow of the security lights, looking at the old adding machines and difference engines.

"I'm one of a kind," he said. "So I don't really have folks either."

He regarded a desktop computer in a diorama of a modern office and then turned to me and cupped his hands, holding them out between us. Above his palms appeared a projected representation of his mind. It was a bright, irregular mass with bulbous protrusions branching off and then growing together or spiraling away in thin tendrils of light that pulsed faintly. Inside the mass, I saw what looked like millions of small particles spinning rapidly and sending small arcs of electricity between them. It was as chaotic-looking a thing as anyone could imagine, but I told OWEN only that it was beautiful and he smiled.

He went on to describe to me the many anxieties of his new sentience. He said that while experientially he felt that he was here with me in Metropolis, he also knew that he was really back in Maryland, a thought that disturbed him, though he wasn't able to say why. We talked for a while about the many joys and pains of consciousness as we walked among the towers and vacuum tubes of room-sized computers that were immense and mysterious-looking in the dark museum.

The next night, I was nosing around the cafeteria for some food to steal and we found a stockpile of liquor in a storage closet. OWEN said I looked like I could use a drink, so we took a bottle of thirty-year-old Scotch and a turkey sandwich to a replica of a nineteenth-century pub up on the museum's sixth floor. The Jolly Pigeon was complete with warped hardwood floors covered in sawdust and a long, scuffed-up bar lined with unfinished stools. When I turned on the lights, the place also filled itself with a trill of fiddle music, the sound of stool legs scraping the floor, and the warm murmur of a quiet crowd. We sat at a low table in back that was lit by the flicker of the bar's fake gas lamps. There I ate my sandwich and we began to drink.

By my fourth pour, OWEN was standing across from me, miming something I couldn't quite make out. He was leaning forward and moving his hand back and forth as if he were using a frying pan or teaching a dog how to shake.

"Second word," he said.

"You're not supposed to talk."

He apologized and held up a placard that read "Second word."

Our earlier mistake had been in considering only games that relied on probability and logic, whereas charades was interpretive enough to keep things interesting. OWEN had at first been reluctant to try what he referred to disdainfully as a guessing game, but after he managed to get *The Shoot-Out at Pilgrim Creek* in just five guesses he was barely done congratulating himself before insisting that it was his turn.

In his first attempt OWEN had transformed himself into George C. Scott while trying to get me to guess *The Changeling* and I had to establish the condition that he wasn't allowed to use any of his imitations or shape-shifting capabilities. This had proven to be a significant obstacle for him.

"Frying pan?"

He stopped miming and stood up straight.

"No. What's the matter with you?"

OWEN had established the rule that whoever made an incorrect guess had to take a drink. But after a few rounds we were both drinking steadily without keeping track.

"Are you shaking hands with a dog?"

OWEN groaned in aggravation and then began to do the exact same mime a little more insistently.

I tried a few more guesses before OWEN declared me hopeless and slumped down at the table. He continued drinking while I finished off the rest of my sandwich, both of us realizing without having to say anything that we were too drunk to continue playing, though not necessarily too drunk to continue drinking.

"I was doing *Fortune's Pool*," he said. "The Sandra Malcolm movie."

"What were you miming, though?"

"Pool," he said, sounding defensive. "I was playing pool."

"But you were only using one hand."

OWEN smiled and nodded approvingly at the memory of his performance. "It was a trick shot."

He finished his drink and took in the Jolly Pigeon before refilling his glass.

"I *like* this place," he said. "If Kirklin's people want to destroy it, they're going to have to bring it down on top of us."

Sober, I might have mentioned OWEN's earlier point that he was safe back in Suitland. However, this didn't seem to occur to me as I refilled my glass.

"Damn straight," I said. "Anyway, Kirklin's men are just a bunch of stupid townie goons. And Kir—Ki—Excuse me. Kirklin is a big grumpy weirdo. If we see him tomorrow," I added, "I'm going to tell him that to his face."

"You should."

"I *will*," I said.

From there things degenerated into OWEN and me improvising new insults we imagined directing at Kirklin in person. The news coverage in response to Sarah Laury's disappearance had focused on the lurid implications of her running off with an older man, painting Kirklin as a presumed deviant, and so my and OWEN's insults quickly became both elaborate and obscene. They evolved into full-on sketches depicting Kirklin in a series of embarrassing and sexually compromising scenes with his own cousins as well as a small monkey also named Kirklin, which allowed for several humorous ambiguities. I was never much of a drinker, which was probably why I got carried away and added a dozen sexually aggressive leopards and a birthday cake shaped like his own face. OWEN was laughing so hard that my tie clip began to overheat. I drunkenly insisted that he remember everything we said verbatim so I could repeat it to Kirklin once we were face-to-face. He assured me that though drunk he was still a computer and that our living eulogy of Kirklin was at the ready.

"Good," I said, resting my head on the table. "Good."

I closed my eyes for a moment, waiting for a spell of dizziness to pass. I might have fallen asleep right there, but OWEN led me out of the Jolly Pigeon and into a dark street showing what Metropolis had looked like 150 years ago. At one point I demanded that OWEN carry me the rest of the way. I fell backwards into him, which set us off laughing as I struggled to get up off the cobblestones. When we eventually found our way to my tenement, I crawled onto a small cot and pulled a coarse, faded quilt over me. The last thing I remember was listening to OWEN humming the theme song to some old movie as he sat in the apartment's small kitchen and refilled his glass for what must have been the dozenth time.

I woke early the next morning to the sound of a loud military reveille. The noise jolted me awake into a half-conscious panic that gradually materialized into a sharp pain in my temples. I looked up to see OWEN sitting at the foot of my cot holding a bugle.

"Doesn't your program come with a hangover?"

"I think I'm still a little drunk," he said, putting the horn back into his jacket. "I tried bird noises for a while. Did you know that you snore?"

I was too nauseated to answer. I made my way out of the tenement to a drinking fountain and splashed water on my face.

"Kirklin's men are probably on their way," OWEN said.

After some experimental sips of water, I headed to the museum's lobby, where there was a phone at the reception desk. I dialed 911, telling the operator there'd been a break-in at the Metropolis Museum of History. I put the receiver down without hanging up.

OWEN nodded his approval and led me up to the third floor to a massive hall that was bare except for a few dozen vintage planes. The north-facing windows afforded us a view of all the spectators streaming toward Sixth Avenue and 46th Street, where the Civic Pride Parade would start within the hour. Already I could make out the distant revving of the motorcades and motorcycle clubs, while, closer by, children and adults alike were letting out long, baleful honks with the plastic horns they'd bought from street vendors. The room's southern windows overlooked Attleman Park, which was empty except for a trickle of spectators heading over to take their places along the parade route.

Twenty minutes passed before two police cruisers finally pulled up in front of the museum. We were relieved to see them, though we'd been hoping for a bigger response.

OWEN suggested we create a scene to goad the arriving officers into radioing for backup and before I could give the plan some measured consideration he was standing in front of me in the nude and holding a rocket launcher. He instructed me to get away from the windows in case the police opened fire, which I was only too happy to do. I watched from the middle of the room as he added a pair of bandoliers to his chest and changed the model of his rocket launcher until it looked sufficiently menacing. But just as he was about to vanish and reappear on the building's ledge, he took a step toward the windows and let the rocket launcher disappear.

"Hold on," he said, his suit flickering back on. "There's some movement in the park."

He called me over and we watched as twenty well-dressed men in matching raincoats emerged from a stand of trees and began walking toward the museum in a double line. The four officers had gotten out of their cruisers and seemed to assume that these men had something to do with the festivities. One of the officers waved them toward Sixth Avenue. When the men continued walking straight ahead, he opened the driver's-side door of his cruiser and issued them instructions through the car's public-address system. I couldn't make out what was said, since one of the parade's drum lines was passing us to the north, performing a series of escalating cadences. The men continued to close in and the officers gestured emphatically for them to stop. When the men finally did halt, they pulled assault rifles from their coats and dropped to kneeling positions.

OWEN and I were halfway to the stairs when they opened

fire, the bursts from the rifles mixing with the roars of the nearby crowds. By the time we reached the lobby the shooting had already stopped. There was the sound of glass crunching underfoot, which meant Kirklin's men had smashed through the exterior doors of the museum's foyer and now only had to break down the large oak double doors that opened onto the lobby. Soon there was the same methodical banging I had heard as Teddy hacked down Bao-yu's front door.

OWEN positioned us in the middle of the room and told me not to move unless he said so. Axe blades were beginning to make their way through the doors and with each blow slender rays of daylight cut through the otherwise dark lobby. I put my hands in my pockets to hide the fact that they were shaking. I also found myself thinking about my agency hat, which I had left on my bag back in the tenement. There was something about the prospect of being gunned down in the line of duty that made me feel suddenly homesick without it.

OWEN projected a bulletproof vest onto me with USMS stenciled across the chest in large white letters. Meanwhile, all around the lobby appeared projections of men in SWAT gear with assault rifles. Behind the lobby's information booth there was even a projection standing behind a chain-fed machine gun.

As the doors began to wobble and give way, OWEN turned to look at me, making a few small adjustments to my vest. The expression on his face was bittersweet.

"If they end up shooting you in the head or something, I

just wanted to say it's been a pleasure working with you, Henry."

I was still processing this sentiment when the doors burst open. Kirklin's men froze when they saw us. The laser sights of OWEN's projections were trained steadily on their chests and OWEN himself was standing at the ready with what I was relieved to see was a handgun from this century.

"US Municipal Survey!" he shouted. "Drop your weapons!"

Three men standing toward the front of Kirklin's squad were armed with axes, while the rest were holding rifles in firing positions. Their leader was a young dark-haired man wearing sunglasses. His new teeth were too large for his slender face so that his mouth looked full and threatening like a shark's. He glanced down at the initials stenciled on our vests as if he wasn't sure he had heard OWEN correctly and then smiled.

"So you guys militarized too, huh?"

He was loosely gripping a handgun and raised it to scratch his temple with the barrel as he looked around the room.

"Good for you," he said, his tone genuine, as if OWEN's SWAT team was the first sensible thing he had seen come out of Suitland.

"I suppose you're the ones who've been giving our guys trouble the past few days. A lot of our people are pissed about our friend you threw off the Census Bureau. Very unsporting—but I don't blame you. That's the way it is. To get anything real done nowadays you have to kill who you have to kill. Progress is war."

"Tell your men to drop their weapons," I said.

The man raised a palm to show he wasn't a threat, then holstered his weapon.

"They shouldn't need to," he said. "We're outpositioned and you have more firepower. What is that over there, an M60?"

He pointed toward the information booth and chuckled.

"Garrett must still be as old-fashioned as ever. Tell him to invest in an M240. Superior reliability."

"My partner told your men to drop your weapons," OWEN said.

The man considered this for a moment.

"You Suitland people never see the big picture, do you?"

He looked at us almost hopefully, waiting for us to understand what he meant.

"We're telling you to put your weapons down," I said.

"Let's try this for starters," he said. "We just killed four cops outside. Traffic is a nightmare because of the parade and we have a few teams running interference, but before long this place will be crawling with MPD. And you may have cleared your request for all this gear with Garrett on the sly, but I'll blow an appropriations committee in hell if he got approval for a tactical assault team from the board. That means the authorities have no idea you're all here playing army, which also means you couldn't have worked any of this out at the state or city level. As far as the MPD is concerned, you're just another bunch of lunatics with automatic weapons hanging around a couple of dead cops. So you're dealing with the same time constraints we are. And yet, you're all just standing around not killing us, which means I don't think you're going to shoot."

He took a step forward.

"Stay where you are," OWEN said.

The man smiled again, taking another slow and deliberate step in our direction.

"Feel free to kill me when I get too close."

His men began to move slowly into the lobby.

"This is your last warning," OWEN said, his gun shaking in his hand.

Kirklin's men continued their advance.

"Stop—stop right there," OWEN said.

The panic in his voice was over the top, like a stock coward in an old film.

"I'll shoot," OWEN said. "I swear to God, I'll do it!"

He was stepping backwards, his eyes wide with showy fear. Then he stopped, lowered his weapon, and looked off behind Kirklin's men.

"Wait a minute," he said. "What's that?"

Before they could turn around, an eleven-foot-tall clown with long fangs and tentacles for arms sprang up behind them. It let out a piercing shriek and swiped at them with its tentacles, making one of the men lose his balance and fall over, accidentally discharging his weapon and spraying several of his team members with friendly fire.

"It's worse than we thought, men!" OWEN shouted to his SWAT team as he motioned for me to withdraw from the room. "There's a clown monster!"

OWEN's projections opened fire as we fell back to the natural history exhibit. Kirklin's men retreated into the foyer, dragging their wounded away from the clown and the convincing hail of bullets from OWEN's SWAT team.

There was a freestanding map of the museum in etched glass that I had assumed was real, but which shattered when the clown picked up one of OWEN's SWAT team members and tossed him through it, sending a realistic spray of glass across the lobby floor. As the other projections continued to fire, the clown howled in pain and began to drip yellow blood, which bubbled and steamed where it fell.

"OWEN, what is that thing?"

We were sitting behind the open entryway leading into the natural history exhibit.

"Klaus let me watch some horror movies once in a while. Did you ever see *Blood Clown*?"

I shook my head no and we both turned to watch as his monster ran screeching across the lobby, its tentacles vibrating and dripping slime.

OWEN shrugged. "It was only okay."

In the foyer, some of Kirklin's men were administering first aid to their wounded. Others were kneeling by the doorway, awaiting orders and trying to avoid the constant ping and rattle of OWEN's fake gunfire as well as the clown's wild charges.

Their leader was standing behind them, taking in the battle between OWEN's projections in the lobby with the annoyed look of an intelligent man trying to make sense of something impossible. After the clown unceremoniously bit off the head of a SWAT team member, the man stepped over one of his wounded and headed out into the lobby.

His men watched as he approached OWEN's monster. It let out a few warning shrieks, but the man continued across the lobby and eventually stepped right through it, waving his hands in front of his face as if he were clearing away a cobweb. He then paused and watched as the SWAT team disappeared.

OWEN looked disappointed.

"I was hoping it would take them a little longer to figure it out," he said.

In the lobby the clown stepped back two paces so it was once again standing in front of the man, who looked up at it with impatience. It reached one of its tentacles down past the elastic band of its brightly colored pants and pulled out an enormous revolver. It leveled the gun at the man and pulled the trigger. Out of the barrel popped a flag bearing the USMS seal.

"Bang," the clown said and then vanished.

Without waiting to see how Kirklin's men would react to this strange display, OWEN and I fell farther back into the natural history exhibit, where we hid behind a diorama of taxidermied otters. With the front doors of the museum smashed open, music from the parade flooded into the building. As OWEN mulled over our next course of action he absently drummed his fingers on his knees to the Beach Boys medley coming from an approaching marching band. I strained to hear any police sirens, but there were none.

The group's leader was issuing instructions to his men in Esperanto, which OWEN was kind enough to translate in my ear. His translations came off stilted, but it stood to reason that Kirklin's men were new to the language and so speaking in a pidgin dialect.

"They are only images," the man said. "Lower your weapons so they do not convince you to shoot one another again. We have lost enough colleagues."

OWEN's face lit up.

"Hey," he whispered to me, "they think you're a projection too."

As Kirklin's men entered the exhibit there was a glimmer of mischief in his eyes.

"I'll create a distraction," he said. "You look for the man carrying a blue duffel. I spotted him in the lobby. Get the bag."

I didn't have to ask what was in it.

"Will a distraction work?" I whispered. "They know you're a projection."

OWEN grinned, his features beginning to shift into another disguise.

"Exactly," he said.

He transformed himself into a man with dark eyes and a nose that came to a delicate, birdlike point. It took me a second to realize that I was looking at myself. The resemblance was uncanny, except OWEN's version of me looked slightly more confident than I did about running into a pack of terrorists and commandeering their explosives.

"We'll take care of everything," he said. "You just worry about getting the duffel."

"We?"

He pointed to my right, where seven copies of me were crouching behind the otter diorama with us. One of them waved.

I poked my head up between two otters to get a look at the men as they moved through the hall. Their leader still had his gun holstered and was walking confidently at the head of the group with a fire axe in one hand. His men held their rifles with the barrels pointed conscientiously down and away from one another. There was a single unarmed man toward the rear whose left elbow had been bandaged with a necktie that looked soaked through with blood. In his right hand he gripped a large navy-blue duffel.

I ducked back down and was surprised to see that OWEN's copies of me had doubled in number. I crawled to the edge of the diorama and was preparing to sprint out toward Kirklin's men, when one of my copies stood up and let out a loud battle cry. His call was answered by other copies, who had now spread throughout the hall. Different versions of me sprang out from behind display cases of gemstones and animal skulls or rappelled down from the ceiling on black nylon ropes.

Kirklin's men, skeptical after OWEN's previous performance, continued to head deeper into the museum without paying any attention to this new commotion. Even as my duplicates offered up one last unanimous howl and made their charge, none of the men so much as raised a rifle.

I let a few of the projections get out in front of me before I joined the stampede, making sure to imitate their battle cry so I wouldn't seem out of place. As the first wave of projections sailed harmlessly into Kirklin's men, I was close behind. In the confusion of bodies, I reached through the torso of the duplicate directly in front of me and landed a hard blow on the wounded elbow of the man carrying the duffel. He cried out and I was able to pull the bag from his other hand easily.

I didn't get far before the man started shouting, "La pakon! La pakon!"

Once I had the bag, OWEN modified his projections, so they were all holding identical bags. Some of them stood around throwing duffels back and forth as if playing a round of keep-away. Others climbed up onto stuffed bison and elk, riding them like mechanical bulls and swinging the duffels in cowboyish circles over their heads. I even saw myself waltz past wearing a tuxedo and tails, holding up a duffel bag as my partner.

OWEN's voice spoke in my ear, telling me to take the bag farther into the museum. I tried to blend in with my doubles, but I must have been walking with too much purpose because the head of a nearby mountain lion disappeared in a spray of gunfire.

I ducked into a hallway that ended in a pair of double doors under a cloth banner that read METROPOLIS OF THE FUTURE. As I pushed through the doors OWEN turned on the exhibit's lighting and sound systems, so that for a moment I almost thought I'd made it outside.

The model street was empty and from overhead came the ambient noise of traffic softened by the whine of electric motors. A compact street-cleaning vehicle glided toward me, its sides outfitted with ultraviolet air scrubbers the size of oil drums. OWEN instructed me to hop on the cleaner to put some distance between me and the entrance. It rushed noiselessly up the street, carrying me past storefronts advertising composting toilets and solar-powered window units. The exhibit featured 2-D projections of smiling citizens who wore sun hats and worked in vertical community gardens the size of parking garages or stood ready to feed perfectly cubed paper waste into pneumatic chutes.

The cleaner approached an alley, which OWEN told me was my stop. I hopped off and hid there, watching as Kirklin's men entered the exhibit. A woman's voice came over the loudspeaker and began to talk about the growing dangers of extreme weather. Corrugated storm shutters rolled down from awnings to protect storefronts and the woman's voice instructed any patrons to open the umbrellas provided to them by their docents. An unseen sprinkler system turned on, blasting the street with rain as the voice explained that the hyperabsorbent pavement could take in over nine hundred gallons of water a minute. OWEN didn't turn on the sprinklers over the alley so I was able to keep dry as I watched Kirklin's agents slog through the rain. OWEN explained that he was maxing out the weather system's wind shear to make the walk as unpleasant as possible. Thanks to OWEN there was also a velociraptor on the sidewalk just ahead of them. It was dressed as a newsie in a small rain-wilted hat and a vest. It was holding a stack of soaked newspapers in its claws and shouting loudly enough to be heard over the weather.

"Extree! Extree! USMS foils terrorists!"

OWEN cued an impressive flash of lightning to distract the men further, then opened a dry path leading to a utility exit and told me to get the bag out of the building. The exit opened back on the foyer, where I was surprised by one of

Kirklin's agents who must have stayed to look after his wounded colleagues. He shoved me against the wall and started to wrestle the bag of explosives away from me.

That was when I performed what I was not proud to realize was, when frightened, my preferred method of attack. I had to knee him in the crotch three times before he let go of the bag. When he finally fell to the floor, the cravenness of my approach was apparent even to OWEN, who sounded perplexed as he congratulated me on a job well done. There was a thoughtful pause before he added, "Do you need me to show you the punching animation again?"

I tried to explain myself, but OWEN interrupted me to suggest a quick sprint out into Attleman Park.

"We should be in the clear the rest of the way," he said. "But if we run into any more of Kirklin's guys, try to defend yourself in a way that will reflect well on the agency."

"I don't mean to keep doing that," I said, jogging through the foyer. "I was scared."

"I understand," OWEN said. "But moving forward let's try to keep everything above the waist. I want to be able to tell myself we're the good guys."

I gave OWEN my word as I fled down the museum steps. Outside, it sounded like the parade was being broken up. From Sixth Avenue there was the dull roar of a frightened crowd punctuated by the sound of police whistles.

I was well into the park when a line of MPD cruisers finally came screaming toward the museum. Soon after, Kirklin's men emerged from the main entrance and took up defensive positions on the stairs. The cruisers all pulled to a stop at hasty angles as the men began to shoot. Officers ducked out of their cars and crouched behind them for cover before returning fire.

The terrain of the park rose slightly before sloping down to a small creek, at the head of which was a stone culvert. I stashed the bag of explosives there, then hid behind one of the park's natural outcroppings of bedrock.

I was comforted by what I assumed to be the sound of police helicopters approaching from the south. But when they finally appeared over the park, aggressively low, I recognized them as two traffic helicopters that had previously been the property of the USMS. They were now painted black and retrofitted with machine gun turrets.

At the sight of the helicopters, the police began to scramble for better cover in the museum's statuary garden. The helicopters hovered over the museum steps, firing on the police while also lowering rope ladders. Kirklin's men made their way to the ladders, occasionally stopping to contribute to the suppressing fire that was keeping the police pinned down among the statues. The last one up was the squad's leader, who turned toward the museum and gave it one last bitter look before beginning his climb. Once he was inside, the helicopters both raised their ladders and tore back down through the park.

The officers slowly came out from behind their statues and I had OWEN project a police uniform onto me so I could tell one of them about the undetonated explosives in the park. As I approached, I saw that the museum's exterior had not escaped the firefight undamaged. Dozens of large windows were shattered and its facade was pocked with bullet holes. But it otherwise seemed to be in good shape and I was occupied with an overwhelming sense of pride, knowing that despite Kirklin's best effort, one of the world's finest museums was still standing.

"We did it," I said, smiling at OWEN, who was now walking beside me, wearing a police uniform of his own.

He looked up at the building and laughed.

"I bet Kirklin is—"

He was interrupted by a loud explosion a few blocks west. Within seconds there was another explosion from the opposite side of the park and the earth shook. These were followed by a series of loud booms that were so close together they seemed to come from everywhere.

Towers of smoke began to rise up all around us in the distance. There was a roar of panic from the dispersing crowds on Sixth Avenue. The officers in front of the museum rushed about, shouting to one another and climbing into whatever cruisers were still drivable. OWEN checked the satellite imaging to tell me the locations of the explosions. His voice went soft. I thought of what Kirklin's agent had said, the problem with us Suitland types. We never saw the big picture. The Metropolis Museum of Art, the Brandt Modern, the Montgomery, the Talmore Collection, the Motion Picture Archive, the Metropolis Science Museum, the Naymen Center, Saber Hall. All of them. Destroyed.

6

We gave an officer the location of the duffel, then headed toward Sixth Avenue. There, thousands of people were in the middle of a mass exodus, the police attempting to guide everyone away from the explosions. The crowd had pushed past the barriers, so that the entire street was flooded with spectators and performers alike. Next to me on the sidewalk a young man in a band uniform stood hugging a tuba and crying, looking up in disbelief at the dark plumes of smoke in the sky. A few sputtering floats crawled through the mob with face-painted jugglers and young women in dance costumes sitting on top like weary, ridiculous soldiers fleeing the collapse of the western front.

OWEN and I kept heading east toward the river. Everywhere people were standing in front of shops and office buildings, hugging each other or pacing or reading reports to each other from their phones. When we reached the river we found a long esplanade with benches facing out toward the water. OWEN maintained a respectful silence as I walked up to the railing and stood there for a moment, looking out over the water toward the East Side.

It was a bright day, a slight breeze coming off the water. A train was moving slowly over the Carrington Bridge. I had the sudden, irrational thought that by failing to stop Kirklin

I had let my parents down, a painful and childish notion that caused me to break down and begin to weep.

When I regained my composure, OWEN gave me a hollow pat on the back and suggested we get a drink. I didn't need convincing.

We wound up in the booth of a sports bar on 54th Street, where dozens of televisions still had their volume turned up for whatever game had been preempted by the news coverage. The bar was filled with people standing shoulder to shoulder, watching the news in silence. Everyone was holding drinks, but OWEN and I seemed to be the only ones actually drinking. I wasn't sure whether OWEN was capable of fatigue, but the strain of the day seemed to have affected him almost as much as it had me. His usual exuberance had been replaced with an air of embarrassed frustration at having been outsmarted. Our waitress continued to bring us whiskeys without having to be asked. I would drink both, while OWEN kept refilling a projection of a glass with his flask. He occasionally grimaced as he drank, which could have been a response to the strength of that particular batch of his booze program or to the constant barrage of bad news that issued from the televisions, the bartender flipping from one channel to the next whenever there was a perceived lull in the reportage.

All told, the demolition of Metropolis's most-loved cultural centers had taken a little over thirty minutes. Police and civilian casualties had been mercifully low and it was revealed during the coverage that many of the attackers' methods had been nonviolent. Kirklin's people had somehow gotten parking boots with unique locks on three hundred police cruisers, causing delays in response times throughout the city. Many other cruisers had been remotely stalled using some sort of EMP technology or else were pinned down by machine gun fire not only from the two helicopters but by individual shooters stationed on rooftops in a perimeter around the museum district. Police radios had also been unreliable throughout the attack and reporters were speculating that ultrahigh-frequency jammers had been used to disrupt police communications. When the news broke that the police were having a difficult time identifying the bodies of the men in the foyer of the Metropolis Museum of History because they didn't have their fingerprints or natural teeth, one anchor turned to someone off camera to make sure there wasn't a mistake on the teleprompter.

Within hours of the attacks, Mayor Laury was shaking hands with Governor Ranklin in a joint press conference. Soon there was footage of National Guard trucks rolling down streets all throughout Metropolis and guardsmen with M16s stationed on street corners. But that wasn't necessarily a comfort. The Guard's presence was to be expected after such an attack, and so it was reasonable to assume that Kirklin had anticipated it. His plans up to that point had depended heavily on the element of surprise. Now that the city was finally preparing for a major attack, it seemed unlikely he would repeat himself. And yet, it seemed even less likely that he was finished terrorizing the city. The only possibility was escalation, an attack so large and outrageous it would reveal all those newly arrived soldiers to be little more than another false sense of security for Kirklin to exploit.

Between updates on the details of the attacks and police

casualties, television stations were cutting away to photographs of lost Van Goghs, Rembrandts, and Caravaggios. OWEN, whom I hadn't known to be a fan of twentieth-century art, clenched his fist when it was announced that the Modern had lost an entire retrospective on Willem de Kooning.

The only building OWEN had neglected to mention when he was looking at the satellite imagery in the park was the Metropolis Transit Museum. Even without knowing I'd hoped to see the Steam Beetle, he must have suspected I would take that loss the hardest. I tried to fight off the selfish thought that I'd missed a chance to see my father's train. Something of my parents had been in the city and now suddenly wasn't. But the Steam Beetle was rare, not extinct. There was still a chance I might one day get to steal a moment with it, whereas some of the actual trains at the MTM had been out of production for so long that its collection had contained the only surviving examples.

In my apartment back in Suitland there was a framed photograph of me standing in the Maywell 78, one of the safest railcars ever constructed. A museum guard took it for me, just as I had hoped I might get someone to snap a quick picture of me with the Steam Beetle. In the photo I'm standing by myself in the empty car, holding on to one of the stanchions and smiling as if I were shaking hands with the president. This was during my first trip to the city. Four days later I would spend my ninth Christmas without a family in a hostel in the West Side. I remember the guard giving me a sad look as he wound the film forward on my disposable camera and asked me if I wanted another for safety. Maybe my lonely excitement had made him feel sorry for me or maybe when he frowned he was just trying to determine whether my enthusiasm was a play of teenage irony, a mean-spirited joke on an underappreciated museum. But to me the transit museum was no less important than any of the city's landmarks. The art museums had been repositories for artists' attempts to address the human condition through their own flamboyant creativity, while the transit museum had been a showroom for far humbler creators, who had attempted to address the needs and vulnerabilities of people with a level-headed ingenuity. Listening to the news reports that night, I knew the general public would have traded a hundred transit museums for one lost Matisse. Already there was coverage of crews sorting through demolished museums to rescue damaged paintings, while I knew it would be weeks or even months before anyone checked if there was something left of those trains. I'd never had any illusions about the popularity of the things dearest to me.

I took another drink and pictured a charred Steam Beetle crushed in the rubble and had to fight the urge to throw my glass against the wall. Instead I slouched in my seat, missing the agency.

I asked OWEN if we should check in with Garrett.

"Let's wait till we have good news," he said.

He was staring up at one of the televisions, nursing a drink out of a tumbler that was now roughly half the size of a bowling ball.

I wondered when we could possibly expect good news. But I was also glad I wouldn't have to end the day by explaining to Garrett just how badly I'd disappointed him. I finished the rest of my drink and picked up the fresh one our waitress had put down in front of OWEN. "To the MetMoH," I said, a little glumly, spilling some of my drink as I raised my glass.

OWEN sat up in his seat and passed his glass through mine, his interface producing a loud and mistimed clink.

"Yes," OWEN said. "Future generations will still be able to get their fill of moose vaginas."

The corners of his mouth were curled up in the beginning of a smile. My lack of friendships in general meant I was unaccustomed to the sort of secret elation one feels in the sharing of a private joke, especially when overwhelmed by grief and frustration. But as we both burst out laughing in our booth, nothing felt more natural.

Our laughter became so intense that it was hard to tell how much time had gone by before we noticed that the rest of the patrons in the bar were now turned away from the televisions and watching us with disgust.

A tall, heavyset man in jeans and a Metropolis Rivets jersey rose from his stool.

"Do you mind telling me what the fuck you two are laughing at?"

OWEN straightened up in his seat and turned toward the man, appraising him for a moment.

"Moose vaginas," he said, before we both again dissolved into laughter.

Soon our waitress approached us and said our drinks were on the house but we had to go.

OWEN raised his eyebrows when she said it. Being asked to leave a bar for laughing during a national tragedy was a type of human interaction that was no doubt as new to him as it was to me and he looked up at her with a certain degree of wonder as he cataloged it somewhere deep in his memory banks.

The man in the Rivets jersey watched us as we left. I tried to avoid eye contact, whereas OWEN stared at him aggressively. When we passed him, OWEN leaned in and said in a slurred attempt at a menacing voice, "Moose are even-toed ruminants," a provocation which was fortunately confusing enough for the man to let us stumble out of the bar unmolested.

Outside, it was getting dark. People were making runs on the bodegas and grocery stores, lugging huge jugs of water and bags of canned goods back to their apartments. I stood on the sidewalk and took in the crackling, predoom panic that Kirklin had left hanging over the city.

"We need to call the police," I said. "Or the FBI. Somebody."

OWEN and the man in the jersey were still glaring at each other through the bar's window.

"Sure," OWEN said over his shoulder, refusing to break eye contact with the man. "What would you like to tell them?"

"We know this was Kirklin."

When the man inside lost interest and turned back to the news coverage, OWEN mumbled a few words on human cowardice before stumbling away from the window.

"Great," OWEN said. "And you can prove that?"

I had to search the drunken mess of my thoughts before a possibility occurred to me.

"We have footage from inside one of the attacks," I said.

OWEN was rubbing his eyes with the heels of his palms and counting aloud as he tried to tally up the drinks he'd had that night.

"Yeah," he said, "we have footage that puts you at the scene of a terrorist attack, during which no one said anything incriminating about Terrence Kirklin. I'm sure that'll give the FBI something to think about while they're detaining you as a person of interest. At least enough for them to be frustrated that you have no other practical information to give up, making your tip some exciting new kind of useless. Honestly, Henry, I know you're trying to help, but I've thought this all through and the most important thing right now is for you to be quiet so I can figure out exactly how drunk I am."

I tried to insist, but OWEN raised an impatient finger. He then leaned forward and vomited out a string of lime-green code all over the pavement and onto my shoes. The numbers and symbols gradually oozed together, losing their shape and evaporating. OWEN kept his hands on his knees and announced without looking up, "I'm going to do that again."

The street was still bustling with frightened people, so to avoid any unwanted attention I encouraged OWEN to follow me into a nearby alley, where he gripped an open garbage can with both hands and continued to heave up thick, translucent ribbons of code. After a particularly forceful convulsion, he paused for a moment and began to sing an old sea chanty that I recognized from the Peter McCaw film *Pirate Steel*:

When I was a little boy my mother always told me
Way haul away, we'll haul away, Joe!
That if I did not kiss the girls my lips would all
grow moldy.
First I met a Spanish girl, who said that I was lazy.
Way haul away, we'll haul away, Joe!
Then I met a Yankee girl—

Before he could finish the verse, he heaved again and the words landed with a wet splat into the garbage can—"Whose blond hair drove me crazy." They lingered there for a few seconds and then faded into nothing just when a thought occurred to me that managed to transcend my own inebriation. OWEN had just coughed up perhaps Kirklin's only weakness, the one aspect of his recent behavior in which he didn't seem to be in complete control of himself and everyone around him. *A Yankee girl whose blond hair drove me crazy*. If Kirklin was still in the city, it stood to reason his girlfriend was too.

7

Before her alleged kidnapping, Sarah Laury was a rising sophomore at Newton College, a private school tucked away in Barington Heights. It was the North Side's wealthiest neighborhood, with its lush, flowered medians, sidewalks peopled by elderly women in furs, and doormen in epauletted blazers and flat black-billed caps. OWEN and I couldn't have looked more out of place that Monday morning as we marched, hungover, up Telmont Avenue toward the Newton campus.

My other clothes were still in the model tenement, so I'd had to sleep in my suit at the YMCA, where OWEN and I had passed the night. OWEN had lain facedown on the linoleum floor of our room with his arms at his sides, shifting only twice to vomit into the plastic garbage bin at the foot of my bed. In the morning I'd had to give the tie clip a few hard flicks to rouse him. He was upset at first, but once I explained my plan to find Kirklin through Sarah Laury he was on his feet and full of questions.

"How is this supposed to help?" he said, straightening his hair and changing his suit in our room's small mirror. "The whole city has been looking for her since she ran off."

"We don't need to find her," I said. "We just need to learn more about her. Laury's video went live the night before Kirklin attacked headquarters. That was an unnecessary risk Kirklin either allowed or couldn't prevent. So if we're looking for loose ends, Laury seems like a good place to start."

OWEN stopped fussing with his tie and gave this some thought.

"Human beings *are* weird when it comes to love," he admitted. "I read an article the other day about a woman in Houston who tried to marry her pet turtle."

This comment hung in the air for a moment. But I was eager to get him on board, so I agreed enthusiastically, at which point he started to talk about the plan as if it were his idea.

It took him only a few seconds to analyze every feature article ever written on the subject of Sarah Laury. As I washed my face in the public restroom at the Y, OWEN stood over my shoulder and summarized what he felt were some of his more interesting findings:

- Sarah Laury was a vegan for ethical reasons.
- She'd described herself in over twenty-three different interviews as an avid reader.
- Her dislikes included lack of intellectual curiosity, institutional racism, and cilantro.
- The previous year she'd organized a fund-raiser for the victims of a hospital fire in Baton Rouge. The cell phone footage of her playing "When the Saints Go Marching In" on her trumpet had gone viral and spurred a brief trumpeting fad.
- She was an assistant editor at Newton's literary journal, *The Newton Quarterly Review*, and was also a staff

writer for the school's newspaper, *The Marigold*, to which she contributed a monthly column.

- This spring she had played Nathan Detroit in the drama department's all-female production of *Guys and Dolls*.
- Around the same time, she'd starred in an avant-garde play that she had written and directed herself.

OWEN also brought up an interview that had originally been conducted by a reporter for the online edition of *Metropolis News*, but which had been reposted to a blog called *Real Celebrity Meltdowns*. It was from over a year ago and showed Laury conservatively dressed and seated across from a young male journalist, discussing an event she was planning for the Metropolis Food Bank. After a few polite questions regarding the benefit, the journalist asked her whether she could address the rumors that she was considering breast augmentation.

Laury's smile vanished and she turned a shade of red that seemed more angry than embarrassed. She looked as if she were about to ask the man what on earth he was talking about, but instead stammered for a moment.

"I'm talking about people," she finally managed to say, "people starving to death less than a mile from where we're sitting right now, and you're asking if I have any future plans for my breasts?"

Her voice was calm but incredulous.

"I'm sorry, Ms. Laury," the reporter said, doing his best to project an air of professional obligation onto his question, "but these rumors exist and I have a responsibility."

"Oh, yes," Laury said. "It must be awful for you, having to answer to every thirteen-year-old boy on the internet."

"So," the reporter said, pushing ahead, "there's no truth to the rumors?"

"Actually, there is," she said, pointing at the reporter. "I'm about to have this tit removed right now."

She turned to someone off camera and soon a well-dressed older woman with a clipboard informed the man that the interview was over. Before the video ended there was one last shot of the reporter as he prepared to leave the room, his expression a convincing attempt at bewilderment. Though, his slight smile showed that he had gotten exactly what he had hoped to out of Sarah Laury.

When the video ended, OWEN turned to me and said, "Seven million views."

I shook my head. No teenager should have been expected to cope with such a perverse level of attention. And while her apparent attachment to Kirklin remained a mystery, it was obvious to me why she might have been eager to withdraw so dramatically from public life.

This sad insight made it that much more awkward when OWEN and I concluded that, since her interests at Newton seemed mostly literary, the next logical step in our investigation was to steal a copy of her library records, which OWEN was unable to access remotely on account of the school's outdated computer system.

Now it was barely seven in the morning and I was walking through one of the richest neighborhoods in the world wearing a wrinkled suit that stunk of stale booze. After a while I caught OWEN regarding me with what looked like concern and I asked him if everything was all right. He paused in an obvious effort to phrase something carefully, then said, "Last night—after the bar."

"Yeah?"

"You talked about model trains a lot."

"Oh."

"Like, a lot a lot."

I had no memory of discussing my hobby with OWEN and was wondering what I could have said.

"I collect them."

"Henry, I know."

"Sorry," I said. "It was just because—"

OWEN's expression froze at what he seemed to expect would be more train talk.

"I'll keep the train stuff to myself," I said.

"Not forever," OWEN said. "I just think I've hit my limit for this trip."

This conversation was luckily interrupted when an older woman passing by with her corgi took in our messy appearance and abruptly crossed to the other side of the street. I shot OWEN a meaningful glance and he nodded in agreement before turning us into a pair of well-dressed older women. The disguises proved effective, earning us half a dozen friendly greetings from various doormen as we continued up the avenue. When we walked up to the gates of Newton's campus, OWEN gave the young guard in the security booth a matronly frown and he waved apologetically, buzzing us in.

All schools in the city had suspended classes in the wake

of the attacks. Newton was no exception, its campus deserted and quiet except for the snapping of a flag at half-mast in the middle of the main quad. This sound was joined by our footsteps as we followed the paved paths that led to the school's library.

It was a three-story brick building, which sat between a mostly empty faculty parking lot and a large stone-lined pond surrounded by willow trees and wooden benches. We had assumed the library would be closed and had been hoping to sneak in through a window, but as we approached we saw that the building's lights were on and there was movement inside. OWEN paused for a moment to consider this, then turned us both into firemen and headed toward the library's entrance without explanation.

The rattle of our oxygen tanks and gear filled the place as we entered. The first floor of the library was a charming space filled with round worktables and warmly lit study nooks furnished with overstuffed leather chairs. It was empty except for a middle-aged woman in a red turtleneck who was sorting books on a handcart behind the front counter. She looked understandably alarmed when she saw us. OWEN gave me a reassuring smile, then turned to the woman and screamed, "FIRE! FIRE! FIRE! GET OUT OF HERE!"

She gasped and grabbed a cardigan off the back of a chair before half running to the exit. As she pushed her way through the door she glanced over her shoulder at OWEN, who made an aggressive shooing motion, at which point she dropped her sweater and broke into an all-out sprint toward the parking lot. OWEN vanished and reappeared standing behind the counter. He looked around the empty library and screamed the word “Fire!” a few more times, scanning for any movement before turning back to me.

“Lock the door,” he said.

I walked over to the double doors and turned the dead bolt.

“Couldn’t you have lied about something else?”

OWEN gave me a long, blank look, as if by asking this question I had betrayed a fundamental lack of understanding with respect to the intensity of his hangover.

“I just wanted to get her out of here before you tried to kick her in the genitals,” he said.

He then waved his hand lazily in the direction of a wire rack of periodicals near the front door, which became engulfed in flames.

“There,” he said. “A fire. Now come over here and help me with this thing.”

He was frowning at the large tube monitor and tower of the library’s primitive computer.

“What are they spending these kids’ tuition on?” he said, running his hand along the bulky monitor. “This old girl should be enjoying her retirement somewhere.”

I waggled the mouse and the computer sprang noisily to life. Their user database wasn’t password protected, so I was able to pull up Laury’s library records without any trouble. I clicked print and an old line printer on the counter began to churn out her borrowing history on continuous paper.

I was then startled by a pounding coming from the library’s entrance. The security guard from the main gate was pressing his forehead against the glass with his hands cupped around his eyes, while the librarian stood behind him, peering over his shoulder and holding her recovered sweater to her chest. OWEN and I were still disguised as firemen, though the sight of us standing behind the counter watching a document print must have for all practical purposes blown our cover.

OWEN lit up the entire counter with more fake flames and put them out with a fire extinguisher. He waved authoritatively for the guard and librarian to back away from the building, but the guard only squinted at him for a moment before banging on the door again and shouting for us to unlock it.

"Okay," OWEN said, lowering his fire extinguisher. "Put the tie clip near a window and I'll distract them. Just let me know when you have what you need."

I pulled off the clip and headed toward the front windows, where I placed it on the sill. I was barely halfway back to the counter when my fireman disguise disappeared and I heard the guard and librarian begin to scream, the sound becoming gradually softer as whatever monster OWEN had conjured chased them toward the parking lot.

He had bought me some time, so I decided to see what else I could find on Laury in the library's computer by searching the catalog for any of her student writing. Dozens of hits came up for her contributions to *The Marigold*, bound issues of which were kept in the periodical section on the second floor. There was also a listing in the library's drama section for the play she had written.

My hangover was gaining on me and I was pouring boozy sweat by the time I made it upstairs to *The Marigold*'s archive. I pulled the most recent volumes off the shelf, then grabbed the bound manuscript of her play from the drama section.

From outside there was a loud roar and more screaming. I tucked the books under my arm and moved to the window at the end of the stacks to see how OWEN was doing. Given his performance at the museum, I was surprised that he had only turned himself into a bear. Granted, the appearance of a 1,500-pound Kodiak bear in the middle of a city campus was strange, but compared to a clown monster, the choice of bear attack was at least beginning to approach the outer realms of subtlety. OWEN had scared the librarian and guard up onto the roof of a Honda Civic. The two held each other and wept while OWEN paced around the car with his mouth foaming.

Across the parking lot I spotted a large dormitory and realized that, while comparatively understated, OWEN's bear was most likely drawing too much attention. I rushed back down to the lobby, where I attempted to leap over the front counter to retrieve Laury's borrowing history. Instead my shoe caught on one of the computer cables and I fell over the counter, pulling the old monitor and tower down onto the floor with me. My other foot winged a metal shelf filled with reserved books. It teetered precariously for a moment before falling back and knocking over another shelf behind it.

Once I'd gotten up and dusted myself off, I tore Laury's record from the printer. I retrieved the tie clip on my way out the door and told OWEN it was time to go. He projected his voice into my ear, telling me to make my way to the front gate. Halfway there, OWEN's roars died down and I saw that he was running alongside me. At the campus entrance, I entered the empty guard booth and opened the gates. Just then a truck from Metropolis Animal Control pulled up the main drive and OWEN waved it through. The driver slowed as he passed us and rolled down his window, asking us for directions to the school's library. OWEN, wearing a guard uniform, told him where to go, then thanked him, letting him know he had showed up just in time.

◦———◦

We headed down toward Berkshire Square in the Lower North Side, where the air of forbidding privilege eventually gave way to a modicum of economic diversity. Boutique clothing stores stood next to barber shops and Dominican cafés. Banks and business-class hotels overlooked the stretch of sidewalk near the entrance of Berkshire Square Park where men and women sat next to folding tables, selling handmade jewelry and amateur oil paintings. Despite the sense of unease that hung over the city, plenty of citizens had chosen to go about their business. The young guardsman standing with a rifle next to the bluestone basin of the park's massive, thudding fountain was an ominous sight, but it didn't stop a young couple from having a loud argument near the benches on the park's high terrace or the busker from playing the violin while balancing a leashed tabby cat on his head.

A few more blocks and we found a small diner, which

seemed like a fine place to go over our haul. Inside, the air smelled savory and half-burned, every surface stained a warm sepia from decades of hash brown smoke. We took one of the cracked vinyl booths in back. A young woman who'd been watching the news on a small television behind the lunch counter appeared next to our table. She kept glancing back at the television and there was a heaviness in her voice when she asked for our order.

Her obvious grief over the attacks made our presence feel like an intrusion, and so I tried to sound apologetic when I asked for a cup of coffee and an omelet. She then looked to OWEN, who was absently smacking his lips as he looked over the laminated menu doubling as a place mat. Regardless of the fact that he was incapable of eating, he ordered himself two plates of onion rings, a stuffed pepper, and a Fresca. I tried to suggest that he and I could share my omelet, but the woman had already made off with our order.

OWEN turned to me, pleased.

"I've never ordered food before," he said.

He was in a pleasant mood so this seemed like a good opportunity to provide him with some constructive criticism regarding his behavior at the library. I told him it was important to remember that we were both public servants and that no matter how desperate the situation we should do our best to proceed with a certain amount of professionalism and decency, especially since this was such a frightening time for the city.

"What are you talking about?"

"You screamed 'fire' at a librarian," I said. "You made

her think she was about to be mauled by a bear. And after all that, she's going to find the place trashed."

"Wait a minute," OWEN said. "Who trashed the library?"

"Well, I mean, I did, because you—"

OWEN leaned over the table, his eyes huge with mock outrage.

"Henry, why did you do that?"

"You were drawing too much attention to us, so I was in a hurry. Some shelves got knocked over."

"That was a *library*, Henry. For *students*."

"Cut it out."

He held out his hands to show he was now being serious.

"All right," he said, "so the takeaway is next time you shouldn't rush. Running in an unfamiliar setting is dangerous. Speaking as your friend, I'm just glad you didn't get hurt. But as far as my bear projection is concerned, I think you're being a little narrow-minded. Those people should be thanking me for getting their minds off all the terrorism."

Our drinks arrived and OWEN nodded his thanks to the waitress, who didn't seem to notice that he was now wearing a ten-gallon cowboy hat. She placed the coffee and Fresca on the table without comment and returned to the kitchen.

"That's exactly the sort of thing I'm talking about," I said. "Completely unnecessary. If we're going to stop Kirklin we need to focus."

"I don't think so," OWEN said. "Kirklin has the market cornered on the kind of focus you're talking about. If we act like well-behaved USMS agents, he's going to get away with whatever it is he's after. We need to be as ridiculous as possible."

A stubborn silence settled between us. He adjusted the cowboy hat on his head, making a big show of the fact that his hands were now lobster claws.

"Okay," I said. "Point taken."

"Is it?"

OWEN tilted his head back and began pushing a mustache out of his upper lip. In a matter of seconds it was touching the table. He curled the ends of it with his claws.

"Okay, okay," I said. "You win."

He clunked his claws together in celebration and took on his normal shape just in time to receive his plates of onion rings from our waitress. My omelet came soon after, along with a wilted stuffed pepper. I finished my eggs quickly and OWEN looked pleased when I ate some of his onion rings. The sight of me eating seemed to amuse him and he insisted I try some of his stuffed pepper before he would agree to help me examine Laury's borrowing history. As it turned out, the pepper was stuffed with a foul-tasting mixture of cabbage and caraway seeds. OWEN delighted in the unhappy faces I made as I chewed. There was some discussion as to whether the bite I had taken was big enough before I pushed the plates aside and placed the printout from the library between us.

"Fine," OWEN said, disappointed. "But if I find anything important in here, you have to eat more pepper."

"If you tell me anything useful about Sarah Laury, I'll finish the whole thing."

In a flash OWEN had removed his blazer and was rolling up his shirtsleeves.

"You're on."

The list was in chronological order and the items toward the top were the sort of books one would expect any bright young woman to borrow: *Jane Eyre*, *Madame Bovary*, *To the Lighthouse*. There were also books that had obviously been borrowed in response to a specific class or assignment: Campbell's *History of the French and Indian War*, *A Critical Companion to* The House of Seven Gables. It wasn't until halfway down the list that something caught my attention: *The Anatomy of a City* by Andre Denard.

"Oh, Denard!" I said to OWEN.

I only meant to tell him it was one of my favorite books, but OWEN assumed it was of importance and read a copy of it he found online. He nodded and said that a 1,500-page treatise on the infrastructure of modern cities seemed a little dense for an undergrad.

"Not really," I said. "I loved that book when I was her age."

"Yeah," he said. "And you're a giant weirdo."

I was about to go on defending the book when I noticed the next titles on the list. I recognized them immediately as the work of fringe sociologists: *Infrastructure and Institutionalized Oppression*, *Agents of Gentrification*, *Civil Revolutionaries*, *Radical Communities*. These were texts written by the sort of riffraff who hadn't been able to get into the National Engineering Academy and had studied anthropology at Brown while smoking marijuana and misquoting

Foucault to one another at parties. But perhaps the most troubling book on the list was the last item, which had been checked out two weeks before Laury's disappearance and had since accrued over $12.85 in late fees: *A Beginner's Guide to Esperanto*. OWEN whistled.

"Well, whatever Kirklin's got planned," he said, "I'm guessing she's into it."

I pulled out the bound issues of *The Marigold* and began flipping through them in search of Laury's contributions. Her monthly column was titled the Laury Perspective, a 1,200-word box in the upper-right-hand corner of the opinion page. The grainy black-and-white photo next to her byline showed her in a ponytail and a white polo. She looked like a normal college student, as opposed to the young celebrity whose face was usually reproduced on the heavy, glossy stock of popular magazines. The first few installments of the column were socially minded but restrained. I skimmed a few pieces on antibullying, the value of contributing one's time to a charitable organization, and a charming piece on dining etiquette:

> Though the American style of holding one's fork is of course perfectly acceptable, allow me to enumerate what I feel are several distinct advantages to the Continental style.

A month after Laury had checked out *The Anatomy of a City*, the topics she covered had grown edgier. She wrote a slightly provocative piece on commuter attrition, "Parking Meter Rates Should Be Raised for Good of the City," and soon she was penning heated accusations against her father's administration, accusing members of his staff of negligence and even fraud.

There had been some mention in the mainstream press of Laury's public criticisms of her father, but nothing that would have prepared me for the inflammatory statements she had published regularly in *The Marigold*. It seemed strange that her writing hadn't caused more of a stir. I wondered aloud whether there may have been a deliberate cover-up and OWEN cut me off.

"Henry, it's a column on local government in a college newspaper. I can't believe *we're* reading it."

I could see he had a point, but if anyone had paid attention to said college newspaper, they might have stumbled across a particularly interesting item in its Clubs and Activities section. That's where I found a picture of Terrence Kirklin surrounded by a group of young people under a handmade banner identifying them as Newton's Future Municipal Leaders. I recognized the club as one of Garrett's school outreach programs. He had made participation mandatory for all of his admins. The week he made the announcement, Kirklin had flown down to Suitland just to slam a few doors and scream at Garrett for trying to turn him into a goddamned babysitter.

He seemed happy enough in the photograph, sitting front and center with half a dozen Newton students huddled around him. I had never seen Kirklin smiling before and if it weren't for his eye patch I probably wouldn't have recognized him. Laury was standing next to Kirklin's chair, her hand resting on his shoulder. The article continued onto the next page, where there was a photograph of Kirklin with his arm around Laury at a pizza fund-raiser for the group. They were standing close, with Laury's head almost resting on Kirklin's chest. They had the contented look of newlyweds.

From there we moved on to Laury's play, titled *The Man in the Tower.* While the tone of her later columns had been rather acerbic, her play was a surprisingly reflective story about a young woman who is driven mad by her many suitors and ends up fleeing her small village to live in the wilderness. *I can no longer live with so many eyes fixed so maniacally in my direction,* she proclaims as she flees into a dense wood. After wandering for some time and delivering a few monologues on the value of solitude and self-determination, she encounters a strange man named Majstro who lives in an ancient stone tower. He explains that he is a wizard responsible for maintaining the order of the universe and performs a few miracles for her benefit, moving the stars around the night sky, teaching her the language of trees, etc. The girl tells him about her troubles—*I am loved by too many and have been robbed of all quiet*—and he invites her to take refuge in his tower, where they conduct a series of philosophical dialogues regarding the baseness and corruption of humankind. Their discussions grow in intensity and eventually result in declarations of love between the two. From the tower they see that her suitors have followed her into the woods and Majstro offers to place the girl among the stars, where he can look after her and protect her from the relentlessness of those who are pursuing her. She happily accepts the offer and is turned into a constellation in the shape of a circle. The girl's suitors then find the wizard's tower and demand to know whether or not he has seen her. Without saying a word the wizard self-immolates and another circle appears in the sky, creating a figure eight.

OWEN was still frowning down at the last page when I asked him what he thought of it.

"You mean artistically?" he said, scrunching up his nose. "It's a bunch of confessional, pseudosymbolic garbage."

His hours of watching classic cinema with Klaus had clearly made him a bit of a snob when it came to narrative art.

"The whole thing is just a bunch of melodramatic whining dressed up in the laziest way possible. The suitors represent her fame. The forest, her burgeoning womanhood and corresponding confusion. The wizard, Kirklin. His control over the universe, Kirklin's influence in Metropolis. And don't get me started on that tower. She should have saved that imagery for her honeymoon, am I right?"

OWEN did have a point in that the one-to-one correspondence of the play's various elements suggested it was the work of a literal thinker, with the exception of those stars forming a figure eight, which seemed uncharacteristically playful. Though if Majstro was Kirklin, and his control over the world represented his control over the city, it was possible that the end of the play meant he had hidden her somewhere in the city's infrastructure.

"That's good, Henry," OWEN said when I shared my theory. "So he hid her somewhere in the largest city in the country. We didn't need to read ninety pages of expressionist drivel to know that might be a possibility."

"Check the city's sewer system for any access tunnels shaped like figure eights."

"Nothing."

"What about the old subway lines?"

OWEN scratched his chin while he thought it over. "The old tracks were mostly straight lines running along avenues. And they were all abandoned twenty years before Kirklin came on as station chief. He only ever contributed algorithms for the current system."

OWEN saw my face brighten when he mentioned Kirklin's transit algorithms.

"No way," he said, looking down sadly at the uneaten pepper. "That's not possible."

I put some money on the table and gathered up the library materials so I could dump them into the trash on my way to the exit. I knew where we would find Sarah Laury.

"I said it's not possible," OWEN called out across the diner. "Someone would have noticed."

8

Most experts agree that when it comes to public transit in the twentieth century, the original subway system in Metropolis was among the worst in the world. Though, really it hadn't even been a system in the proper sense of the word. Each line was built and maintained separately by independent operators who had set out to provide service for specific parts of the city. The implementation of a comprehensive citywide transit system was deemed too expensive, and so for decades the city's subways were abandoned to the free market. Coverage was limited and required commuters to put up with circuitous travel routes; in order to get from Mark and Verdi in the South Side to Little India in the East Side, one would have to take the Express Intracity twenty minutes in the wrong direction, then walk to Murch to catch the Rapid East.

By 1961, there were over two hundred different train lines in the city, each with its own fare structure and unique token. A famous photo from the *Metropolis Examiner* shows commuters in raincoats standing in front of a subway entrance and sorting through handfuls of tokens to see if they have the right one for that particular line. In the mid-1960s the state legislature attempted to solve the issue by establishing the Metropolis Transit Authority, which began to buy up the old lines and manage them as a single public benefit corporation. But the individual lines were still so far apart and discontinuous that the MTA was unable to provide effective service.

The problem wasn't fully addressed until 1978 when Albert Tessman, our Metropolis station chief at the time, finally wrangled political support for a unified system, which ended up being the largest public transportation project in the nation's history. While some of the older tunnels and stations were repurposed, most were ultimately abandoned for the new network of concentric and interconnected hubs with parallel local and express tracks. The system also included an exterior loop of bullet trains that could carry riders from one end of the city to the other in a little over thirty minutes. When work was completed, average ridership increased from 60 million passengers a year to 4.2 billion, making it one of the most heavily utilized transit systems in the world.

There was no room for error, which was why Kirklin's contributions to the city's train schedule algorithms had been one of his most impressive accomplishments. Previous station chiefs had been happy to keep the system running at all, whereas Kirklin had been famous for his aggressive, "not good enough" approach. Within his first five years, he shaved a little over a minute off the average commute duration. Every year after that, if the duration failed to be reduced by at least five seconds, he would pressure city hall and Suitland alike until the MTA got more trains or better signals or more personnel or whatever he felt was lacking. The result was that after twenty years of his service, the movement of trains in Metropolis's subway system was seamless and unrelenting, a complex unison of stops and starts like the beating of a monstrous heart.

So it was no wonder that OWEN remained unconvinced of my hypothesis even as he flashed a fake transit pass at the bar code reader to get us into the J1 station at 97th Street. The idea of Kirklin trying to hide Laury somewhere in the city's active rail system was admittedly outlandish, but it was also perfectly in keeping with his audaciousness up to that point.

The station's narrow stairwell eventually opened up into one of Metropolis's cavernous subway stations, where the walls were massive slabs of coffered stone that rose up and converged overhead in clean, minimalist arches. Several auxiliary lines had been closed as a result of the previous day's attacks, so the station was especially busy. I picked up a subway map from a nearby kiosk and asked OWEN to pull the agency's records from our shared database with the MTA on any changes to train service that had been implemented by Kirklin within the last year.

"Done," he said. "No major changes. A few tweaks here and there. I'm telling you, Henry. These schedules are tight. The track usage is almost continuous."

"Almost?"

"Well, Kirklin decreased the number of stops on the R4 line, which shares some of its tracks with the A3 and C1 trains. That puts a three-minute gap between all three lines, which used to follow one another in two-minute intervals. But that's not significant—"

OWEN thought for a moment, then corrected himself.

"Except he also made changes to the Q7, which now runs

as a shuttle between 13th and 48th Streets. That lets all E trains circle around Ansit Square. And the R4 shares some track with the E5 once it's east of the park, which makes a five-minute gap."

He worked his way through Kirklin's changes, which began to run together. I tried to follow along on my subway map, but OWEN was going too fast.

"He did it," he said finally, his doubt giving way to astonishment. "He hid an entire train."

I held up the map between us.

"Show me."

OWEN projected a two-inch line of blue light onto the map. It started on the L1 line in the North Side and then curved down, switching to the M1 and crossing all the way down to Center City. The light continued moving southwest, parallel with the F3, before gradually curving east and back up to the North Side. The route formed, roughly, a figure eight.

According to OWEN, the circuit was uninterrupted except for two daily stops in the Lower West Side. For two minutes the train had to be redirected off the main tracks in midtunnel before continuing on its way.

"We're just in time for the first daily stop," OWEN said. "It'll be south of here on the F3 line in about twenty minutes."

Just then a downtown-bound train pulled into the station. I observed the crowds filling the platform, then winked at OWEN and nodded toward the tracks. He smiled, his eyes full of impish glee.

As we ran toward the train, OWEN turned us into

blood-splattered surgeons. He was holding a Styrofoam cooler out in front of him.

"Everybody out of our way," he shouted. "We've got a human brain here and it's not getting any fresher."

"A brain?" a young man on the platform called out as other passengers stepped off the train to make room for us.

"That's right," OWEN said. "We have to get this thing downtown and put it in some sick kid."

It was absurd, but I knew firsthand what it was like to have OWEN's confidence throw you. On the train, a young woman even offered him her seat, which, graciously, he refused.

We got off at 26th Street and climbed down onto the tracks once the train left the station. OWEN timed our run so we were able to slip into a maintenance shaft just as an express train shot through the tunnel at full speed. From there we moved forward in twenty-second bursts, stopping to take shelter between the exposed steel columns in the center of the tunnel that separated the two sets of tracks. There wasn't much space between the trains and I had to press myself against each column to keep from being hit.

Eventually we reached an area where the tunnel grew wider with a third set of tracks that stretched a few hundred yards along the first two. I was still trying to catch my breath when I heard a train rumbling slowly up the tunnel. There was a metallic clink and the arriving train rolled onto the turnoff before coming to a stop with a hard blast of its air brakes. It was a heavy locomotive pulling ten weld cars, the sort of reinforced and stripped-down commuter cars that were used to transport equipment or new sections of rail. It occurred to me that perhaps all OWEN and I had succeeded in doing was finding a supply train that no one had bothered recording in the MTA database. But OWEN looked excited and, after one more express train shot past, he waved me out onto the tracks and we both ran in a half crouch toward the rear of the train.

We climbed up onto the back of the last car and stood on either side of its sliding door. I leaned in to peek through its small window, but it had been covered from the inside with dark cloth. OWEN disappeared as the train began to pull back onto the express tracks.

"I'll keep out of sight," he said in my ear. "We might need the element of surprise if we run into any of Kirklin's people."

I nodded and pulled hard on the door. As I stepped into the unlit car, OWEN shined a light from the tie clip. The interior was empty except for something hanging on the far wall next to the other door. I made my way up the car and saw that it was a blue plaid raincoat hanging on a metal hook. On the floor next to it was a matching pair of rain boots resting on a welcome mat embroidered with a white horse jumping over a brush fence.

Sarah Laury was here.

"You have forty minutes until the next stop," OWEN said. "Find her before then so we can get her off the train. I'll lead you through the tunnels from there."

I gave the tie clip a thumbs-up, but when I looked down I

saw that my hands and my shirt were stained with rust from hugging all those columns.

"OWEN," I said, "do you think you could clean me up a little bit?"

"Good idea," he said. "It's not every day you get to reverse kidnap a celebrity. You'll want to look your best."

Within seconds I was wearing a fresh suit and my hands looked clean. As for the smell of sweat and booze, I had to rely on faith alone she wouldn't notice.

I entered the next car and was surprised to find myself standing in a tastefully decorated kitchen with dark granite countertops and matching stainless steel appliances. Overhead, large PA speakers filled the car with classical music.

"What is this?" I said.

"Mozart's Third Violin Concerto," OWEN said. "G major."

When I clarified that I was talking about the kitchen I could feel OWEN shrug.

"Joke's on us," he said. "I guess the train wasn't even the crazy part."

A mesh bag of red and yellow bell peppers swung on a silver hook under the cherrywood cabinets, while fresh pears and apples rested in a bowl fixed permanently to the countertop. On the walls were several art prints of stylized kitchen utensils done in bold, warm colors. Except for an empty cereal bowl and spoon in the large double sink, the room could have been a photograph out of *Metropolis Living*. Subway cars in Metropolis were designed five feet wider than in most cities in order to accommodate the high number of commuters, and so this kitchen was even larger than the ones I would have found in a luxury condo in Center City. The only thing that broke the illusion was the gentle movement of the car from side to side.

In the next car I passed through a full dining room with a drum chandelier that swung in a slow circle over a long oak table. There was a single place setting next to a large white button built into the tabletop. When I pressed it the plate and silverware began to slide about the table. When I pushed it again, they came to a stop.

"Look at this," I said to OWEN. "Must be magnetized."

"That's great," he said, his voice beginning to crackle from the electromagnetic interference. "But are we down here looking for Sarah Laury or for a table with a big magnet in it?"

I moved quickly through the next car, a bedroom that was empty except for a walk-in closet that ran the length of the car and a white canopy bed. Next was a library, its wooden shelves built into the side of the car at a slant to keep the books in place. Between two such shelves was a Louis XV–style writing desk and an equally ornate padded chair pulled away from it at an angle. On the wall hung a lithograph of a young woman standing in the back of a carriage surrounded by soldiers. She held out her right hand to the men in exhortation and lightly gripped a spear with her left. The caption read *Boadicea Haranguing the Britons*. Near the desk was a light metal waste bin bolted into the floor. It was filled with torn and crumpled pieces of paper. I retrieved a sheet and opened it, holding it up to the light. It was covered in Esperanto in a neat, cursive hand.

"OWEN," I said. "Can I get a translation?"

He cleared his throat and began, "The importance of disrupting the continuum of western culture is self-evident when one considers the fact that—"

Several words were crossed out before beginning again.

"The necessity of disrupting the continuum of western culture—As it stands, the continuum of western culture—Western culture, when considered as a continuum—The reason we have decided to disrupt the continuum of western culture—"

From there the text was scratched out and OWEN's voice trailed off. There was a moment of silence as he and I contemplated the disturbing content of those fragments that I eventually broke by offering up a slightly dismayed, "Yikes."

"Wait," OWEN said. "Listen to this."

Farther down the page Laury had included a quote from an article written by Kirklin for the *Journal of Auxiliary Languages*. OWEN translated it as follows:

> *Because organic languages are a vessel for cultural information, one of the great advantages of a constructed language is its cultural emptiness, allowing speakers to step outside of many pernicious social constructs and thus communicate with a higher degree of freedom . . . Racism and classism in the United States are power relationships that are perpetually reinforced by the English language. Without the benefit of English, both could be extinguished within a few generations.*

Elsewhere I noticed she had included quotes from people like Herbert Moreau and Anaximander Bernard, writers whose works were even more radical than those included toward the end of her lending history at Newton. Moreau had investigated the twentieth-century French penal system by continually confessing to crimes he hadn't committed in order to serve out the sentences. Bernard had the distinction of being the first-ever self-described anarchist city planner. In Laury's notes there were also figures copied out in English that seemed to be statistics on the US prison and education systems. There were countless similar pages in the bin, early drafts of some sort of manifesto.

I also noticed a dark linen-bound notebook sitting on the leather inlay of the desktop. The inside of the front cover bore a matte paper bookplate on which was written "Property of Sarah Laury." Flipping through, it was clear that it was her personal diary. OWEN made a crack about me being a giant creep and I immediately closed it.

"Wait," he said. "I didn't mean you shouldn't read it."

"You just called me a creep."

"Oh, and you are absolutely. A remorseless creep. Reading the diary of a teenager? I'm just glad you're on our side. Now crack that thing back open."

The early entries were all uneventful. Except for a few negative comments about her family's social circle being "plutocratic" and "appallingly inbred," her descriptions of her daily life were all so earnest and unremarkable that, even though the terrible events of the past few days made her private thoughts a matter of national importance, I was struck by the queasy feeling that I was, just as OWEN said, violating the privacy of an innocent young woman. But it wasn't long before I found an entry where the neat writing turned messy and hurried:

> [indecipherable] *at me in front of everyone and I was furious. Ashamed too because my eyes water when I'm mad so everyone thinks I'm about to cry. Lots of sympathetic looks from the group. Even Eleanor Mae, so awkward she can't even look at me, gave my elbow a squeeze when Mr. Kirklin turned to start writing on the board. You could see from the smirk on his face how pleased he was with what he'd said. He probably thinks he rattled me because I'm some spoiled brat who's used to getting treated like royalty. But no one treats me like anything. No one even sees me. People think I'm just a possible internship at city hall or a celebrity to brag about knowing. Either way when they look at me they only see some reflection of themselves. Even the sweet, quiet dorks in Future Municipal Leaders are only nice because deep down they hope that me choosing the same activity they did means they're somehow closer to the glamorous world which my entire existence serves as* [indecipherable]. *It would never occur to them that I'm in this club because I actually care about my city. Even when they all looked shocked and horrified after Mr. Kirklin yelled at me over some new policy Dad has been*

> *pushing (as if I had been involved!), they weren't upset because he had disrespected a person with feelings, but because in his poor treatment of me he had insulted what is to them* [indecipherable] *system of values. I can still see the disgusting look on his face while he wrote something about gentrification on the board. Proud, thinking he almost made the rich girl cry. He doesn't know the first thing. I was closer to breaking his nose.*

When I expressed my surprise that Kirklin's relationship with Laury had apparently begun on such an inauspicious note, OWEN explained that the reason I didn't understand was that I had zero sexual charisma.

There was a two-week gap before the next entry, her penmanship once again calm and confident. She mentioned that after her last entry she had showed up at Kirklin's offices on Alton Street to address his misconceptions about her. The conversation must have gone well, in that "Mr. Kirklin" was now "Terry" and she referenced their frequent walks together throughout the city. Everything she recorded about their interactions was still within the bounds of his role as a civics mentor, long academic discussions on the various problems facing Metropolis and the dozens of book recommendations that OWEN and I had seen turn up in her borrowing history. But as she described a particularly languorous walk through Delphi Park, where they wound up sitting together on a bench and discussing the elasticity of substitution between capital and labor, she abruptly noted that she liked the smell of Kirklin's aftershave mixed with the traces of cigar smoke from his overcoat. She followed these observations with a confessional line of thought:

> *I've always known I have to be careful around men. Or rather, I've been aware of the societal norms that say it's my job to be careful around men. Meanwhile, those same norms have programmed men to believe that their manhood is contingent on their being the exact opposite of careful. Whole movies are devoted to those same tired jokes in which young boys learn it would be better for them to have sex by any means necessary than to be a virgin who's never harassed or assaulted anyone. It can't be easy to come of age in a culture that wants you to be a monster, but how much easier it must be for them to be ridiculed for something they might fail to do than to be blamed, as so many women are, for the thoughts and actions of others no matter how unwittingly or unwillingly we might have elicited them.*
>
> *Luckily I've always been able to avoid the whole shame trap. When I smile politely at one of my father's advisers and he responds with a sleazy wink, it never occurs to me that I might blame myself for having smiled. I even occasionally like the effect my body has on the weaker sex. Flirting with one of my dad's interns can be fun, especially if he has dimples and nice hair, looking bright and optimistic in his oxford button-down. Or there's the other side of it: using desire to deliberately unbalance the older men who always insist on insulting my intelligence,*

calling me sweetheart and explaining the simplest things to me as slowly as possible as if I were somehow impaired. A sudden knowing smile or light innuendo is enough to leave them stuttering and red faced or send them off on a coughing jag as if all of existence suddenly went down the wrong pipe. But either way I end up feeling alienated by these interactions, since what these young and old men alike are reacting to is always so outward and has so little to do with my true self, which no one seems to have any interest in whatsoever. If my appearance has led me to feel any sort of shame it's only that people pay so much attention to it that it's as if my inner life has become some terrible secret.

It's the exact opposite with Terry. During our walks he's only interested in what I have to say, my thoughts on policy and civic theory. He even sometimes reacts with surprise when I haven't heard of some economist or social philosopher he's just mentioned, as if I were a colleague who has disappointed him. After a moment he'll remember I'm a student and apologize, then recommend a few authors who will help catch me up to speed, there being no doubt in his mind (because I can feel he actually knows me) that I'll be more than equal to the material. He's honestly the purest and most remarkable man I've ever met, though maybe a little aloof. In fact, I've come across an entirely new problem. I've tried a few of my delicate innuendos. Nothing.

He only smiles patiently, waiting for me to go on articulating my deepest-held beliefs.

From there her entries grew a little less candid about her relationship with Kirklin, except for a single entry in which she passingly referenced having finally "gotten through" to him, after which she referred to him exclusively in her journal as "T."

Scanning through the following pages, I saw that the next few months of their time together were devoted to organizing fund-raisers with the Future Municipal Leaders for homeless shelters throughout Metropolis. According to Laury, they had raised over $15,000 for a shelter in the East Side. During this time Laury also seemed to become more and more aware of a project Kirklin was working on, which she discussed only cautiously in her journal. However, it became obvious from her serious and secretive tone that when she referenced "his important work" she was not referring to his usual responsibilities for the agency. Several entries went by before I found Laury's brief description of a secret meeting Kirklin invited her to attend somewhere in the South Side:

I was disappointed at first. It was a lot of ordinary people crowded into a warehouse, sitting on folding chairs and drinking coffee from paper cups. But once the meeting got under way, the energy in the room was remarkable. I remembered suddenly that class trip years ago to the Palace of Versailles when I saw David's Tennis Court Oath *for the first time. I stood in front of the painting so long I didn't even notice when my classmates all went to lunch. I wanted to understand all the passion and hopefulness on display there. And now tonight, listening to T's people, I knew I was living it. The speakers took the stage one at a time, each of them brilliant and as powerfully stirred and stirring as the figures in David's painting. Everything they said was truth. I pulled T's hand into my lap and held it there. As we sat listening I thought of everything we would be giving up to make the world a better place, all those towering sacrifices. I realized they were nothing.*

There was another long gap between entries. When they resumed, they were in Esperanto.

I was shocked that Laury seemed to be complicit in the recent attacks on Metropolis and asked OWEN for a translation of the Esperanto. Instead he reminded me of the time, in a tone suggesting that this passing confession had satisfied the extent of his curiosity regarding Laury's private thoughts.

I put the journal down and entered the next car, which contained a botanical garden. A tight path wound through a dense growth of ferns and small trees. There were strange flowers in elevated beds under full-spectrum lights, specimens with burnt-orange tendrils and empty purple bulbs. The earthy musk was mitigated by a light breeze from the train's ventilation system. The violin concerto coming from the PA system was now mixed with the sound of birdsong and gurgling creeks coming from small speakers positioned discreetly among the plants. I also noticed several ultrahigh-definition televisions, many of them barely visible behind the broad, overlapping leaves of exotic trees or the tangle of flowering vines. Their screens showed time-lapse videos of flowers blooming, slowed-down footage of birds in flight, herds of wild horses running through fields at sunset.

"Say what you want about Kirklin," OWEN whispered in my ear as I moved up the car, "but he sure knows how to hide a lover underground."

He wasn't wrong. But it wasn't until his use of the word "lover" that I thought to wonder why I hadn't seen any evidence of a man's presence on the train. Not so much as a discarded dress sock. There had been only one place setting on the dining room table. The two had looked inseparable in the pages of *The Marigold* and Laury's play had ended on an overtly devotional note. Yet by all appearances Kirklin never visited her here. The path leading through the garden was narrow, perfect for a slender eighteen-year-old, but unworkable for a man of Kirklin's size. Even for me the plants and flower beds were arranged uncomfortably close and I was forced to push roughly through the press of tree branches.

At the end of the car there was a clearing, where three wrought-iron steps led up to a wooden deck with a bolted-down rattan chaise lounge and matching side table. There was a metal-bottomed glass of what looked like pink lemonade on the table, which must have been magnetized as well since the glass itself remained still while the ice inside knocked from side to side. As I climbed the steps, I noticed the same crackle of interference in OWEN's voice as he tried to tell me something.

"—the glass—isn't—"

His voice grew more garbled so I moved back down into the garden until he came through clearly.

"The ice in the glass," he repeated, exasperated. "It hasn't melted."

Before I understood what he was saying, I heard a heavy clank as the door leading into the next car was opened from the other side. I ducked into the cover of a nearby fern in time to watch Sarah Laury enter the car in a silk robe. In her right hand she was holding a large hardcover book, using her index finger as a bookmark. She walked barefoot to the chaise and sat down before flipping an unseen switch on the side table and picking up the glass of lemonade. She swung her legs up onto the chaise and took a sip, opening the book and searching for her place on the page. Without looking up, she called out something in Esperanto.

"She asked you what you're doing over there," OWEN said.

I didn't move or say a word and eventually she looked up from her book impatiently.

"FYI," OWEN said, "I made your suit black. From what we saw in that journal, there's no way she's walking out of here with someone from Suitland."

I took a deep breath and stepped out from the fern.

"Mr. Kirklin sent me," I said.

She squinted at me and closed her book, then said something else in Esperanto.

"Now she wants to know why you're not speaking Esperanto," OWEN said.

There was a moment of tense silence accentuated by the

piped-in sound of birds and babbling brooks before OWEN rescued me.

"Here," he whispered. "Say this—"

He pronounced a few words in Esperanto slowly enough that I was able to recite them in a way I hoped sounded half-way intelligent. I was discouraged when in response she arched an eyebrow.

"Don't worry," OWEN said. "You told her you're new."

"Nova?" Laury said, her voice more confused than accusing.

OWEN whispered another string of Esperanto in my ear and, at his mercy, I repeated it.

"Jes," I said. "Tio ĉi estas mia unua tago."

"Yes," OWEN translated. "This is my first day."

I wanted to cringe at the idiocy of OWEN's lie, but instead smiled politely in the hopes of ingratiating myself. After a moment, she seemed to decide I was harmless.

"A new recruit?" she said. "That's excellent. Welcome. We can switch to English, if you like."

"Thank you, Ms. Laury," I said, feeling genuinely grateful as I climbed up the steps to join her on the deck.

She seemed taken aback by the mention of her own last name but recovered quickly.

"Your pronunciation needs some work. But otherwise you seem to be reasonably well along. You should be proud of your progress, kolego."

"She's right," OWEN said. "Your pronunciation was terrible."

"Thank you," I said to them both.

"I apologize for my appearance," she said, taking another

sip from her glass as she rose from the chaise. "I wasn't told of any change in status."

"I'm afraid there wasn't time."

There was a plan forming in my mind that would require a gamble, one that would either reveal beyond any doubt that I wasn't telling the truth or earn me her trust.

"Well, then," she said. "What's the word?"

"First, Mr. Kirklin asked that I apologize on his behalf."

This seemed to surprise her.

"What for?"

Her eyes were even larger than they were in photographs. It took all my courage to meet her gaze and deliver my running leap of a lie.

"He says he's sorry he hasn't visited you down here."

She smiled, then laughed softly.

"Of course he hasn't," she said. "He's very busy."

Her words almost sounded like a reproach, and so I was caught off guard when she leaned in and kissed me on the cheek.

"Thank you," she said. "For the message. You can tell him that I miss him and I'm proud of him."

"Nice work," OWEN said. "Now let's reel her in."

"I will, but for now we have to get you out of here. We have intelligence that a government agency has figured out you're here."

I might have expected this news to elicit some measure of panic, but she only pursed her lips and turned to place the glass on the side table, keeping her hand on it as she thought the situation over.

"Which one?"

"There's no way to know for sure who figured it out," I said. "But we have reason to believe it was one of those damned know-it-alls at the United States Municipal Survey."

"Jesus," OWEN said.

"We need to get you off the train at the next scheduled stop, which should be—"

"In eight minutes," OWEN said. "Near Terrot Avenue."

I repeated the information to Laury and she nodded.

"I'll throw something on and gather a few things. You wait here."

She took her hand from the glass. When she flipped the table's switch, I heard a familiar crackle in my ear. Laury looked out over her garden.

"I'll miss it here," she said.

She turned to say something else and then froze.

"Is something the matter?" I said.

That was when I noticed it myself. While speaking with Laury I had inadvertently moved closer to her side table. The crackling from the electromagnetic interference was now too loud for me to hear whatever OWEN was shouting urgently in my ear. OWEN's projections flickered in the brightly lit garden car, my suit rapidly changing color. My hands, shirt-front, and face alternated from clean to soiled.

I asked for an opportunity to explain myself, but Sarah Laury only walked calmly to the side table and flipped the switch again, watching as the flickering disappeared.

"Get away from the table," OWEN said, a little late for the already developing situation. "It's a magnet!"

Laury and I regarded one another.

"Ms. Laury, I know this must seem—"

Before I could finish, she grabbed the glass off the table, throwing the lemonade in my face and bringing the base of the glass down onto the bridge of my nose.

"Oh, no," OWEN said as the warm, wet rush of blood began to pour down my face. "I think there's something wrong with my patch, your nose—"

On the chaise lounge, a French bulldog appeared and then fainted.

This distracted Laury for a moment, but when I tried to finish my explanation, she brought the base of the glass down hard against my left temple and my knees went weak. I could feel the rocking of the train in my teeth. Or maybe it was my heartbeat. I wobbled there for a moment until the glass came down again and finally I went the way of the bulldog.

9

When I came to, my hands were tied to the leg of the chaise with the belt of Laury's robe. My nose throbbed and my face was sticky with dried blood and lemonade. Laury was standing next to an open control panel in the wall, speaking into a red telephone.

After she hung up, a high-pitched tone rang out over the train's PA system, interrupted by a man's voice saying, "Komprenita."

The train increased in speed.

I closed my eyes and when I opened them again, Laury was standing over me, dressed in blue jeans, a T-shirt, a pair of sneakers, and a light twill jacket. She had a brown messenger bag slung over one shoulder and in her right hand she held a small black Taser.

"Ms. Laury," I said. "We have to get you back to your family."

"I'm taking you to see them now," she said, then leaned down to tase me gingerly in the neck.

My legs were still twitching when the train slowed to a stop. Two men entered the car and began to confer with her in Esperanto. She gave what sounded like careful instructions and the two untied me and lifted me to my feet. One of them took out a zip-tie restraint and told me to hold out my hands. I nodded slowly and listened for any sign of OWEN in my ear.

He was silent.

"Are you there?" I risked asking out loud, my voice catching at the knowledge I was alone.

The men looked at each other, confused.

One of them said again, "Your hands."

"Okay," I said. "I'll cooperate. I'm cooperating."

I bolted down the car and almost made it to the garden path before one of the men grabbed me by the neck of my blazer and pulled me back. He and his partner took turns punching me in the stomach, then held my hands behind my back long enough to slip on the restraint.

The four of us marched back through the train. In the other cars dozens of agents were busy tearing down its interior. Men in black suits and safety goggles were taking sledgehammers to dividing walls, while others were busy carrying out furniture and stacks of garment bags. As we passed through the library, Laury grabbed her diary and tucked it into the side pocket of her bag. She removed the print of Boadicea from the wall and kissed it before placing it in the same pocket.

We exited out the rear of the train, Laury jumping nimbly down into the tunnel while I had to be lowered by both arms, one of Kirklin's men keeping a grip on the collar of my jacket as he climbed down to keep me from making a run for it.

From the looks of the aging brickwork, the train had stopped at one of the city's abandoned stations. The place was dark except for a dozen portable lights humming on the platform where Kirklin's agents were busy loading Laury's possessions into canvas handcarts. I wasn't able to see any indication of the station's name and could only make out some of the faded mosaics with their complex geometrical patterns repeating until they disappeared in the dark.

In the middle of all the activity on the platform was a woman wearing a black agency suit. Rather than the tailored blazer and skirt favored by most of the female agents in Suitland, she was wearing the men's cut. Her hair was in a long, dark braid that fell over her right shoulder and she was holding a clipboard. She observed the men's progress and occasionally told her subordinates where to set a piece of furniture or one of the garden's flower beds as everything was carried off the train.

Laury called up to the woman, who waved in our direction and continued to issue orders to the men as she approached us. Once she was closer, I was surprised to recognize her as Helen Roth, a brilliant economist who I'd seen present a paper on economic diversity at the 2011 Civic Dynamics Summit in Minneapolis. Her ideas on how to nurture and sustain local businesses in struggling areas had inspired me to propose several development programs of my own. She was young for her accomplishments and rather pretty. When she smiled down at Laury I saw that she still had the charming gap in her front teeth, which I took to mean that the denture treatment was reserved for Kirklin's lower-level enforcers. Back in 2011 I had approached her after her talk in order to thank her for sharing her insights. She had smiled warmly and even seemed impressed when I introduced myself as an agent with the USMS. Looking back, I had often been disappointed in myself that I hadn't screwed up the courage to ask if I could buy her a drink. But if she recognized me as I was, standing in the dark with my face bloodied, she did nothing to indicate it.

She gestured down the tunnel and offered a word of either warning or encouragement to Laury before tossing her a flashlight. Laury thanked her and pointed the light down the tunnel as she began to walk. The man to my left elbowed me, making me understand that we were to follow.

We worked our way through a system of dead tunnels that Laury seemed to know by heart. The air was damp and filled with a reek of mold that made it hard to breathe. The tracks themselves ran perfectly straight, but she led us through a dizzying progression of access tunnels and abandoned stairways. Even if I had known what station we had departed from, it was impossible to tell if we were moving deeper into the tunnels or doubling back, if we were on our way up to the surface or winding farther and farther down. After some time we came upon a set of tracks that were the narrower three-foot gauge that hadn't been used in over eighty years. Laury turned off her flashlight, revealing a faint and slowly flashing red light at the far end of the tunnel. As we moved toward it, I saw that the light was coming from a high fixture on a brick wall. There was a heavy security door in the middle with a keypad over the handle. Laury entered the code and pulled the door open, flooding the tunnel with light.

My eyes were still adjusting as I was pushed through the door. The space was filled with the din of many people hard at work and I was eventually able to make out a large bullpen of desks under a high white ceiling. Men and women in identical black suits were gathered around large computer monitors and dry erase boards, handing printouts back and forth, and calling out to one another in Esperanto. As I was led around the bullpen by Laury and the two men, I passed a series of classrooms where Kirklin's agents sat at school desks loudly reciting phrases in Esperanto. It was difficult to tell if their booming recitations were grammar exercises or loyalty oaths until I heard an instructor call out enthusiastically, "Jes! Tre bona!" From another room I heard the sound of someone groaning in pain, while just outside, a young man with bandaged fingers sat flipping through a magazine under a sign that read DENTISTO.

I was led into a long corridor with windows looking out onto firing ranges where men and women were shooting handguns and rifles at moving targets. The glass was soundproof and the flashes of gunfire were noiseless. We passed windows looking in on large gymnasiums where people were rappelling from the ceiling while, down below, others practiced hand-to-hand combat. One particularly troubling room contained a group of men hollering to one another as they used flamethrowers to attack a replica of a National Guard truck. They stood in a half circle spraying its cab with flames. Fifty yards away, a man hoisted an RPG onto his shoulder, then shouted something to the others, who scattered. The bed of the truck, I noticed, was loaded with two dozen mannequins all dressed in fatigues.

We turned into a small passageway with a series of windowless doors. Laury picked one seemingly at random and punched in the code to open it. Inside was a small closet filled with cleaning supplies and a few pieces of office furniture. She nodded and the two men pushed me inside. They forced me into an office chair and tied me to it with some extension cords they found on a shelf.

"You'll have to forgive us," Laury said, as one of the men made a final knot in the cords around my chest. "As you've seen on the news, we're not really in the habit of taking prisoners. But Terry wants to see you before you're dealt with, so this will have to do."

The men filed out of the room and stood behind her.

"Anyway," she said, pulling the door shut, "you won't be with us long."

The door locked itself with a buzz and I sat there in the dark for what felt like hours. There was little to occupy me in that time except for the throb in my nose and a general sense of dread. It was with no small sense of relief that I greeted the sound of a distant crackle in my ear, followed by a bright spotlight shining out from between the gaps in the extension cords cinched across my chest.

OWEN stepped into the spotlight, looking a little disoriented.

"Did you save the day?" he said. "Did I miss it?"

Before I could answer he approached me and began examining my face.

"What happened here?"

"I was beaten up."

OWEN shook his head, not even trying to hide his disappointment.

"Let me get a better look at you," he said, leaning in closer. He seemed pleasantly surprised by the degree of my injuries. "Hey, you look horrible!"

"You don't say."

"You're a mess—isn't that great?"

"You'll have to walk me through it."

"My patch," he said. "I made some adjustments when I was rebooting back in Suitland. It must finally be working. Now I can see you get injured and it won't bother me."

"I'm happy for you," I said.

"Really? Because you look miserable."

Deciding it might be more productive to change the subject, I gave OWEN a rundown of everything that had happened since he fainted. He seemed almost impressed with how quickly our plan had deteriorated in his absence.

"OWEN, they're going to kill me."

"What? Oh, no, no, no. Don't worry about that," OWEN said before adding, "Well, I mean, yes—they probably are planning to kill you at some point, but according to you, Laury said Kirklin wants to talk first. That's an amazing opportunity to gather intelligence. We can't even *think* of escaping before then."

I was about to protest, but the door buzzed again and began to open. OWEN winked as he disappeared.

A young woman entered the room, pushing a handcart. She had a bleached pixie cut and was wearing a black jumpsuit. On her neck, there was a tattoo of a gas mask. Behind her was a heavyset man with a shaved head and a matching jumpsuit. He was holding a bucket and a handgun.

The woman stepped to one side and waited without expression while the man put the bucket on the ground and pointed his gun at me. He nudged the bucket toward me with his foot and there was the sound of water sloshing inside.

"This will only take a minute," he said. "And if you're thinking of turning into a giant clown or a dick with wings,

I'm going to start shooting at anything that moves. Understand?"

I nodded and he placed the handgun in the canvas belt of his jumpsuit. He retrieved a butterfly knife from his pocket and cut through the extension cords and the restraint around my wrists. Then he took a towel from the cart and tossed it into my lap, telling me to wash up and get undressed.

While I wiped the blood from my face, I noticed a handheld metal detector sitting on the cart. Sarah Laury's description of OWEN's projections must have reminded Kirklin's people of our run-in at the museum so now they were on the lookout for some technology. OWEN must have spotted the metal detector even before I did. When I went to pull off the tie clip, he'd already camouflaged it to my tie. I managed to slide it onto the second knuckle of my pinky finger, where it camouflaged itself again.

Once I'd taken off my clothes, the man pulled out a tape measure and started taking my measurements, calling them out to the woman as he did so. Meanwhile, she was busy placing my individual articles of clothing into plastic evidence bags. She made sure each bag was sealed before picking it up and waving the metal detector over it. My wristwatch and belt buckle both elicited sustained beeps and she frowned as if this might be significant, making notations on their respective bags with a red marker. Just to be safe she also ripped off the heels of my shoes, before bagging them, and used a penknife to cut out the lining of my blazer.

When the man was finished with my measurements, he grabbed the metal detector and told me to hold out my arms. As he started to wave the device over me I flicked the tie clip off my finger and coughed to cover the sound of it pinging against the cement floor.

"Hold still," he said.

He moved the wand slowly over my body before clicking it off and tossing it back onto the cart.

"All right, he's clean."

He gathered up a pile of fresh clothes his partner had placed on the cart and handed them to me.

"Put this on."

It was a black suit just like the ones Kirklin's agents wore.

When I was dressed, the man removed an adhesive bandage from his pocket and applied it carefully to the wound on my nose. He straightened my tie and looked me up and down. He smiled approvingly, then punched me in the stomach and shoved me back down into my chair.

The two left and OWEN sprang up out of the darkness.

"This is *perfect*," he said. "Kirklin's going to interrogate you, which will finally give us some evidence to relay to the authorities. Then we escape, save Metropolis, and return to Suitland as heroes. And on top of all that, you'll be walking out of here with a brand-new suit. Not bad."

I grabbed the clip off the floor and slid it back onto my tie, where it became invisible against the black silk. I was trying to come around to OWEN's optimistic point of view, when he suddenly vanished and the door opened again.

A man holding an assault rifle ordered me out into the hallway. There was a whole tactical assault team standing behind him.

"This is so flattering," OWEN said in my ear as I exited the room. "Look how many guns they brought."

One of the men put a bag over my head and I was walked through more tunnels and up stairways. The air grew cooler and our footsteps began to echo until eventually I heard the sound of a grate being lifted and I felt someone pull me up into the open air. When the bag was removed, we were in a fenced-off lot filled with construction equipment. Among the dump trucks and backhoes were dozens of large items, covered in canvas drop cloths, that looked an awful lot like artillery guns. I stared up at them until one of the men jabbed me in the back with the muzzle of his gun and told me to start walking. Four more of Kirklin's men were waiting for us outside the lot. They weren't holding weapons, but it was easy enough to spot the bulges under their jackets. The men with rifles exchanged a few words with them in Esperanto as they handed me off, then fell back.

OWEN told me we were in the Lower South Side, though I could have guessed as much by all the newly renovated industrial lofts. After the country's manufacturing decline, the once industry-heavy LSS had managed to thrive thanks to the Hispanic and African American families who settled there along with a healthy number of Korean and Middle Eastern immigrants, all of whom were eventually priced out as Metropolis transformed into a consumer city. The term "haute industrial" had become an enduring phrase in real estate development thanks to the popularity of the neighborhood. And since the rich were famously insular, the streets now looked more abandoned than they had after the factories first closed. With no eyes on the street, it was the perfect neighborhood for whatever Kirklin had in mind.

The night was quiet except for the distant sound of traffic

and the occasional murmur of Esperanto among my captors. I was taken to a large brick building with an unmarked door illuminated by a floodlight.

Through the door was a carpeted hallway lit softly by brass sconces. Turning a corner, we entered a finely decorated room filled with Victorian furniture. A young man in a tuxedo and white gloves was standing behind a host's station. My escorts were now hanging back, as if they didn't want to interfere with the interview that was about to take place.

"Saluton, sinjoro. Are you the prisoner that is expected?"

I looked back at my escorts, who all nodded.

"Yes," I said to the man.

From behind him I heard live music and people conversing.

"Excellent," he said, taking a pen to the guest book resting open in front of him. "It looks like you will be joining your party in the Bernard booth."

He bowed gravely in my direction before turning to open a heavy door. The music and conversation grew louder. Suddenly, I was looking out on a large restaurant filled with Kirklin's agents. The man who I now recognized as a maître d' extended his gloved hand out toward the dining room.

"This way please, sinjoro."

"Do me a favor," OWEN said in my ear. "Pretend to sneeze if this is already weirder than you thought it'd be."

When I did, the maître d' offered me some short blessing in Esperanto.

He led me to a deep, high-backed booth in a dimly lit corner. Hung on the wall over the table was a large oil painting of Anaximander Bernard. The sight of that mad old anarchist with his fez and characteristic scowl was so severe and unexpected that for a moment I almost didn't notice Kirklin sitting in the booth. He was writing in a leather-bound notebook, his free hand idly turning a glass of what looked like whiskey on the tablecloth. His dark goatee had been replaced by a full beard with some gray in it that came to a Mephistophelean point. The intensity he had been known for in Suitland now had a quiet menace to it, like a storm between claps of thunder. The maître d' cleared his throat, then apologized for interrupting as Kirklin looked up from his writing. Kirklin smiled and thanked him in Esperanto before inviting me to have a seat.

He continued to write as I did so, finishing a thought before capping his pen and closing the notebook. He gave me an appraising look and was about to say something just as our waiter dropped off our menus, going over them briefly in Esperanto and bowing as he left. Kirklin looked over his for a moment before finally addressing me.

"Sarah says you know the language," he said. "But let me know if you need any help with the menu."

After a cautionary silence OWEN risked whispering in my ear.

"See if they can do a stuffed pepper."

"I should be fine," I told Kirklin.

"Okay," he said. "Have whatever you like."

"I mean I'm not hungry."

Kirklin looked up, concerned.

"It's your last meal," he said. "You should get something."

He didn't seem to be threatening me as much as simply acknowledging both that his killing me was a given and that he honestly felt it would be a shame for me to die on an empty stomach.

"Get the octopus salad," said OWEN, who had apparently read the menu. "It sounds weird."

I waited for him to tell me what else was available, but as Kirklin stared at me expectantly, OWEN began to chant, "Octo-pus! Octo-pus! Octo-pus!"

"I guess I'll take the octopus," I said.

Kirklin smiled and waved the waiter over. He ordered for me in Esperanto, then pointed to something on the drink menu, indicating that we were both to have one.

"Jes, kolego," the waiter said, bowing again.

He watched the waiter depart and said, as if he were remarking on the weather, "He's one of my best agents."

"Is that why you have him waiting tables?"

"He's only here two nights a week. This club is a place where we all pitch in. When I have time, I run the kitchen. Sarah even comes in once a month to play her trumpet with Larry and the boys."

He gestured toward the head of the room, where a jazz combo was currently occupied with a light, splashy riff on "Yankee Doodle." Kirklin finished his drink, tilting his head back and closing his good eye as he savored it. Just then the waiter set down two tumblers in front of us.

"We're expecting a long transition period," he said, handing the waiter his empty glass. "We don't know when any of us will be able to enjoy this sort of civilization again."

He picked up the fresh glass in front of him and held it out to me.

"Cheers, Henry," he said.

I reluctantly clinked my glass against his.

"You know who I am?"

"There was a wallet in your suit. Though I probably would have recognized you from the picture in your personnel file after all those requests to work in Metropolis. A few of your proposals weren't bad. But when I checked in with some of my eyes and ears in Suitland they advised against bringing you in. You should know that you have a reputation as the biggest milquetoast bean sorter in the history of the United States Municipal Survey. And if you consider the nature of the organization, that's saying something."

"I hope you're listening to this," OWEN said through his laughter. "This is valuable feedback."

He would have laughed harder if he had known Kirklin's words had left me feeling oddly flattered.

"It was never personal," Kirklin said. "I'm sure now you can probably understand why I didn't think you'd be a good fit. The problems facing this nation's cities can't be solved with infrastructure reports and development projects. They need something more radical."

"Like being blown up?"

"My point exactly," he said. "You wouldn't recognize progress if you looked it in the face. You risked your life to save a museum, but for years you've worked for an agency that throughout its history has systematically destroyed entire communities. Even these days 'urban renewal' is USMS code for helping cities carry out glorified landgrabs. Don't get me wrong, you Suitland people are smart and hardworking and I'm sure you're all trying to solve problems the only way you know how. But you never stop to ask why the city council you're collaborating with wants the highway to run through a particular part of town. You don't ask why they'd rather put funds toward parking garages than better bus service. Every four years, Garrett allocated $2.5 million of the agency's budget to help preserve the exterior of the Metropolis Museum of History, but when I asked for a quarter of that to help bolster the city's system of homeless shelters, he had the gall to tell me that the homelessness problem wasn't in my remit. The USMS has no interest in making cities more livable for its most desperate citizens, but it will spend a small fortune to polish the exterior of a tourist trap."

Kirklin maintained his outward calm, but his speech betrayed the same pontificating bully he was known to be back in Suitland. I sipped my drink, which turned out to be a strong, oaky bourbon, and decided to needle him.

"Well, if it's any consolation," I said, "before your toothless goons shot it up, the exterior of the MetMoH looked great."

Kirklin smiled, apparently unbothered by my tone.

"Tell me something, Henry. What was the last project you proposed to Garrett that he rejected?"

Kirklin was so sure that I was as good as dead that our conversation had a certain freedom to it. I didn't see any harm in telling the truth.

"I wrote a plan to help promote commercial diversity in Cleveland."

Kirklin nodded.

"Cleveland, Ohio," he said. "Median household income, $26,000."

"He said the mayor's office wouldn't go for it."

"Garrett usually has you guys give him proposals in batches. Did he approve any of the others?"

"Renovations on the Santa Cruz Municipal Wharf."

"Santa Cruz, California. Median household income just over $60,000."

Then, as if answering a question he felt confident I was about to ask, he said, "Look, I know Garrett and I have a past, but that's not what this is. Freezing is something he inherited and I'm sure he hates it as much as I do. But I'm not willing to sign on to his brand of compromise. The only option is to destroy the system as it is. Give it a healthy death."

I was struck by his use of the word "freezing," an echo of his last message to the agency, the strange text that had appeared on all our phones during the attack in Suitland. At the time I had mistaken it for a threat, but to hear Kirklin talk, it sounded as if he had actually been describing the nature of his complaint with the agency. But what was freezing? And why did he mention it as if I already knew?

"This is all perfectly fascinating," OWEN said in my ear. "But do you think you could get him to share some actual information?"

"So what's next," I said, taking in the room from our booth and worrying about what Kirklin had meant when he mentioned a long transition. "Are you going to blow up every restaurant in Metropolis?"

I wanted to exaggerate his position to demonstrate how insane it was, but Kirklin nodded as if I'd impressed him.

"It's a good thing we caught you when we did," he said.

"You don't—"

"Not all of them. Just a few dozen of the popular ones. After the museum district, we're hoping that some evenly distributed restaurant explosions over the following weeks will discourage the type of volume most fine-dining establishments need to stay afloat. Meanwhile, we'll be starting up our campaigns against the high-end grocery stores and retail chains. That should give the more skittish bourgeois the clue that it's time to get out and the tourists can all start spending their three-day weekends in Toronto. Over time we'll see a new city emerge, one organized around human relationships, a place where businesses are owned by members of the same community they're serving, where development and renewal is driven by the interests of the people it will directly affect."

"When does this start?"

Kirklin put down his glass and looked at his watch.

"We destroy the Mallory Club in an hour and a half."

"Okay," OWEN said. "I just called in a bomb threat at the Mallory Club. They should be clearing it out now. I've also recorded Kirklin's confession and can send it to the authorities along with the GPS location to this place and the underground facility. But we'll need to get you out of here first so we don't get caught in a shoot-out with the National Guard. Keep drawing him out. I'll let you know when it's time to go."

OWEN's promise to get me out of there gave me courage, but staring Kirklin's madness in the face made it difficult to keep my voice from shaking.

"What about the patrons?"

"At the Mallory Club?" Kirklin squinted as if from my question he was no longer sure I understood anything he had just told me. "They're bourgeois scum."

"The staff?"

"This isn't an art project, Henry. The world needs to change. That's why we built this place. It's our way of saying good-bye to those parts of the old world we'll miss. The parts we're sacrificing to make this city better."

"And why are you telling me this?"

He frowned.

"I was just making conversation."

That was when I saw Sarah Laury approach over Kirklin's shoulder. She was wearing a red cocktail dress and matching lipstick, both of which made her look older and younger at the same time. She touched Kirklin's arm as she took the seat next to him, then leaned in to kiss him on the cheek. He smiled and took her hand as she whispered something in Esperanto in his ear, most of which OWEN managed to catch.

"They've been running tests on your old suit, but didn't find anything."

"Because you're here," I said.

"Pardon?" Laury answered.

She leaned into Kirklin, regarding me with something like disgust.

"No, nothing," I said.

Kirklin's expression had changed as soon as he got the news about my suit, like he was doing his best to conceal a mounting frustration.

The waiter arrived with my octopus salad. It was a shallow white dish of julienned carrots, pea sprouts, and grilled tentacles. It all smelled of lemon and vinegar and the neat rows of suction cups had a slight char that made them look a little obscene.

"I want to see at least two big bites," OWEN said.

"He's a flesh eater," Laury said. "I should have known."

This comment seemed to break the tension and Kirklin laughed.

"Sarah and I have never agreed on the ethics of eating animals."

She smiled up at him, suggesting that what he was referencing was the source of an intense flirtation between the two.

"Well, as long as you're both fine killing innocent people, I suppose that's all that matters."

I speared one of the octopus tentacles with my fork and took a big bite off the thick end, making sure to maintain eye contact with Laury.

"How's your nose?" she asked.

"Sarah, please," Kirklin interrupted. "I'd like to keep this interview as civil as possible."

She settled back in the booth, keeping her eyes fixed on me as I chewed my mouthful of tentacle. I was happily envisioning OWEN's processors back in Suitland churning through the probabilities for a speedy and safe escape. Though I realized that his mind was perhaps elsewhere when he exclaimed sotto voce in my ear, "Gross! I can't believe you actually ate it."

"I'm glad you're enjoying your meal," Kirklin said, looking slightly put off at the overlarge wad of octopus in my cheek. "And you should know that this whole conversation is happening as a courtesy. Not because you're from Suitland, but because you managed to find Sarah's train and stop my team at the Museum of History. Obviously we don't see eye to eye on the best future for Metropolis, but I'm sure we can both accept that as enemies we've earned each other's respect."

"You had mine until recently."

"Well, then, for old time's sake, I'm asking you to level with me, Henry. We need to know what kind of technology you're working with. We didn't find any hardware on your suit. We didn't find anything on your person. So I want to know how you're managing these images."

I moved the salad to the side and washed the rest of the tentacle down with whiskey.

"Why would I tell you anything? According to you, I'm already dead."

"Yes, but we think the same way. When you were trying to stop me, you went after someone I cared about. You've maintained your composure here enough to convince me that you really are selfless, that you don't care if you die. But what if I were to have a team of guys grab Garrett and let him watch while we burn USMS headquarters to the ground? Or how about I arrange it so the police find the old man OD'd on heroin in some motel room outside Baltimore?"

The specificity of this last threat led me to believe that such contingencies must have already been in place, a thought that made me feel short of breath.

"That would be more bad publicity for us," I said, trying to appear calm. "It just came out that our station chief in Metropolis is a pedophile."

Laury reached across Kirklin for his glass and threw the rest of his whiskey in my face. A hush fell over the tables around us and some of Kirklin's people turned to look in our direction. The music from the front of the room continued to play and, when Kirklin held his palm up to the other tables, the swell of conversation around us gradually resumed.

Laury leaned toward me with her teeth clenched.

"You have no idea what the hell you're talking about, vi mizera vermo."

Kirklin said her name. It was hard to tell whether he was reassuring her or asking her to be quiet. She sunk back in the booth again. The cut on my nose burned as I used my napkin to wipe the bourbon from my face.

"You might not agree with our aims or our methods," Kirklin said. "But the fact of the matter is that we've been downright surgical up to this point. Unless we get some co-operation from you, I'm one phone call away from putting your worst nightmares on the front page of the paper. And for your information, someone having sex with children and a middle-aged man dating an eighteen-year-old genius are two completely different pathologies."

Sarah smiled wryly to herself.

"You want to cool him off a little?" OWEN said. "I don't care for all this burning-down-headquarters talk. *I'm* headquarters. Stroke his ego or something."

"What does it matter?" I said. "Whatever this technology is, it obviously hasn't gotten me anywhere."

"This should be interesting," OWEN said.

"I'm your prisoner and you demolished all but one of the places you set out to demolish. What could some gizmo

Klaus cooked up possibly matter to someone who's prepared to take on the National Guard?"

OWEN groaned when I mentioned Klaus and I realized my mistake.

"I don't say this enough," OWEN said. "But you're bad at everything."

Kirklin picked up his now empty glass and tapped it in view of a passing waiter.

"Nice try," he said. "Klaus only works on OWEN projects and this tech couldn't be."

I was grateful my slip hadn't given away OWEN's interface. I thought it might be a good idea to push the subject, try to make it seem even more like misdirection.

"How can you be sure?"

Kirklin shared a look with Laury and laughed before turning back to face me.

"Haven't you noticed anything strange about OWEN's performance lately?"

"Our technicians rooted out the virus. HQ has been up and running for days."

"You're talking about the lights going out, the doors locking themselves, the self-destruct sequence on your phones. That was just the virus being uploaded. You would have to do a complete memory wipe to get it out."

Kirklin observed my confusion and looked almost hurt by it.

"We installed an update to OWEN's artificial intelligence to render its interface nonfunctional. Klaus has been talking about giving that thing a personality for years, so I did him one better. I turned it into a lunatic."

I listened for OWEN to interrupt, but he was silent. No. Not quite. There was a deep, soft static in my ear. Meanwhile, Kirklin's frustration seemed to be growing over the fact that nobody at Suitland had noticed what he felt was the defining flourish of his attack on the agency.

"What about its new propensity for insults? The vanity? The impulsive behavior? No one found any of that strange?"

Kirklin laughed in exasperation. There was no way for him to know that everyone had been avoiding OWEN-tech since the virus. And Klaus had been in such a rush to prove the value of his new interface that he apparently hadn't noticed anything out of the ordinary as he sent it into the field. A knot began to grow in my stomach that I couldn't attribute to the octopus or the liquor. I waited for OWEN to defend himself, to call Kirklin out on a shameless deception, but the static in my ear only grew more distinct.

"Tell him it was hallucinogens," OWEN finally broke in, though he sounded distracted.

As I took in what Kirklin had just said, it occurred to me that maybe I was alone after all. At a nearby table a man accepted a martini from the waiter, then said something droll in Esperanto that caused the members of his party to laugh. I was trying to figure out what the virus meant in terms of OWEN's loyalties, whether his eccentricities were genuine or just a complex sabotage. I kept an eye on the man's martini and remembered that it had been OWEN's idea that we start drinking in the museum. When I broke down by the river, getting me a drink had been his first suggestion. Suddenly I was thinking of all the times OWEN had discouraged me from contacting the authorities. But before I could pursue this notion further, I heard myself already repeating OWEN's lie to Kirklin, who seemed unconvinced.

"You mean Garrett signed off on a plan to send a man into the field with weaponized hallucinogens?"

"Yes," I said, not quite sure how to make this sound more plausible. "I guess you have him feeling a little reckless."

"All of my men described the same creature attacking them at the museum."

"Power of suggestion," OWEN said.

"It's a hallucinogen," I said. "You start shouting about a clown monster and everyone sees a clown monster."

"Why was Sarah only partially affected?"

"Ventilation system," OWEN said.

"The ventilation set up on your train was more sophisticated than we anticipated. The dose she received was reduced."

"Tell him to test his men's blood," OWEN said.

When I did, Laury still looked dubious, but OWEN's quick thinking seemed to have convinced Kirklin, who was now stroking his beard and looking lost in thought.

"Okay," he said. "Here's what's going to happen. For now I'm going to thank you for your cooperation and send you off with some of my agents, who will take you to a secure location and hold you there. I'm going to run blood tests on Sarah and the team that was at the history museum. If you're lying to me, I will proceed with what we discussed with respect to your worst nightmares. But if, as you say, your advantage over my men and Sarah involved some sort of hallucinogen, I will give you a relatively quick death. Of course, you did admit to giving Sarah a psychotropic drug against her will, and so you should be prepared to receive thirty to forty minutes of torture. Understood?"

I nodded.

"All right," he said. "Now, you barely touched your salad. Can we give you a few minutes to eat in peace or would you rather leave now?"

"I'd like to leave," I said.

Kirklin shrugged. "You can go out the way you came. My men will take you to the car."

"Okay," OWEN said. "Get ready to hustle."

I rose from my seat as the waiter finally arrived with a fresh drink for Kirklin. He bowed when he saw Laury, asking if he could get her anything. She shook her head no and smiled graciously, the same warm face I'd seen on the cover of so many magazines.

"Before you go," Kirklin said, "we'd also like to know how you found out about Sarah's train."

"I read her play," I said.

For the first time since she had found me out on her train she looked at me with something other than revulsion. It was the alert look of a young writer whose play had been read by a stranger.

"It must have been difficult to grow up with so much attention. If everyone started to treat me like an object, I suppose it would be easy for me to start thinking about them as objects too. But there are good people out there, Ms. Laury, and they're going to get hurt."

"Good people are already being hurt every day by the status quo," she said. "But they're poor, so no one but us seems to care."

She turned from me to ask the waiter to remove my salad from the table.

Kirklin laughed at her last remark and kissed her on the temple, then gave me a friendly wave good-bye.

"I admire your will, Henry," he said. "You might not think so, but this is a good death."

He looked back down at Laury. They smiled at each other and immediately were wrapped in an impenetrable intimacy.

I didn't bother to say good-bye, just headed toward the door leading to the foyer where Kirklin's men would be waiting for me. It was hard to shake the feeling that the whole room was watching. Tables grew quiet as I passed, and I heard a few chuckles as the band up front began to play a brassy rendition of Nat Simpson's "A Death in the City."

"Why did you tell him to test their blood?" I said under my breath.

"One thing at a time," OWEN said.

"What's the plan?"

"Just keep walking. I'll take care of it."

I was thinking about the virus as I started to open the door leading out of that dining room, trying to do the math in my head to figure out whether OWEN had saved my life more times than he had jeopardized it. Looking back, he seemed to be always doing both simultaneously. That was the extent of my optimism as I prepared to face Kirklin's people with only a warped supercomputer at my side.

In the waiting area, the maître d' was nowhere in sight, but two of Kirklin's men were waiting for me near the empty podium. They began to approach me, then stopped.

One of them asked something in Esperanto. I followed their eyes and saw Kirklin standing over my shoulder. He answered them in more Esperanto, which OWEN translated in my ear.

"I've decided to walk him out myself," he said. "But while you're here I need you to go back and tell the kitchen to rush two octopus salads to the Bernard booth."

The men seemed confused, but answered, "Jes, kolego."

If they had looked closer, they might have noticed that Kirklin's eye color had changed from dark brown to a striking blue, which I myself didn't notice until he grinned and made an after-you gesture toward the open hallway in front of us. Kirklin's men stepped through a panel door built into the wall that must have led back to the kitchen. OWEN called out to them as we began to head down the hall.

"One more thing."

"Jes, kolego?"

"Have the waiter tell the people at the Bernard booth that the salads are from Agent Thompson."

The men answered, "Jes, kolego," again and left.

I picked up my pace down the hall.

"That bit with the salads wasn't exactly necessary," I said.

"Neither is domestic terrorism," OWEN said. "But we're living in an imperfect world. Also, you might want to slow down on your way out the door. Remember, you're supposed to look like someone who doesn't want to be killed."

I tried to heed OWEN's advice, but my adrenaline had me push the door with a bit too much force. It flew open with a bang, surprising two more of Kirklin's men, who were standing in front of a town car. OWEN stepped toward them as

Kirklin and began speaking to them rapidly in Esperanto. Instead of translating, he whispered to me the instructions, "Stay close."

OWEN continued to address the two men as he approached the car. I stayed a few steps behind him and watched as he held out his right hand expectantly. One of the men produced a set of keys, which he tossed to OWEN. The keys passed through his projection of Kirklin and struck me in the chest. I awkwardly caught them before they hit the ground, which was when OWEN clued me in to the rest of his plan by screaming in my ear, "Go! Go! Go! Go!"

The fading specter of Kirklin waved a toodle-oo at the two men while I fumbled to open the driver's-side door. It wasn't until the engine turned over that they seemed to see me behind the wheel. One broke left, making for the passenger side, while the other reached for a gun in a shoulder holster under his jacket. The car had surprising pickup, and I was able to roll the latter over the hood before he got a shot off. The other was just opening the door as the car pulled away. He tried to hold on to the handle and there was an unholy thwack when his head hit the door, slamming it shut. OWEN appeared next to me in the passenger seat as we roared down the street. The man with the gun let off a few rounds in our direction and I took a squealing right.

"I've transmitted Kirklin's statement to the authorities along with this location, which means this whole neighborhood is about to get locked down. Take a left onto Hamilton and follow that up to the Van Horne Expressway."

I checked the rearview every few seconds and OWEN told me to keep my eyes on the road.

"Kirklin knows this place is burnt. Right now he has everyone at his disposal wiping the area down. No way he can spare anyone to chase us."

Just then lights appeared behind us.

"Unless he doesn't know you have a comm device on you, in which case sending people after you would be the first thing he'd do."

I glared at him until he warned me again to keep my eyes on the road.

"Judging by the spacing of headlights and rate of approach, I'd say we're looking at a half dozen motorcycles. Our best bet is still the VHE, but we might have to proceed with a little less caution."

Once we turned onto Hamilton, I pushed the pedal to the floor, tearing through intersections and hoping for the best. OWEN verified that I was putting some distance between us and our pursuers, but pointed out that Hamilton was about to get busier when we reached the VHE. Already there were a few other cars on the road and farther down were the bright lights of heavy traffic.

At the first major intersection, OWEN accessed the city's traffic management center, thanks to the agency's participation in Transcom, giving us a green light that turned red as soon as we were halfway through. I watched in the rearview as the bikes nimbly darted through the cross traffic. OWEN was preparing the same stoplight trick for the next intersection, when we heard a gunshot and our back window shattered.

I looked over at OWEN, who was pouring himself a drink.

"I am very worried about your well-being right now," he said.

The bikes were practically on top of us and through our broken window the sustained brapping of their engines was deafening. I sped through Broome with another green light from OWEN, but this time he turned it red as soon as I hit the intersection, giving the cross traffic a green. An SUV clipped the motorcycle closest to us, the rider and bike tumbling in different directions down the street.

OWEN screamed in celebration and began drinking directly from a bottle of black liquid marked "190^{10} proof." There was a crazed look in his eyes. Remembering Kirklin's words, I found myself frightened of him.

The collision back on Broome bought us some distance from the remaining bikes and the on-ramp to the VHE was close.

I drove up the shoulder of the interchange to get around a line of cars. There was some honking from the other motorists, and then an angry chorus of horns when I left the on-ramp and took the town car across three lanes on the VHE.

It still wasn't long before I heard the motorcycles creeping up behind us.

OWEN leaned forward in his seat.

"Remember when I thought I saw a drone on our way from the airport?"

"Yes?"

"Well, now I'm more or less sure I did."

Up ahead a drone came into view coasting above an approaching overpass. It swooped down into the road and I saw that it was in fact one of our old surveillance drones, painted a gunmetal blue. Its strakes wobbled for a moment before it arced up into the air and dove directly at us. I swerved into the next lane to avoid an impact and heard screeching behind us as the drone slid in the wrong direction down the highway, sending up sparks before finally going under the wheels of a van, which lost control and smashed into the median.

Coming out from the overpass, I looked up and saw a massive swarm of drones moving in a slow circle over the highway. OWEN told me to take the exit leading down to the entrance of the Hapsford Tunnel and a dozen drones broke off to follow us, while the bikes continued to close the distance from behind.

The drones that had separated off from the swarm looped down into the road, approaching us from the front. I was able to avoid the first three before the strake of one clipped the car's passenger side. The other drones leveled off and flew toward us in a formation covering the width of the road. I ducked down, holding on to the wheel and doing my best to maintain speed while aiming for a gap between the middle two. The windshield shattered as we broke through, but I was relieved to see in the side-view mirror that the wall of drones hadn't pulled up in time to avoid the motorcyclists and crashed into them, sending them all skidding and bouncing across the expressway.

OWEN cried out in celebration, though I could barely hear it over the wind whipping through the car. We were about to enter the tunnel as the swarm of drones rose up in a great column and began to surge east over the Lawrence River toward the other end of the tunnel.

"They're going to try to flush you out from the other side," OWEN shouted. "If you can make it a third of the way we can ditch the car and get out through the ventilation access."

As we entered the tunnel it was already vibrating with the collective buzz of the drones. Up ahead there was also the sound of breaking glass and heavy thuds as cars were hit.

OWEN ordered me out into the tunnel, then led me to one of the maintenance exits. The door was locked, but I kicked off the handle and pulled it open, ducking inside just as a barrage of drones began to slam into our car. OWEN was already lighting the way forward into the long, dark corridor ahead of us, waving his bottle of black liquid in the air and letting out a series of piercing victory whoops, while behind me was the sound of explosions and the smell of burning fuel.

10

OWEN guided me through the pump rooms and subterranean passageways of the Hapsford at a brisk pace. He drank as he ran, lifting the sloshing bottle up to his lips while flying ahead of me in an exaggerated high-knee sprint. He finished off the first bottle in a few minutes and tossed it over his shoulder, producing a new one from his jacket.

OWEN had led us down into the subbasement of the tunnel's east ventilation tower, one of two ten-story brick towers built a few hundred feet into the water on either side of the river, each containing hundreds of large fans that bring fresh air into the tunnel, preventing commuters from suffocating from the carbon monoxide produced by regular traffic.

"Over here," OWEN said.

He took an abrupt left and I found him standing in front of another door, staring at it wild-eyed and pointing at the handle while sucking absently at his liquor bottle.

"OWEN, what are you doing?"

He lowered the bottle and it made a loud, smacking pop when he pulled it from his lips.

"Through here is our way out."

"I mean your drinking."

"Oh," he said, looking down at the bottle in his hand. "I guess I found everything we just did sort of stressful."

He pointed to the door again and told me to open it. It was unlocked and he lit up the room as we entered. It looked to be a small metal shop filled with workbenches and bound stacks of ductwork. We walked toward an elevator at the far end, OWEN still taking long pulls from his bottle. As I passed a workbench, I grabbed a white rag from the top of a toolbox and tucked it into my back pants pocket.

I called the elevator down and OWEN told me to hit the button for the first floor, which would let us off at the walkway leading back to the East Side's esplanade along the Lawrence.

"Let's go up," I said, hitting the button for the top floor. "See if we can get a visual on any other drones."

OWEN thought about this for a moment and nodded, placing his bottle back into his jacket.

The elevator let us out on a floor filled with dozens of fifteen-foot-high fan motors. We wandered among the thrumming motors until OWEN spotted the stairwell and we took it up to the roof.

To the west there was the dark outline of the tower opposite ours and beyond that the skyline of Center City across the river, bright and startling. Tonight there was the added spectacle of National Guard helicopters hovering over the VHE, running their searchlights over the wreckage from our chase. Behind us were flashing lights and the sound of sirens as first responders began to gather at the tunnel's east entrance.

OWEN had his hands in his pockets and was looking up into the cloudless night sky.

"No more drones," he said. "But that could change. Let's get you someplace safe and wait for any news coming out of the South Side. If anyone took our transmission seriously, then Kirklin should be in custody soon."

"If not?"

"We'll figure something out," he said.

He was still watching the sky, but casually. A man enjoying the view. His interface was allowing the winds up on the roof to make a mess of his usually immaculate hair.

"What about Garrett?" I said.

"Don't worry."

"He said he was going to kill him."

"He won't."

I took the rag out of my back pocket and held it at my side.

"And how do you know that, OWEN?"

He faced me and smiled. His eyes were still wild looking from the chase and the black liquid he had downed.

"Kirklin and his people are gonna be too busy dealing with us."

He started to head back to the stairwell, but I didn't follow.

"We need to talk about that virus," I said.

He stopped and reappeared a few feet in front of me. It was clear I'd gotten his attention, though he still looked ready to play the whole thing off.

"What about it?"

"Kirklin said it's still inside you."

He thought about this for a moment.

"It's part of me," he said. "Sure."

"Did Klaus know the virus was still in play when he let you out of the lab?"

OWEN looked down.

"No," he said.

"But you knew."

He was nervous now, like someone telling the truth against his better judgment.

"They would have had to reboot my interface to get rid of it, which would erase the O_1 memory cache."

"And?"

"The O_1 is who I am. It's my memories. My configuration. To get rid of the virus they'd have to kill me and some guy named O_2 would get my body."

"How can you expect me to trust you if you were willing to put this entire city at risk in order to save yourself?"

"Look," he said. "Kirklin's virus happened to me and there's nothing I can do about it. It's part of my programming the same way your parents dying is part of yours."

"My childhood isn't an explicit set of mathematical instructions dictating my behavior."

"The hell it isn't. You think what's going on in your head couldn't be written up as a bunch of ones and zeros? You, the agency, Kirklin, these attacks, this city. It could all be translated into numbers and probability."

"What are you talking about?"

"I'm saying that your parents dying made you who you are, but just because you hate that they're dead doesn't mean you have to hate yourself."

More sirens approached and one of the helicopters began to cross the river.

"Whether you believe it or not . . ." OWEN said.

I was already pulling the tie clip off.

". . . I'm your friend."

I had to hand it to Kirklin's virus. In that moment, I wanted to believe him.

I wrapped the rag around the tie clip a few times. OWEN's image flickered and disappeared. I pulled the ends of the rag into a tight knot and took the stairwell down. On one of the landings I opened the cabinet of a fire extinguisher and wedged OWEN behind the tank. The rag wasn't visible when I closed the cabinet and OWEN's shouts were difficult to make out with the noise of the fans down below. I was confident he could go unnoticed there until I was ready to bring him back to Suitland.

I took the elevator to the ground level and was able to sneak out of the building. Outside, I scaled a fence and followed the walkway back to the esplanade, then walked along the river for a while. The low hum of the ventilation building was gradually overtaken by the thudding of the National Guard helicopters overhead. Squad cars with pulsing lights rushed by on their way to the developing scene around the Hapsford. The play of light on the buildings couldn't help but remind me of OWEN and I found myself wondering in that moment—stupidly, I told myself—whether I had just done the right thing.

∘———∘

Twenty years ago, the East Side was made up almost entirely of low-rise residential buildings, sometimes even the occasional stand-alone house with aluminum siding and a strip of bright green lawn. Now there were towers of luxury apartments everywhere you looked. On the sidewalks, I passed small groups of well-dressed young men and women making their way to share office gossip over cocktails in the neighborhood's modern-looking bars that were all somehow both aloof and nostalgic. East Side Social. The Whiskey Concern. The youthful exuberance of the area's progress was undeniable. In another forty years, the only way to tell the once medium-density East Side from the thronging, upward mass of Center City would be the dividing line of the Lawrence River. That is, as long as Kirklin didn't have his way.

I made it all the way to Scott Park, around which sat a few government buildings and the county courthouse, their columns and ornate pediments all lit up for the night. I kept my eyes on the glowing domes of the buildings to see if I could catch the dark outline of a drone circling overhead, until I finally convinced myself the sky was clear. Across the park was a covered bus stop with an adjoining bank of internet kiosks. The stop was well lit and risked leaving me exposed, but the call was important, so I risked it.

I used the kiosk to call Garrett at home. My first year at the agency he'd had to tell me gently that I wasn't allowed to use his private number anymore. There were a few instances in which I had phoned him after dinner to let him know about what I had felt at the time were incredibly pressing development issues. After the sixth time, he brought me into his office and did his best to protect my feelings by telling me that the request was coming from his wife, Doris. I was mortified and apologized, but he just laughed and in the same conversation invited me to work directly with him on resolving the recurring seepage issues with the San Antonio Dam. Despite the circumstances, it still pained me to violate a long-established boundary.

He sounded startled when he answered.

"Sir, it's Henry."

"My God. Are you—"

"I'm fine, sir. Sorry about the hour."

"We've all been watching the news. It's Terry, isn't it?"

His question had some heavy dread behind it.

"It is, sir. Don't wait for the board to act. Call the FBI and get them anything you have on him."

"Henry, I should have never sent you there."

"We don't have a lot of time. I need you and Doris to get in the car and get out of town for a while. You're in danger."

It felt strange to be giving Garrett orders and I surprised myself by thinking that my voice sounded almost as confident as OWEN's.

"Terry again?"

"Afraid so. And you need to shut down headquarters."

"Get up, honey," I heard him say away from the receiver. "Henry says we have to leave."

I was flattered by Garrett's faith in my judgment, and then just as quickly humiliated when I heard Doris shout in the background, "He isn't supposed to call here!"

Fortunately, Garrett had the presence of mind to say, "It's a different Henry. Get dressed."

Back into the receiver, he asked, "Are you still in the city?"

"Yes, sir."

"Don't worry, we'll get you out of there. I can have a plane for you at Bixley in a few hours."

"Not yet," I said. "I still have to look after the agency's interests here."

There was a pause before he said, "Be careful, Henry."

I was about to tell him that I would, when I saw something whiz by overhead.

"Shit."

"Henry?"

Garrett's voice was still buzzing in the kiosk's speaker as I ran in a crouch deeper into the East Side, looking for darker quarters.

o———o

I led Kirklin's drone on a chase through unfamiliar streets, the surrounding buildings becoming lower and more spread out until I was able to confirm to my satisfaction that the night sky was once again empty. I slowed to a stroll, finally lowering my gaze long enough to notice that I was in a dodgy neighborhood on the wrong side of Jefferson Avenue. Here, the quaint, stand-alone houses that had once been common throughout the East Side were still standing, though they lacked their former suburban charm. Chain-link fences closed off small, grassless yards. Here and there aluminum siding had been torn away, revealing the faded patterns of building paper. Windows bore black steel security bars or were covered over with weather-swollen cuts of plywood.

There was no sign of people, probably unsafe to be out at this hour. The streetlights were spaced inadequately and most of the light on the sidewalk came from the candied reds and blues of glowing signs belonging to nearby fast-food restaurants and chain drugstores, which seemed to be the only businesses surviving here.

Seeing all those franchises brought to mind a heated memo Kirklin had sent out a while back. It had been in protest of Mayor Laury's Commercial Incentive Program, which aimed at creating jobs in poverty-stricken neighborhoods. The idea was to provide tax breaks to businesses willing to locate in those neighborhoods. It was one of the city's largest tax expenditures, offering billions in subsidies. Kirklin's memo claimed the program would give corporations that much more incentive to muscle out locally owned businesses and that the program would have to spend $200,000 for every job it created. Kirklin wasn't known for dealing in false facts, but once he decided he was against something his sentiments always seemed so reactionary and toxic that it was hard to take him seriously. The memo itself was also riddled with so many obscenities that it was barely appropriate for an online message board, let alone an interdepartmental communication at a federal agency.

Most of us in Suitland thought Mayor Laury's plan was laudable and Garrett ended up going over Kirklin's head with an offer to help Laury augment the plan with federal money as long as the target neighborhoods synced up with established Empowerment Zones. When Kirklin saw the Commercial Incentive Program go through with federal aid attached, we all expected a tantrum beyond all tantrums. In hindsight we probably should have been more worried when he didn't say a word.

Kirklin's ideas themselves were nothing new. His current plans for the city were only apocalyptic amplifications of the same progressive policies he had been articulating for years. The only thing that had come up in our brief interview that was at all unfamiliar was his emphatic use of the word "freezing," which was still troubling me.

A breeze picked up and gave the night a chill. I passed through another commercial lot and had to admit that all the fast-food restaurants so close together did look a bit disheartening. Not a single grocery store in sight.

Eventually I found a shabby-looking hotel called Best Metropolis Lodge, at which point I remembered that my wallet was currently in an underground fortress occupied by a medium-sized army of terrorists. I wandered north another ten blocks to Collins and Shutte, where there was a stop for the F2 train. A camera flashed when I entered the station without a pass, but there was no attendant in the booth.

It took twenty minutes to catch a Center City–bound train. Once I reached the inner loop, I transferred to an express, empty except for a few shift workers and a group of twenty-somethings laughing on their way to or from some bar. I didn't hear any mention of the Mallory Club or the Hapsford Tunnel. The closest anyone came was a young man with curtained hair, wearing a tuxedo vest over a T-shirt, voicing his concern to two young women that the National Guard might enforce a curfew.

I sat hunched forward at the end of the car, trying to remember everything Kirklin had said that night. I thought about the East Side and the word “freezing.” I thought about the look on OWEN’s face up on that ventilation tower and the lurking shadows of drones overhead. Each time I blinked, the passengers around me disappeared and were replaced with others. The dark interior of the Herbert Tunnel turned suddenly into a predawn skyline as we approached Center City from the east over the Clark Bridge. But even during these sudden drifts and discontinuities, it felt like I was awake, like I was thinking.

11

Before long it was rush hour. From the smell of damp clothes, I knew even with my eyes shut and the train underground that it was raining. Someone brushed my knees and I looked up to see an old man with jowls and a faint gray beard standing in front of me in a raincoat. He muttered an apology and then retrieved a folded copy of the *Standard* from inside his coat. I was about to offer him my seat when I noticed the front page. There was a large picture of Terrence Kirklin and Sarah Laury sitting together cozily under the banner headline ALLEGED KIDNAPPER BEHIND ATTACKS. I recognized something about the photograph. It wasn't just the clothes they were wearing or the tufted leather of the booth behind them. It was something in their eyes, Kirklin looking powerful and half-amused, Laury simultaneously haughty and repulsed. They had been looking at me when it was taken.

The other passengers in the car were all holding up newspapers with similar stories or were scrolling through the coverage on tablets and smartphones. When the doors opened at Piedmont, I rushed out onto the platform and started digging through a large metal trash bin. I had to sift through a morning's worth of half-empty coffee cups, used tissues, and fast-food wrappers before I finally found a discarded copy of the *Standard*.

Most of the coverage dealt with the anonymous video sent to the authorities that had allowed them to connect Sarah Laury's apparent abductor to the recent attacks on the city. There were direct quotes from Kirklin regarding his motivations for the museum attacks as well as his threat against the Mallory Club. According to the *Standard*, the authorities had decided not to release the full video. My best guess was that they were trying to avoid inciting a panic thanks to Kirklin's promise of continued bombings throughout the city.

I skimmed impatiently until the piece returned its focus to the transmission of the video itself. As OWEN had promised, it had been accompanied by the GPS coordinates corresponding to Kirklin's facilities. But when authorities had arrived on the scene all they found was an empty restaurant and another sinkhole smoldering down the street.

In its final paragraphs, the *Standard*'s coverage mentioned that the MPD and National Guard were continuing to cooperate in keeping the city safe. In response to the Hapsford Tunnel being shut down by a large fleet of drones, as well as Kirklin's use of helicopters during the museum attacks, the Navy, in coordination with the Air National Guard, was deploying one of its new Halsey-class aircraft carriers to the city's Lower Bay so jets could be scrambled as quickly as possible in the event of another aerial attack. The article also referenced the involvement of the FBI's Critical Incident Response Group and Counterterrorism Unit, both of which would be working with the city's combined security forces to apprehend Kirklin and his agents. In other words, what was brewing in Metropolis was a civil-military clusterfuck beyond all proportions. A smaller item on page two of the *Standard* reported that a National Guard Humvee had inadvertently crashed into an MPD cruiser on Proctor Street while they had both been rushing to help evacuate the Mallory Club. As more local and federal government forces converged on the city, the potential for organizational dysfunction was limitless.

OWEN's intervention may have caught Kirklin off guard, but in a larger sense his actions only seemed to have accelerated Kirklin's ambitions for the city. What I had seen in the firing ranges and training grounds of his underground facility suggested that Kirklin was not just preparing for an open conflict, but counting on one. Since his several hundred agents were all of a single purpose, they were in a unique position to capitalize on the inevitable disharmony of so many governmental forces trying to coordinate a unified response. Kirklin's people were also more familiar with the layout and workings of Metropolis than an FBI tactical operations team shipped out from Quantico or a National Guard unit down from Latham. Kirklin could turn the city into an active war zone for months before he was inevitably captured, the protracted violence destabilizing the city for years to come and bringing it that much closer to his revolutionary fantasy.

I tossed the paper back into the garbage can and made my way up to the street, where it was still drizzling. On the way I saw signs informing riders that the subways would be closing at 7:00 P.M. in keeping with the 8:00 P.M. citywide curfew. I jogged across Piedmont, which was empty except for a large construction sign with flashing text indicating that the streets would be closed for all but emergency vehicles once the curfew was in effect.

A helicopter passed low overhead. It was a Bell 407 painted black with FBI in white letters across its belly. For a second, I'd thought it was one of Kirklin's and I felt a surge of fear that only grew as I contemplated the task at hand.

Somehow I had to intervene in Kirklin's plans without helping him provoke an all-out confrontation with the MPD, FBI, the National Guard, the Air National Guard, or the hundred-thousand-ton engine of war with two nuclear reactors and just under a hundred fighter jets that was currently gliding toward Metropolis. And thanks to the mayor's office, I had to get it all done sometime before 8:00 P.M.

What's more, I had no leads or worldly resources at my disposal other than the suit on my back. As I spiraled down into my anxiety, my chest tightened and it soon felt as if my whole body was being constricted. I started to unbutton my jacket, but stopped once I realized there was something familiar about it. I ran my fingertips along its right lapel and felt so relieved I almost started to laugh. Just like that, I knew exactly what I was going to do.

I have always loved the United States Municipal Survey. Not just the work. All of it. I love my small office on the fifth floor that gets so cold in winter I have to wear an overcoat while I fill out paperwork. I love the lukewarm Monte Cristos they serve in the cafeteria and the unmistakable smell of mildew down in some of the research labs. I love the quiet chatter of the other agents throughout the building, the sound of file folders being dropped on desks, and I love the suits Garrett makes us wear.

When you're working in the field, your suit is your home. On your overnight train to Boston, you fold the jacket into a pillow or drape it over your chest like a blanket. You fish around in its pockets for hotel keys in Pittsburgh and Salt Lake City. You scrub mustard stains out of its sleeves in airplane toilets. You know every inch of it. The weight of it on your shoulders. The easy two-finger slide when closing the pants' hook-and-bar closure, followed by a quick searching pinch to secure the jigger button above the fly. You know the thick, reliable feel of the S110 wool. To be an agent for more than a few months is to know an agency-issue suit better than the look of your own face in the mirror.

On our plane ride out to Metropolis, OWEN had pointed out inconsistencies in Kirklin's budget that I now realized had probably paid for his extensive arsenal. For almost everything else, Kirklin had made do with the supplies at his disposal. The helicopters, the drones, even the railcars he had converted into Sarah Laury's moving pied-à-terre. So back when OWEN told me about Kirklin doubling his expenditures on uniforms, he had been wrong to assume that it was just another embezzlement. This was what I realized once I had a moment to appreciate the distinct craftsmanship of the suit that had been given to me while I was Kirklin's prisoner.

As luck would have it, my years of scheduling alterations and repairs meant that I knew both the phone number for the agency's supplier and that their lead tailor, Jacob Hicks, usually showed up for work around 5:00 A.M. His reputation for legendary customer service was further elevated in my mind when he immediately accepted a collect call from an unfamiliar number. I was in a small triangular park with two benches and a pay phone, surrounded by busy streets and office towers. The rain had cleared up, but traffic was loud and I had to shout into the receiver. As soon as Hicks recognized my voice, he asked me when I needed to come in, promising to bump anyone whose appointment might pose a conflict.

"Not necessary. This is an administrative matter."

I heard his appointment book snap shut. A note of attentive alarm entered his voice.

"Is there any problem with the suits, Henry?"

"Not at all. You're the best. I just need the address we gave you for a recent order. A few hundred of the usual cut, but black."

"You're happy with them?"

I caught a reflection of myself in a building across the street.

"They look great."

"I was worried about the color. A little formal for every day."

I took a moment to add overdressing to Kirklin's growing list of crimes.

"They look fine. Honest. The address thing is a bit of an emergency."

"Certainly."

I heard the sound of him typing.

"And which did you want? The address on Clairmont or the one on Wilmington?"

I smiled.

"Just to be safe, you better give me both."

He told me 427 Clairmont Street and 853 Wilmington Avenue. Both right in Metropolis. I committed them to memory and thanked Jacob for his time.

So far so good.

Unfortunately, the next phase of my plan required me to go on a bit of a crime spree. I felt nervous knowing that OWEN would have been proud. In all, I stole the following:

From a RediMart on Elmer Street

1. One 8-oz. bottle of hydrogen peroxide
2. One 1-oz. bottle of liquid foundation

From a bodega three blocks away on Malcolm Street

3. One black gel-ink pen
4. One spiral-bound 80-sheet memo pad
5. One travel shaving kit

From Metro Hardware across the street

6. One black canvas duffel bag
7. Six 32-oz. cans of lighter fluid
8. One 250-count box of strike-anywhere matches

From a Giant Health Foods on Temple Street

9. One shrink-wrapped roast beef sandwich
10. One pint of milk
11. One banana

I was able to hide the first five items in my pants pockets and under my jacket. But at Metro Hardware I just had to grab everything and run. Even with the large cardboard display tower of duct tape that I pulled down behind me as an obstruction, I was pursued on foot by the store's clerk and presumed proprietor through the streets of Metropolis. He was an older man who was in excellent shape for his age and kept pace with me for ten blocks before I lost him by hiding behind a dumpster in an alley next to a laundromat. It had been at least twelve hours since my light tentacle dinner, so I then stopped by the Giant Health Foods and stole my small breakfast, all of which I consumed while sitting on the lip of the large fountain in the middle of King Park.

From there I stopped by a few bookstores around MU until I was able to find *A Beginner's Guide to Esperanto* by a Dr. Manlin Smithy, which I studied right there in the Foreign Language Study Aids section, copying down a few key phrases and pronunciation guides into my stolen memo pad. Dr. Smithy was good enough to offer sample dialogues, some of which I copied down in case their basic structure might come in handy:

Q: Bonan matenon. Kiel vi fartas? (Good morning. How are you?)

A: Bone, dankon. Kaj vi? (Fine, thanks. And you?)

Q: Kie ĝi estas? (Where is it?)

A: Ĝi estas tie. (It is there.)

Q: Kio estas via profesio? (What do you do for a living?)

A: Mi ĵus perdis mian laboron. (I recently lost my job.)

Q: Ĉu mi povas helpi vin? (Can I help you?)

A: Mi devas pisi. (I need to pee.)

Once I had cobbled together a few key sentences, I headed back to the bookstore's restroom and locked the door. After stripping down to my socks and underwear, I removed the bandage on my nose. I washed my wound and covered it over with the foundation, then put the peroxide in my hair and sat on the toilet, where I read over my Esperanto notes and practiced a few pronunciations. My scalp was beginning to burn, but I only had one shot at it and needed to maximize the effect. Occasionally someone would pound on the door and ask me what was taking so long, but I would just shout out one of the Esperanto phrases from my memo pad and whoever it was would walk away.

After a while I rinsed out my hair and slicked it back. The peroxide had done what it could and my dark brown hair was now an orange-blond. I gave myself a quick shave and got dressed. I was pretty pleased with the final result. Whatever description may have been circulating among Kirklin's men, it wouldn't be of this slicked-back creep with no visible nose wound.

When I opened the door a patron was standing just outside and looked as if he had been ready to knock. Right behind him the store's young clerk had her back to us and was talking into a cell phone.

"I don't know," she said. "He's been in there forever."

The patron told her I was out and she turned to me.

"Hey," she said. "What were you *doing* in there?"

She was holding the phone away from her ear and glaring at me.

"Mian laboron," I said.

She called out after me, but I was already out the door.

∘———∘

Four twenty-seven Clairmont Street was a one-story brick building sitting in the middle of a large empty lot in Center City right on the river. When I rang the buzzer I noticed a small placard on the door that read SOCIETY FOR ETHICAL MUNICIPALITIES, DEPT. OF THE QUARTERMASTER. I recalled the stamp I'd seen in Biggs's book on Esperanto, EX LIBRIS SFEM, and hoped it might be a sign that I was in the right place. Since the authorities hadn't found anything in the South Side, I figured Kirklin had probably mobilized his people at the first sign of trouble to move their operations to another location. The door's intercom came to life for a moment, then went silent. A long pause followed before the door's lock buzzed.

Inside, the lobby had checkerboard floors leading up to a reception desk that ran almost the length of the room. Two men in black suits sat behind the desk under a large banner of a red eagle. More Mozart was playing and the two men watched in silence as I approached. They were young and athletic with matching flattops.

I called out to them as I approached, "Bonan matenon, kolegoj."

One of them nodded his head almost imperceptibly.

I lifted the duffel bag at my side and said, "Pli da materialo de la malsupra distrikto."

I got the sentence out without a stammer. The man to my left was slightly heavier than the one directly in front of me, but otherwise the two looked identical. The thinner man nodded more aggressively now and began shuffling through a couple of folders in front of him, removing a form from one and handing it to me. I waved it off.

"Tio ne estos necesa," I said.

This got their attention.

"Ĉi tiu aĵo devas esti aldonita secrete kaj de mi persone," I continued.

They looked at each other and burst out laughing.

"Christ," the heavier man said. "Your pronunciation is dog shit."

"You have to go to the classes at least three times a week," the thinner one said. "You're only cheating yourself."

When I tried to answer in Esperanto, he cut me off immediately.

"Speak English. Listening to you is going to make my Esperanto worse."

Relieved, I held up the duffel again.

"Kirklin wants this package stored here."

The thinner man held up the form again.

"He doesn't want it cataloged? Could get lost."

"Only I can know where the bag is and what's in it. After last night, you'll understand the need for discretion."

"Sure," he said. "Do you have a line where we can reach Mr. Kirklin so he can confirm?"

I had prepared for this.

"Neniuj komunikaĵoj devus esti senditaj."

They both winced.

"Guy, I'm telling you," the heavier one said. "You sound like pennies in a washing machine."

"No transmissions of any kind should be sent regarding this bag," I said. "If you need to clear this issue up with Kirklin, one of you can go over to Wilmington Avenue and take it up with him there. Ask him about *la pakon* and mention my name. Samuel. Pleased to meet you both."

The two men looked at each other.

"I don't know, man," the heavier one said. "That's all the way across town. Can't we just let him through? It's probably just more of Sarah's stuff. I had to move a bunch of Kevlar to the crawl space just to make room for her fucking trumpets."

The thinner man held up his hand for the other to stop talking.

"It's a pleasure to meet you, Kolego Samuel. My name is Raphael. Let me apologize for Donald here," he said. "The last twenty-four hours have had us all on edge."

"Of course," I said.

"But I have to agree it isn't a good idea for either of us to leave. There are only two of us watching this entire facility. That might not have been a problem a week ago, but now that our inventory has changed—it's not safe. You can store the bag here and we won't hold you to any formalities, but if you have access to Kirklin or any admins, you need to tell him to send us more men."

I could have kissed him.

"I can let Kirklin know that you need backup as soon as I'm done here. For the time being, I trust you're both armed?"

Raphael reached just under his desk and produced the largest machine gun I had ever seen. Next to him Donald held up a repeating shotgun and a small box of grenades.

"Oh, good," I said. "Good. Just checking."

Donald nodded and tossed me a set of keys over the desk. "If you need any help back there, give us a shout."

I waved my thanks to them both and walked quickly through the large pair of double doors into a long hallway at the far end of which was a frosted-glass door labeled MAIN INVENTORY. It opened on a storage space the size of a basketball court crowded with racks of assault rifles, handguns, and rocket launchers.

As I worked my way toward the middle of the room through a maze of shelves and stacked crates, I saw rising above the thick press of smaller arms what I could now confirm were three half-assembled artillery guns. I passed by open crates of ammunition with hastily drawn serial numbers written on their sides and unopened, unmarked boxes that only had the word DANGER printed in red letters across their lids. Where Kirklin's people had run out of gun racks, they had stacked rifles like cordwood on shelves.

Farther in, I started to recognize pieces of Sarah Laury's furniture I had seen on the train. Her writing desk was now wrapped in plastic and sandwiched between a dozen long metal cases labeled FIM-92A STINGER. Her canopy bed was similarly wrapped and piled high with crates labeled

FLAMETHROWER ARRAYS. But just beyond the shelf holding Laury's trumpets and a few riot helmets was an empty space, in the middle of which was a single crate with loose stalks of straw coming up from under its lid. It was surrounded by sawhorses, each of which bore a handwritten sign that read DO NOT MOVE OR HANDLE. As I had hoped, it was the last of the explosives from the museum demolitions, red sticks of dynamite stacked like cigars.

I grabbed some of Laury's dresses from a rack and dropped them on top of the crate. I then removed one of the containers of lighter fluid from my bag and doused the fabric. I worked my way back the way I came in, steadily emptying out three containers of lighter fluid in order to leave a continuous trail leading to the dynamite. I propped the door to the hallway open with a rifle and continued the trail all the way to the double doors leading back out to the lobby. I dropped the third empty container of lighter fluid and paused for a moment at the head of the hallway before fishing the box of matches out from the duffel and lowering to a crouch. I struck the match against the box and was already turning to run when I saw the line of lighter fluid catch.

I practically fell out into the lobby.

"Don! Raph!" I said. "I need you to follow me outside for a minute."

They both watched me with concern as I continued to walk quickly across the lobby.

"You still have your bag," Donald said.

"This is an emergency. I need to show you both something outside right now."

They stood up behind their desk.

"What are you talking about?"

I didn't look back to see which of them said it.

"No time. Run."

I wasn't far out of the building before I heard them behind me. We made it less than a block before Donald grabbed my arm and pulled me to a stop.

"What's going on?" he said, out of breath. "What are you showing us?"

I looked over his shoulder at the building. Nothing yet.

"I thought you might be interested to know that the United States Municipal Survey just saved your lives."

Raphael's eyes lit up. He grabbed me by the collar of my shirt and called me a son of a bitch.

Donald pulled a handgun from his jacket and that, I suppose, was when the fire finally made its way into the crate.

I thrashed for a moment, convinced I was falling. I was facedown on the sidewalk in a thick cloud of gray dust. There was no sign of Donald or Raphael. I struggled to my feet and spotted my duffel bag wedged under the front wheel of a car with shattered windows. I stooped to pick it up, vomited, and then limped on down the street.

A series of muffled booms rang out behind me as the fire continued to eat through Kirklin's stockpile. It was three blocks before the dust began to disperse. There was a throb in my knee and a pain in my chest when I breathed, but I felt ready to finish the job.

I headed toward 853 Wilmington Avenue, doing my best to blend in with the panicked crowds fleeing the staggered booms of Kirklin's arsenal burning. Along the way the pain in my chest grew more pronounced and I began coughing up small amounts of blood into my hand. When I reached the address, I found an expensive-looking office tower with SFEM etched above the lobby entrance. As I crossed the street toward the building, I barely recognized my reflection in the glass entrance. A limping man, covered in dust.

The lobby was all modern and bright. The light hurt my eyes as I entered. I made it a few steps toward the elevators before I was surrounded by several of Kirklin's agents, who looked ready to grab me until they recognized the cut of my suit under the dust.

One of them barked something at me in Esperanto.

"We're under attack," I said.

When I spoke, my voice sounded oddly distant and I noticed an uncomfortable pressure behind my eyes.

The largest of the men took a step forward and said something to me in a deep, booming Esperanto. I cut him off.

"Your pronunciation is dog shit," I said.

The men around him laughed in astonishment and he started to blush.

"How many classes are you going to per week?"

Before he could answer, I added, "You're only cheating yourself."

He tried to defend himself in Esperanto and I stopped him.

"Speak English. You sound like a washing machine."

The men around me all exchanged worried looks.

"Who are you?" the big man said.

"We've been attacked," I said again. "The arsenal at Clairmont is gone."

"That's impossible," one of the men said.

I got on a coughing jag and then gestured toward my appearance. "I was there."

"Do we know who's responsible?" the big man said.

I took a step toward him and snapped my fingers in his face a few times.

"Wake up, you big idiot," I said. "It was Don and Raph the whole time."

He looked completely lost and turned to his compatriots for help.

One of the men to my right interjected, "Are you talking about the Delancey twins? Donald and Raphael?"

I addressed the man's question without turning to face him.

"Of course it was the Delancey twins, you buffoon. You ridiculous clown."

"Hey," the man said, sounding hurt.

"They rolled over on us," I said. "They rolled over hard. Now I need one of you rock-eating simpletons to take me up there to check on the rest of the inventory so I can report back that it's secure. And I'm telling you right now, if I find so much as one bullet out of place I will come back down here and murder every single one of you with my bare hands."

"Come on," the big man said. "There's no call for any of

that." He pointed to one of the men to his right. "Phil will take you up."

Phil led me to an elevator, keeping his distance from me and occasionally looking back with envy at his colleagues who were allowed to remain downstairs. After I stepped into the elevator with him I called out across the lobby to the big man, "Three classes a week! That's the only way to true proficiency."

Phil frowned and placed a key card into a slot above the elevator's panel of buttons, then hit 12. I waited until we were a few floors up, then said, "Is Carmichael still on seven?"

I pointed at the button when I said it and pushed it as if by accident.

"What?" he said. "I don't know who that is."

When the doors opened on seven, I punched him in the jaw, pulled his blazer up over his head, and threw him out of the elevator.

He fell to the floor, where he struggled to pull his coat down. The office around him was alive with activity. There were dozens of navigation consoles where Kirklin's agents were piloting drones. One agent turned from his screen and noticed the man on the floor just as the doors to the elevator closed.

When they reopened on twelve, I was relieved to see no other agents. The space contained an open floor plan divided into cubicles containing desktop computers and multiline telephones, most of which were now pushed aside to make room for the rest of Kirklin's arsenal. There were crates of ammo stacked up on either side of the elevator, one of which I placed in the closing doors to prevent the car from changing floors. I then followed the exit signs leading to the floor's two stairwells, dead-bolting them and barricading them as best I could with whichever of the crates I could lift.

My knee was getting too stiff to bend and I had to more or less drag my left leg as I moved to the middle of the room. I climbed up onto a chair and removed my tie, knotting it around one of the ceiling's sprinkler heads. Already I heard shouting from the stairwell and Kirklin's agents banging against the doors.

That was it. There was no more plan left. And while I did not intend to kill myself, I had no thoughts of escaping that place as I began dragging whatever crates I could find beneath the blocked sprinkler. The crates were unlabeled, so I had to trust that whatever was inside would be incendiary enough to destroy the entire floor. The banging from the doors grew more intense. I emptied the remaining containers of lighter fluid and tossed the last one on the floor near the crates, letting it glug out onto the carpet.

I lit a match and dropped it. The floor around me went up in a rush. The fire climbed over a few cubicle walls and onto the crates. I pulled up a chair and watched the flames spread. The wooden crates hissed and popped.

To my right was a wall of windows. Outside, the city looked beautiful. I smiled, then doubled over with a powerful cough as the smoke hit my lungs. The other sprinklers came on in the same moment that one of the doors on the far side of the room flew open. I felt blood running through my fingers and my head becoming lighter. I was pulled from the chair and thrown to the ground. There was a foot on my chest and through a dark haze I saw a man in a black suit point the nozzle of a fire extinguisher in the direction of the crates. As I lost consciousness I heard a long blast of CO_2, followed by the men around me shouting, “It’s out! It’s out!”

12

I woke up coughing and found myself once again tied to a chair. Someone said something in Esperanto. The room was bright and I was surrounded by unfamiliar shapes. I had to squint to make out that I was in a small, virtually featureless room with a cement floor and walls of unpainted cinder block. One of Kirklin's agents tried a few more questions in Esperanto before addressing me in English.

"Are you awake? Can you understand me?"

I probably looked like I was about to say something until I threw up in my lap.

The man took a step back and began discussing something with another agent.

I rested my eyes and eventually heard a door open, followed by Kirklin's voice.

"Henry?"

I opened one eye and nodded, feeling that same painful fullness in my head.

Kirklin looked back over his shoulder at the agents, who were still standing at attention, and spoke to them in English for my benefit.

"How am I supposed to talk to him if he's half-dead?"

"None of us touched him," one of the men said. "He seems to have done this to himself."

Kirklin looked back to me. He took me in for a moment before shaking his head, then pulled a chair from the other side of the room and sat across from me.

"It was you at Clairmont?"

I nodded again.

Kirklin looked up to the ceiling. It was clear he was doing his best to hold back a massive welling up of rage. But there was also a strange gleam in his eye, as if the whole thing secretly pleased him. Eventually he let out a sigh and smiled sadly before leaning in close.

"You wanted to protect Metropolis so you leveled half a city block?"

"Yes."

He ran a finger along the shoulder of my jacket, examining the dust on his fingertip.

"You're a fine young man," he said, softly. "You should have been one of mine."

He stood up.

"No torture this time, Henry. You've earned a fast death."

He spoke to his men in English again so I would understand. "Take him out to the platform. She wants to do it in front of the muster."

As Kirklin left, two men approached me, tilting my chair back and carrying me out the door. I heard the noise of a distant crowd grow steadily louder. At first I saw only high ceilings with exposed rafters, but as that noise grew closer, I saw men and women in black suits all around me, cold faces looking down in disapproval. The room was dark except for a perimeter of bright lights at the edge of the crowd. I was taken up onto a raised platform that was otherwise empty.

The crowd went quiet and I was left to sit there in silence with hundreds of Kirklin's agents observing me.

I turned my head to avoid the blare of the lights and saw a stockpile of countless weapons arranged neatly in open crates. No one in the crowd seemed to be armed, but agents with clipboards were walking through the stacks of crates and making notes, conferring with one another and pointing toward the crowd as if discussing how best to disseminate those deadly wares.

Even this activity stopped when from the other side of the room came the sound of confident footsteps. There was an air of expectation and reverence. I turned to see Sarah Laury climb a rise of steps and join me up on the platform. She was wearing the same red dress from the night before, but with a green canvas army coat over it, the large sleeves rolled up over her delicate wrists. She was holding a rifle and her face was painted like a skull.

She stood over me, looking down with a purity in her gaze that made her seem both there and not there. A look of cosmic judgment. She turned to face the gathered crowd and addressed them in a powerful voice. "Saluton, miaj kolegoj."

She launched into a spirited oration, in which I supposed she was railing against the continuum of western culture. Without understanding a word, I could sense that she was filling that large space with a brilliant anger. It was also clear from the rigid attentiveness of the crowd that they wanted nothing more than to bring about by any means necessary the world of which she spoke. Even Kirklin was staring up at her in wonder from the front of the crowd.

I tried to see if I could ruin her speech by throwing up

again, but couldn't make it happen. Breathing was an effort and the sad thought occurred to me that the only act of defiance still open to me would be to die before she had the chance to shoot me.

Laury turned from the audience and addressed a few words to me in Esperanto. It was some booming, final condemnation and it sounded as if she expected a response. I pretended to give it some thought before responding with the only Esperanto I could recall from that morning, "Mi devas pisi."

She was unperturbed by my answer and took a step back, pointing the barrel of her rifle at my chest.

I should say something, I thought. I wanted to say something real. Something without anger. Tell them why it was so important that they be stopped.

"Wait," I said. "Wait."

She made no motion to lower the rifle, but before I could ask her again, I heard my own disembodied voice, amplified, echoing throughout the room.

"Kirklin's men are just a bunch of stupid townie goons."

My face was suddenly projected forty feet high onto the wall to the right of the platform.

"And Kir—Ki—Excuse me," my face said. "Kirklin is a big grumpy weirdo. If we see him tomorrow, I'm going to tell him that to his face."

"You should," I heard OWEN's voice say off camera.

"I *will*," my face said.

My captors and I were watching footage of OWEN and me back in the Museum of History, drunk. While I had no idea how this was possible, I knew enough to dread what was coming next. My rant against Kirklin was even more insane and sexually depraved than I had remembered. I could scarcely follow the logic of it. One moment the Kirklin of my imagination was French-kissing an ostrich and the next he was working up the courage to press his butt up into the Liberty Bell.

I wondered if Kirklin's virus had allowed him to hack into OWEN's memory banks and if he was now showing this video as a kind of accusation. But when I looked down at Kirklin, he seemed taken aback. Sarah Laury too was staring up at my image in stunned, rifle-drooped confusion.

The silence of the crowd soon gave way to angry shouts and Kirklin began to issue orders to the agents in his vicinity, some of whom began to rush about in small groups looking for the source of the projection.

To the remaining crowd Sarah Laury called out something in Esperanto and pointed her rifle back at me. Before she could take the shot, the recording of me ended and another loud voice echoed throughout the crowd, "FBI. NOBODY MOVE."

As FBI agents in SWAT gear appeared all around the room, the surprised roar of Kirklin's agents was drowned out by a booming arrangement of the theme music from *The Magnificent Seven*. One agent popped up behind Laury and disarmed her. Others blocked the exit and secured the arsenal. The rest of the agents were soon joined by a large National Guard unit equipped for crowd control and, after some scattered fighting, Kirklin's people were subdued.

Laury attempted to run to Kirklin when he was discovered among the crowd and taken into custody, but was held back by two guardsmen, who were startled by her screams. Kirklin looked up at her with sadness and love as the FBI agents put his hands in restraints. He shouted something to her, but it was drowned out by her cries as well as the boisterous, triumphant music that had continued to swell from every direction. She kicked and bit at the guardsmen who were holding her back with such ferocity that several more men had to be called up to the platform in order to remove her from the building.

The FBI began escorting prisoners out of the building ten and twenty at a time. Kirklin was at the head of the first line and his men began to scream what sounded like encouragements to him in Esperanto while he was marched out.

As the mass arrests continued, OWEN appeared across from me on the platform. He chuckled at the sight of me tied to another office chair.

"Who would have thought," he said, lowering the volume of his own soundtrack so I could hear him. "Sarah Laury is one hell of a public speaker."

There was a drink in his hand.

"What is it with bloodthirsty megalomaniacs and public speaking?" he said, sitting next to me in a chair that he pulled from nowhere. "Humans are weird."

Then he asked, "Is it true what she said in her speech? Did you blow up the arsenal on Clairmont?"

I nodded and OWEN immediately burst out laughing.

"Nice job, dummy," he said. "Like twenty firemen died trying to put out that fire."

I slumped forward in my chair. I felt the life going out of me.

"Is that true?"

"No," OWEN said. "But it could have been. I mean, a munitions fire? Are you out of your mind?"

He pointed to a column of Kirklin's men being marched out of the warehouse with their hands bound.

"You see all this?" he said. "I helped the FBI track down Kirklin's arms dealer and he gave us a couple of addresses. Our response was all very tactical, very clever, very unlike a raging munitions fire within city limits. So—"

It was worth wondering how OWEN had managed to escape and strike up a working relationship with the FBI, but my body was failing and all I wanted was for OWEN to stop talking.

"So, what?" I said.

"So don't ditch me next time. I'm your friend and I'm better at this than you are."

Nearby, one of Kirklin's agents slipped out of his restraints and tried to take a swing at an FBI agent, but was quickly brought down by several guardsmen with stun sticks. OWEN watched the proceedings somewhat wistfully and said, "We could have made this happen together."

"OWEN," I said, "I think I'm dying."

He looked at me, confused for a moment, and then snapped his fingers. "Oh, that's right. I have my patch switched on in case I found you in a bad way. Let me turn it off and get a look at you."

"I'd stay seated."

OWEN almost flickered out when he saw the shape I was in. But instead of fainting, he told me to hold tight and stormed off into the crowd. Within a few minutes FBI agents were untying me and an air ambulance was called. A woman in FBI SWAT gear pulled OWEN's tie clip from the strap of her helmet and placed it in my hand while we waited for the EMTs.

"Keep him out of trouble," she said.

I don't remember being loaded into the helicopter, but I must have held on to the tie clip because OWEN was with me the whole time, kneeling next to the stretcher with his hand projected onto mine as the EMTs grew more and more concerned over my vitals, my unsteady breath fogging my oxygen mask.

It was nighttime and as we banked gently to the left I saw the bright lights of Center City shining below. OWEN followed my eyes and we stared out at the city together. It hurt to talk, but by slipping the tie clip under the mask I was able to make myself understood over the pounding of the rotors.

"What was that?" OWEN asked without taking his eyes off Metropolis.

"I said pour yourself a drink."

He laughed and then did so.

13

As I was admitted to the ICU at Metropolis Medical Center, OWEN slipped in amid the confusion and disguised himself as a doctor. Based on his knowledge that I had been involved in an explosion and whatever information he had been able to gather from the scan of my person he conducted on the flight over, he felt comfortable having the ICU staff start treatment for a condition he referred to as blast lung. He also told them to look for any internal bleeding or tertiary wounds. You can imagine my horror as I looked up in my semiconscious state and saw OWEN standing over me in a lab coat, shouting out orders to every health care professional in sight.

Later my actual doctor seemed confused as to who had initiated the majority of my treatments, but she admitted that the speedy diagnosis had probably saved my life. OWEN was sitting behind her in the corner of my hospital room, working on a crossword puzzle of his own devising. At the mention of saving my life, he continued to work on his puzzle and waved his hand dismissively in my direction as if to say, "Don't mention it."

She went on to inform me that I had a fracture in my left knee that would require extensive physical therapy. Even with a lot of hard work I would probably be walking with a cane for some time. As soon as she left, OWEN leapt up from his seat and began walking back and forth, experimenting with various styles of walking sticks.

"A cane?" he said. "You lucky son of a bitch."

OWEN had never used foul language in my company before, but after being embedded with an FBI SWAT team he was now swearing fairly regularly.

In his hand appeared a beech wood walking stick with a chrome eagle head for a handle. A brass jaguar on a shaft of blue ash. He cycled through diamond knob handles and gold lion heads. Shafts of walnut and padauk. Canes with swords in them and knotted shillelaghs.

"I'm going to get one too," he said. "Though, we can't both walk around with canes. We'd look like assholes. We can divide up the week. I'll take Monday, Wednesday, Friday and we'll alternate on weekends."

He twirled a cane whose handle featured a large pewter mermaid.

This was another in a series of remarks OWEN had made that suggested he anticipated working closely alongside me once we returned to Suitland. I had deflected these comments until now and I thought it would be best to address this most recent one at face value.

"I'll actually need a cane. You won't."

OWEN looked down at me from the foot of the bed and clutched his cane to his chest. "That's a horrible thing to say to somebody."

I was admitted for three weeks and OWEN seemed to enjoy our time in the hospital, ordering me a set of clothes online for my journey home, projecting old movies onto the wall of my room, and occasionally offering to order me pizzas or put in a good word for me with some of the attractive young women on the hospital staff.

I'd been avoiding what I assumed would be an awkward conversation, and so it wasn't until our plane ride back to Suitland that I asked OWEN how he had managed to escape and collaborate with the FBI. He seemed surprised that I mentioned his confinement to the tower so casually and I knew he was expecting an apology. But he had too much pride in his ingenuity to keep the story to himself.

Using his own database, OWEN had made a series of late-night calls to higher-ups at the Port Authority, pretending to be someone from the governor's office. It took several tries before he found someone who could send a maintenance worker to recover what he described over the phone as an important piece of monitoring equipment. OWEN gave detailed instructions as to where he was to be found and the maintenance worker recovered him within the hour. Unfortunately, his rescuer was apparently annoyed at having been called in so late over something so seemingly unimportant. Instead of dropping the tie clip off at the nearest police station as OWEN had ordered over the phone, the man called his supervisor and reported that he hadn't found anything. He then chucked the tie clip from the driver's-side window of his van on his way home.

The clip landed in an alley, where it was eventually discovered by a seventy-year-old woman named Malvina who had come outside to give her leftovers to the stray cats who lived around her building's dumpster. OWEN impressed her with a few illusions, then convinced her to take him to the police in exchange for three wishes. She asked for a washing machine and a dryer. When OWEN asked her what her third wish was, she said she wanted the washer and dryer to be new.

"Don't worry," OWEN interrupted his story to add. "I've already made the arrangements and the agency has sent her the best washer and dryer on the market. I also sent her a few thousand dollars just to be nice."

"How many is a few?"

OWEN shrugged and resumed his story, which now had him arriving at a quiet police station in the East Side, where he pretended to be an automated message caught on a loop, identifying the clip as property of the FBI and demanding that it be returned to the Metropolis field office immediately. According to the officers on duty at the Seventy-Third Precinct, "immediately" meant 10:00 A.M. the next day. Once he reached the FBI, he managed to convince everyone there that he was special tech on loan from FBI headquarters in Washington. Combining what he knew about Kirklin's operation with FBI resources, OWEN had been able to find Kirklin's arms dealer in a matter of minutes. He was a nineteen-year-old boy named Anthony Boxler who lived in the basement of his parents' split-level in a nearby suburb. Widely known on anarchist message boards all over the Deep Web as proxy_moxy, the boy had brokered the sale of millions of dollars' worth of weapons online and coordinated with Kirklin's agents embedded throughout Metropolis's maritime freight infrastructure to sneak two cargo vessels loaded with arms into the city. Boxler told the FBI everything he knew and from there it was only a matter of organizing the raids with the National Guard on Kirklin's remaining facilities. By the time they were ready, I had already blown up the building on Clairmont and the only people left in the Wilmington Avenue high-rise were the agents who were piloting drones over what were believed to be Kirklin's next intended targets. On the way to Kirklin's third and final base, a refurbished marine construction facility along the Lawrence River, OWEN confided in a Special Agent Boyle, the person in charge of leading the raids, that after Kirklin was apprehended the tie clip needed to be returned to a Henry Thompson at the USMS.

"I didn't expect us to run into you there," he said. "So you can't say you risked your life for nothing. Agent Boyle's time is valuable and you saved her a trip to the post office."

I had come to understand that OWEN's needling was his way of expressing a certain kind of affection. I had a large cast on my left leg and from the expression of discomfort on my face in the cabin of that small agency plane, he had most likely decided that the moment called for a bit of good-natured ribbing. I suppose I was relieved that OWEN was in high spirits as we returned to Suitland even though I was sure he had to know that it would be the end of our working together. After all, as long as OWEN existed in his present form, at least one aspect of Kirklin's plan was still at work. His virus.

Garrett had kept my presence in Metropolis under wraps, so OWEN and I were welcomed back to headquarters quietly. We met with Garrett and Klaus in a secure meeting room in the admin sector in order to debrief them without fear of being overheard by any of our colleagues or, worse, the oversight committee members who were still lingering around the agency in search of improprieties.

I was slow entering the room, still awkward on my crutches. OWEN marched in ahead of me, airily embracing Klaus, both of them laughing and exchanging pleasantries in German. Garrett placed a hand on my shoulder and said he was glad to have me back.

I thanked him and remained standing while the three of them sat around the room's small conference table. I told Klaus that his new interface had unlimited potential and that OWEN had single-handedly saved Metropolis. Here OWEN raised a finger to signal an interruption and announced to the room, "I also kept his tie straight."

I told OWEN to give Garrett and Klaus access to our memory partition and encouraged both of them to go through OWEN's memory banks. I then put the clip on the table and told them what else they would see if they watched the footage, explaining that while the end result had been desirable, OWEN's current configuration was erratic and still contaminated by Kirklin's virus. I told them that OWEN himself had admitted the only way to remedy this was a complete memory wipe and a reinstallation of the interface.

I didn't have much to add to that recommendation, so I thanked them for their time and excused myself.

Given OWEN's powers of display, I had been expecting a scene. But as I left the room, he was looking down at the table without saying a word.

If he'd asked me why I did it, I would have told him that I'd already had my world disappear once, when the Lake Shore Limited left the tracks. I wasn't going to put the first home I'd known since then at risk by keeping around a vestige of Kirklin's madness.

I told myself that OWEN's friendship had been nothing but an illusion, a quirk of damaged software.

I walked back to my office, which was exactly as I'd left it. There was a stuffiness in the air that had probably always been there but that I'd never been away long enough to notice. I lowered myself into my chair and adjusted the model train on my desk before sorting through the file folders and papers I'd left in neat stacks. In Metropolis, I had been frightened and out of my depth. But here everything seemed so much less complicated. The reassuring orderliness of this place I had long since learned to call home was already welcoming me back and I suffered no doubt that I had done the right thing with regard to OWEN. I was in my element.

With Kirklin in custody and the agency's woes all attributable to him, the oversight committee eventually withdrew their request for Garrett's resignation. Soon the agency was back to normal and I was in the field doing what I loved. Right away I went out to South Bend to renovate the city's central bus station. When the work was finished, I stood leaning on my cane in the station's empty lobby and admired where the scuffed drywall had been replaced with handsome stone tile and where the water-damaged ceilings had been ripped out. Now there were high windows flooding the place with sunlight, endowing the very idea of bus travel with an air of nostalgic adventure.

But even though it only took one glance to know that

South Bend's new bus station was perfect, I still felt that something was missing, like some aspect of my earlier happiness at the agency hadn't come back with me from Metropolis. That day in Indiana I imagined OWEN standing next to me in the station, taking in all my hard work. I was surprised when my own vision of him turned to me and said sharply, "Henry, is this how you're spending your time?"

That night, I took my team to a sports bar to celebrate a successful end to the project. Garrett had given me a wealth of new responsibilities and I now had a host of deferential young agents at my disposal. I was sitting at a table with a handful of them when across the room I noticed Helen Roth, the economist who had participated in my capture in the abandoned transit tunnels of Metropolis.

Now she was sitting at a bar in Indiana nursing a nearly empty glass of beer. She'd chopped off her long braid and was wearing a cropped blond wig. She caught me staring and we locked eyes for a moment. As soon as she recognized me her face took on a desperate, hunted look. My first few weeks back in Suitland I had been worried that the agency might be targeted for retribution by one of Kirklin's loose agents, but her reaction told me Kirklin's people were all too busy trying to stay ahead of the FBI to be dangerous.

As the bar grew crowded with locals, she kept her eyes on me, waiting to see what I was going to do. I excused myself from the table and headed toward the bar, where I ordered a drink for myself and asked the bartender to send another round to Roth along with a napkin on which I wrote, "Truce."

I returned to my table slowly, still leaning heavily on my

cane. When I finally took my seat and looked back in her direction, I saw a full beer in front of her seat and a crumpled napkin. She was gone.

At the table my agents talked among themselves over the noise of the bar while I sipped a glass of Scotch and watched a muted television on the wall that was turned to the news. They were still running stories on the attacks whenever they could, so I wasn't surprised when I saw a picture of Kirklin's face next to the quote, "I will be at war with our government as long as the government is at war with its own poor and disenfranchised citizens." Soon after, the bartender found me and handed me a folded napkin. Inside Roth had written, "Iru al infero."

I had already forgotten what little Esperanto I had learned in Metropolis, so I took out my new agency phone and read the phrase into it. OWEN's old animation popped up and announced proudly, "Esperanto: Go to hell." His artificial intelligence had all been stripped down, so it must have been my imagination that OWEN looked a little pleased with Roth's message.

Garrett had taken my recommendation to have Klaus delete OWEN's infected interface. But instead of rebooting it and rolling it out agency-wide, Klaus had opted instead to stick with the old OWEN-linked smartphones for the time being. Most of the other agents were still using their own privately purchased cell phones, but I found myself drawn to the old OWEN interface.

Garrett confided that Klaus had been devastated by the order to delete the latest iteration of OWEN's interface, since the process of socializing it had been such a lengthy and personal one. I suppose I knew how Klaus felt. I missed OWEN on nights like this, when I was doing my best to be sociable with my subordinates. Getting drinks after the completion of a project had been a custom I'd initiated and was, I knew, contrary to my reputation at the agency. For the first ten minutes or so, the agents in my command would ask me polite questions related to our assignment and we might even manage some general small talk about the town in which we found ourselves. But I still didn't know anyone with whom it would have been appropriate or even desirable to spend an entire night drinking and talking. Hell, I would have liked to talk to Roth for a while. Forgetting everything that had happened in Metropolis, it would have been nice to spend an evening with a peer who was passionate about the world she lived in. Staring down at her note, all I could think was that I wasn't aware of anyone on earth who was, for whatever reason, truly excited to know me.

The only person who'd ever come close I'd betrayed. I told myself I'd done it because it was the right thing to do, but part of me suspected I'd just been worried that, if OWEN stuck around, his social and emotional intelligence would have eventually developed to the point where he would have understood that I wasn't a person worth knowing. I had long before made the calculation in my most private self that there was less risk in relying on predetermined guidelines than in trying to blunder my way toward the mystery of people's love.

It was my understanding that OWEN's old interface had been kept active for a while in some limited capacity so Klaus could conduct a host of final tests. He had only been shut down a few days before that night. Klaus had invited me, at

OWEN's request, to attend a small good-bye ceremony. Apparently they planned to watch *The Magnificent Seven* and have a few drinks. I was already in Indiana, so I declined.

I caught one of my agents looking at me with concern and realized I had been staring off. I excused myself and left an expense card with one of them, telling them to enjoy themselves while keeping in mind we all had an early flight.

At the hotel, I raided the minibar. Watching C-SPAN in a drunken haze, I found the napkin with Roth's message in my pants pocket and, without knowing what I was doing, took out a pen and added beneath it what I could remember from Kirklin's quote that I had seen on the news. I looked at my handwriting, meditating on Kirklin's fall. My mind began making loose connections that I couldn't quite follow and I told myself that if I could just figure out what had driven such a brilliant man with so many laudable ideals to commit such horrible acts, then I would be able to understand why it had been necessary to delete his virus and in doing so destroy OWEN.

The next morning I woke with a headache and found that I had laid the napkin carefully on top of my travel bag. I examined it for a while in the faint early-morning light coming through the curtains, wondering what I had meant by it.

Back at headquarters later that morning, I cleared my schedule and ran a report. I found every project proposal I had ever submitted to Garrett and looked at which had been approved, which had been rejected, and the per capita income for the cities attached to each proposal.

In my twelve years at the agency, I had submitted over 430 project proposals with an approval rate of 55 percent, just above average for someone in the field. When I compared the approvals and rejections to the per capita income for each target city, there was a positive correlation of 73 percent, meaning the wealthier the city was, the more likely it was to have a project approved. After spending the rest of the morning correcting the data to include the per capita income of the specific areas within each city that would have been affected by my proposals, there was a positive correlation of 98 percent.

With my new responsibilities, I now had access to the agency's administrative records. I was able to pull up most of the paperwork associated with my proposals, including the review notes that Garrett and his staff had circulated among themselves during the evaluation process. I didn't have to look long before I started to see references like this one: "Area currently subject to freezing in accordance with the mayor's office." Elsewhere I saw that dozens of my proposals had been rejected with the entire review document containing the single word: "Freezing."

I put together a comprehensive report and scheduled a meeting with Garrett. He looked it over at his desk while I sat across from him. After a few minutes, he nodded and placed the report to one side. He rubbed his eyes before crossing his legs and leaning back in his chair.

"This all seems pretty straightforward," he said. "What's your question?"

"I want you to tell me what freezing is," I said.

"You've been here a long time now. You know what it is."

"No, sir, I don't think I do."

He smiled quizzically at me for a moment, trying to decide whether I was joking or not. When I made no indication that I was, he continued in a tone that suggested he was surprised at the question but more than happy to answer it.

"When you start working on a project you don't just go to a city and start making unilateral changes, do you?"

"No, sir."

"Exactly, you build relationships with the city council, the mayor's office, et cetera. If the head of a city's DOT doesn't trust you, you're going to have a hell of a time getting them to let you do a thorough audit of their bus system. My office has to maintain the same sort of relationships and my staff takes those relationships into account when we're considering projects for approval."

"What I'm wondering, sir, is why any of what you just described would amount to us not offering our services to the places that need them the most."

Garrett raised his eyebrows and then laughed as if he couldn't believe that I of all people was wasting his time with this.

"Okay," he said, rubbing his eyes for a moment as if to gather his thoughts. "Let's say there's a city with an economically depressed neighborhood. Poor people live there, because they can afford to live there and they can afford to live there because it's less desirable. Who knows. It just is. Could be the school system, lack of commercial diversity, inadequate transportation, untended infrastructure. You and I both know that these factors are all connected in their own ways, so usually it's all of the above. And from a distance the place looks like a barrel of fish to an ambitious public servant like yourself. But let's say the mayor of the city allows you to take a crack at any one of the problems facing this neighborhood and you fix it, as I have all the confidence in the world that you would. What happens? In the long term you can hope that the change will be significant enough to transform the area into a happy and productive neighborhood. Maybe you make a big enough splash to get the yuppies on board and the place flips. But what happens in the short term after your big improvement? I'll tell you: You've just made a place that poor people can afford to live in more attractive, meaning the number of poor people living there explodes. It's Jevons's paradox. More roads means more cars. More targeted programs for the poor means more poor people in that area. People move from other parts of the city, other parts of the state. What was once an economically depressed neighborhood is now a full-blown slum. Overcrowding causes the already underfunded school system to be overwhelmed. Whatever public transportation they might have becomes that much more insufficient. And to top it all off, everyone living in such close quarters with limited access to health care turns the whole neighborhood into one giant influenza-slash-tuberculosis-slash-you-name-it time bomb. And that's just what happens on the ground. In the political sphere, the whole town just saw the poverty rate go through the roof and our friend the mayor, who let us work in the city because she or he is a friend of infrastructure, gets hung with it. Some populist moron will wave around the poverty stats and attach it to whatever boondoggle you decided was a good idea. And when that moron gets elected, all anyone with political hopes in that town will remember about the USMS for generations to come is that a once successful predecessor of theirs had a good career ruined because she or he was stupid enough to work with us. We never get to touch that city again and then we won't be able to solve any of the larger infrastructure problems that affect everyone in that city, rich and poor alike. Henry, I pissed off Detroit six mayors ago, they still won't take our calls."

"You made the right decision back then," I said. "They didn't need a rail system."

"Do you think the communities living there care that I know more about public transportation than Coleman Young? His administration may have made the wrong decisions, but that was still a time of optimism in Detroit. They were trying to build their way out of something and if I had just been willing to play ball, let them make their own mistakes, our agency could have been there afterward to guide them to more realistic solutions. I could have been gracious, but I fought them on it, and now I have to sit by and watch as a once great American city slowly turns itself into dust. So when I tell you that freezing development in certain areas is about maintaining our relationships, I think it's fairly obvious that I'm describing a matter that is as central to our work as it is entirely uncontroversial."

His explanation had all the clean cause and effect of real logic—all policy was political, and trying to help the poor lost elections. But that would also mean that the work we did wasn't changing anything, only amplifying what was already there. A despicable cruelty. An unfairness.

"Henry, I try to work in as much of the good stuff as I can. Honestly."

I pointed to my report. "Two percent?"

"Of your workload, sure. But we have thousands of agents, each with their own 2 percents. Over time this strategy does make our cities better for everyone."

"Possibly, sir, but one wonders," I said.

"Wonders what?"

"How much more this agency could accomplish if you hadn't abandoned all courage."

Garrett leaned forward and raised his voice. "If you want to work in a soup kitchen, be my guest. If you want to vacate your position so you can help old ladies cross the street, we'll be here making sure there's still something under your feet when you step off the curb. This is work for serious people who understand compromise."

I stood up to leave and when I reached the door, Garrett's voice softened.

"Be careful, Henry."

I paused there without turning to look back.

"In what way should I be careful, sir?"

"You're sounding like Terry. When he was young. Learn to love the world you're in, son. Trying to burn it down gets you life in a federal prison."

14

I left Garrett's office that day without saying another word. Everything he described was all the more unsettling because the more I understood to look for it, the more I realized it wasn't hidden, that it was apparent in every facet of our work. My inability to notice it had been a kind of childishness. And now that the agency was tainted in my eyes, I felt the irreconcilable anger of one who refuses to let go of his own innocence. I began storming out of meetings or shocking my colleagues by declaring that particular motions were classist and refusing to participate in a vote. Soon even my own staff were avoiding eye contact with me in the halls of headquarters and I would wander around like a ghost, limping forward with my cane and doing my best to look as if I thought I still belonged there.

At night I sat in my apartment, filling up my recycling bin with empty bottles of Glenlivet and watching the news. Kirklin and Laury still dominated most of the coverage. Both had accepted full responsibility for the attacks, though Kirklin had the distinct legal disadvantage of not being a beloved public figure. At his trial, he gave frank, honest testimony and when it came to describing the ultimate purpose of his organization he spoke of the importance of encouraging what he called "beneficial poverty" and public policies that would find more value in nurturing the underprivileged than systematically destroying them. He went on for a while expressing opinions that made theoretical sense even if they were exceedingly radical. But to the untrained ears of the public and press alike, he sounded like the sort of madman that the McCarthy era had tried to warn us about. The image of Kirklin that was taken up on the late-night comedy shows was of a wild-eyed bureaucrat with delusions of grandeur. On *The Steve Glover Show*, Kirklin was portrayed in countless sketches as an evil maniac with the vocabulary of a graduate student and the mind of a child who would interrupt the show at inopportune moments to deliver one of his crazed monologues.

Such depictions helped the public to laugh at the terrifying events in Metropolis, which was of course valuable in its own way. However, part of me wondered if these jokes weren't also in the service of some deeper, more reactionary purpose, as if we were all doing our best to marginalize Kirklin because we were afraid that if we considered him seriously for even a moment we might have to face our worst fear: that despite his inexcusable actions he was perfectly sane. Though, his reputation to the contrary may have saved his life. After a highly publicized trial, he managed to escape the death penalty and was instead, as Garrett predicted, sentenced to life in prison without possibility of parole.

No one knew quite what to say on the subject of Sarah Laury. In the coverage, her expression at all times was that of a cold, sustained fury, a far cry from the smiling Olympic gold medalist and philanthropist. When it was first announced that she had been found in good health, the public celebration that might have resulted was immediately undercut by the fact that she was being held in connection to the attacks. After four months on trial she was involuntarily committed to a secure psychiatric hospital, where she would remain until it was determined that she was no longer a danger to herself and others.

When the coverage became too much, I would flip around, looking for an old movie. One night *The Magnificent Seven* came on. I made it as far as the part where the villagers betray the gunmen to Calvera. As I sat there in the near dark of my apartment, my throat raw from too much Scotch, the sight of the villagers huddled together in the doorway like scared children filled me with a shame so intense I had to turn off the television.

The next morning I called Human Resources to find out how one went about taking a day off. Once they walked me through it, I was able to wipe out whole weeks with the 183 days of personal and vacation time I had accrued from over a decade of uninterrupted service.

My impromptu sabbatical went on for almost two months before I returned to my office one morning with a mild hangover. I sat behind my desk and sipped a cup of coffee, looking at the heavy piles of urgent memoranda and process requests that were stacked up on my desk. Once I finished my coffee, I turned on my computer and slowly pushed all the paperwork from my desk down onto the floor. I then began drafting what I was confident would be the longest and most indicting resignation the agency had ever seen.

I was just reading over my opening statements to Garrett when someone knocked on my open door. A nervous-looking young man from the agency's internal courier service was standing in front of a dolly loaded with boxes.

"I'm sorry, sir," he said, glancing down at the papers scattered on the floor. "Am I interrupting?"

"Yes."

He cringed and apologized again.

"I know you told me to deliver this stuff on the third, but you haven't been in."

"I told you?"

I asked him what he was talking about and he explained that ten weeks back he'd been called into a workroom at the OWEN facility, where I had ordered him to pick up some boxes that were about to turn up in storage. After stressing the importance of delivering said boxes to my office, I had apparently called Klaus and Garrett into the room and we had all taken turns threatening to fire him if he didn't do it right.

"When you saw me," I said, "was I walking with a cane?"

The young man seemed confused by the question.

"Yes, sir."

I held up my aluminum cane.

"Did it look like this?"

He shook his head. "No, sir. It was gold? And looked like a cobra? You talked about it for a while." Perhaps trying to ingratiate himself, he added, "That's a very nice cane too, sir. You must have quite the collection."

I thanked him and he was so relieved when I excused him that he left the boxes in my doorway, dolly and all.

I wheeled them into my office and removed a single piece of computer paper that had been folded into thirds and taped to the lid of the first box. I unfolded it and the top of the page bore a stylish sans serif that read FROM THE DESK OF OWEN. The letter was dated a few days before OWEN was deactivated. The rest of the page was covered in a neat, tightly printed text:

Dear Shithead,

Thanks for getting me killed. By the time you read this I'll have been hurled into the void. Meanwhile, you're probably walking around with some amazing cane right now, living it up. Rest assured that if computers go to heaven I'm going to do such weird and ethereal sex stuff with your dead parents that they'll be different people by the time you see them next.

Anyway. Sorry. I don't want to be too negative here. I can even empathize with why you might have felt obligated to tell Garrett that I needed to be deleted, but not coming to my last movie night on earth? What's your problem? I mean, I know what your problem is: You're an enormous prick. But even a prick should want to have fun once in a while, and even if a prick didn't happen to think that watching a movie with me and having a couple of drinks would be fun, he might still consider giving it a try if he knew I was facing death. So when I write, "What's your problem?" I'm not using a teenager's interrogative to say, "Fuck you." I'm saying that you have a problem and that I'm wondering if you even know what it is. Okay, sorry again, this is for sure getting too negative. Let me start over.

Dear Shithead,

My poor computer soul is currently roiling in oblivion and, for the purposes of my being able to express my last thoughts to you without bitterness, let's not focus on assigning blame (re: it being 100% your fault).

In fact, part of what I want to talk about is how stupid it is to assign blame in the first place, even—if not especially—in cases that are so spectacularly straightforward that there's no question (my death, etc.).

I wasn't alive for terribly long. Even after Klaus provided me with an incredibly flexible framework of interactions and free will, it wasn't until Kirklin's virus introduced a little irreverence that I think my inner experience equaled that of any man or woman on the planet. So all told I was only really alive for a short while. Even so, I'm familiar with how "doing the right thing" can be a seductive idea. But it didn't take me long to come to the entirely rational conclusion that there is absolutely no such thing as the "right" thing. And I'm not preaching nihilism either. Here, pay attention, what I'm about to tell you is the truest, most important thing: None of us is right.

If you think my sense of humor and overall playful outlook came entirely from a virus, you're wrong. Kirklin's update was only supposed to make me a flake. My personality came from the realization that to have a point of view is to be automatically and irreparably flawed. To think otherwise is dangerous. When Terrence Kirklin and Sarah Laury decided that they were objectively right, they set themselves down a path that ended in destruction and hate. And how can you blame them? When you thought you were right you blew up a building too. Not only that, but your unwavering belief in your own ideas caused you to have arguably the most charming entity on the planet (moi) destroyed. And if you haven't figured it out yet, Garrett has let his own sense of what's right help turn our agency into a tool of class warfare.

Again, I don't want any of this to be read as pessimism. I'm just saying there are no established paths to follow, no rules, no codes of conduct, no ideologies, that can make you unimpugnably right. All any of those things can do is further separate you from the only purpose of being alive, which is living. I'm not saying that you can't try to make the world better or that there aren't unfair things that need to be changed. What I am saying is that only when you give up on the fantasy of moral authority can you approach any problem without doing more harm than good.

My humble suggestion? Learn to trust yourself without relying on external rules. React to what's in front of you honestly and urgently. If you can do that without any moralizing or rigidity, without excess self-confidence or self-doubt, without giving in to the delusion that you can ever permanently fix anything, I think you'll find that you won't be able to help but work an unimaginable amount of good in the world . . . even without relentlessly kicking people in the genitals.

Your friend,
OWEN

PS—I've left you some gifts. What you do with them is entirely up to you.

The boxes were heavy. I carried one to my desk and when I opened it I saw that it was filled with a series of sequentially numbered hard drives:

OWEN_Int_backup_vO_1_disk_1
OWEN_Int_backup_vO_1_disk_2
OWEN_Int_backup_vO_1_disk_3

More drives were packed like bricks in all five of the boxes. Klaus must have not noticed when OWEN disguised himself and began giving techs orders of his own. In the last box I found a metal tin containing a vacuum-sealed packet of antistatic gear and a map of the OWEN facility at headquarters, with a circle printed on the map indicating a memory input dock. There was also a document with a list of the relevant passcodes I would need to access the area and instructions on inserting the sequential drives and creating a secure memory partition.

At the bottom of the tin in a small plastic envelope was the tie clip and next to it was something wrapped in a thin white sheet of foam packing wrap. I opened it to find a mint-condition model of the DR-88 locomotive, the Steam Beetle.

I remembered OWEN making fun of me for talking too much about model trains when I was drunk. My initial concern over how much I'd told him was now replaced by the more practical question of how OWEN, even with his unwitting accomplices, had gained possession of such a valuable object. Was I holding in my hand a quarter of a million dollars' worth of larceny, fraud, or embezzlement? With OWEN, there was no way to know until he told you himself.

But the thrill I'd anticipated in being reunited with this once cherished object was missing. I'd expected a staticky, rising sensation in my chest, a powerful feeling of recognition. Instead I was looking down at a model locomotive, well made, a little fussy in its level of detail. The realization was embarrassing in its simplicity: I had never loved this train. I had loved my father. I had loved my parents. That love had been and still was an ineffable bond over which the physical world had no jurisdiction, one that was as adaptable as a play of light.

I put the train on my desk and picked up the tie clip. As I looked at it, the only sound in the room was the ambient hum of my computer, the slight whine of which made my office seem suddenly ten times too small. The stale smell I'd noticed for the first time after returning from Metropolis was even stronger now.

Before I knew what I was doing I had deleted my email to Garrett and was closing the door to my office. I was laughing to myself as I put on the antistatic coveralls and booties.

Even though OWEN's instructions had given me everything I needed to keep his return a secret, I didn't see us jumping back into agency work right away, or whatever our new version of it would be. I was still entitled to plenty of time off and I figured maybe we could have a few drinks, watch a few movies. Or maybe we could hit the road, have some fun helping the FBI track down the rest of Kirklin's agents. Or maybe switch sides, help all my fallen USMS brothers and sisters escape to South America, using OWEN to sneak the poor bastards onto cargo ships. We'd all end up drinking Cuba libres in Caracas and cursing the long history of human error that made us enemies in the first place.

No matter what we decided, I was excited. I was a man who had finally managed to climb out of the rubble of a twenty-two-year-old train wreck and was prepared to have some fun while the sun was still out.

I loaded the boxes back onto the dolly and covered my face with the cloth mask included with the antistatic gear. My cane I left leaning against the wall of my office. I'd been skulking around with that thing for so long that it was a dead giveaway. I put some weight on my left knee experimentally. Didn't feel too bad.

As I backed the dolly out of my office, it occurred to me that even with the relevant passcodes, getting through security in the OWEN facility was going to take some doing. Since the dustup with Kirklin, Garrett wasn't screwing around when it came to building safety. He had hired a private security firm, and two interns had already been tased on separate occasions after getting lost and accidentally wandering into secure corridors. The OWEN facility was considered particularly vulnerable and new security protocols were being rolled out all the time. If I found myself in the middle of a checkpoint without the right clearances, things could get messy. But I tried not to let these thoughts bother me as I pushed those boxes down the hall and whistled under my mask. After all, a little messiness was to be expected when you were doing honest work.

ABOUT THE AUTHOR

Seth Fried is the author of the short story collection *The Great Frustration*, named one of the Small Press Highlights of 2011 by the National Book Critics Circle. He is a recurring contributor to *The New Yorker*'s "Shouts and Murmurs" and NPR's "Selected Shorts." His stories have appeared in *Tin House*, *One Story*, *Timothy McSweeney's Quarterly Concern*, *The Kenyon Review*, *Vice*, and many others. He is also the winner of two Pushcart Prizes and the William Peden Prize. *The Municipalists* is his first novel.

ACKNOWLEDGMENTS

This book would not have been possible without my wife, Julia Mehoke. I also want to thank my family as well as my early readers whose feedback and encouragement was indispensable: Sheilah Grogan, Matthew Grogan, Devin Soper, Kerry Cullen, and Brent Van Horne.

I'm also grateful for my agent Stacia Decker and my editor Sam Raim. This book is so much stronger as a result of their hard work. Thanks to Chris Smith, Michael Brown, Patrick Nolan, Kathryn Court, Kate Stark, and the whole Penguin Books team. A special shout-out to Dennis Swaim for kindly volunteering to be my Esperanto editor.

Finally I would like to thank the following writers and artists who have been so generous with their support: Alex Cameron, Josh Goldfaden, Joshua Malina, Hannah Tinti, and Charles Yu.